Praise for BILL DALY

'Daly evokes Glasgow with a masterly touch'
ALEX GRAY

'Impressive ... a vivid new voice in Tartan noir'
MAGGIE CRAIG

'A stylish police thriller ... includes a beautifully formulated
"locked room" mystery ... a cracking read'
DAILY MAIL on *Double Mortice*

'Brilliantly gripping and fast-moving ... and the characters all
have a rich credibility'
EUROCRIME on *Black Mail*

'Daly effortlessly incorporates the seedy underbelly of the
city... *Black Mail* can proudly sit alongside books by far more
established writers in the Glasgow noir field ... A highly
enjoyable debut' **crimefictionlover.co.uk**

CUTTING EDGE

Bill Daly

Published in Great Britain in 2016 by Old Street Publishing
c/o Parallel, 8 Hurlingham Business Park, Sulivan Road
London SW6 3DU

www.oldstreetpublishing.co.uk

ISBN 978-1-910400-35-7

The right of Bill Daly to be identified as the author of this work has been asserted by him
in accordance with the Copyright, Designs and Patents Act 1988.

10 9 8 7 6 5 4 3 2 1

A CIP catalogue record for this title is available from the British Library.

Typeset by JaM

Printed and bound by CPI Group (UK) Ltd, Croydon, CR0 4YY

For Anne and Malcolm

CHAPTER 1

Sunday 19 June, 2011

Waiting in a queue of traffic at a red light, he saw the car in front of him start to roll back down the incline. He gave a sharp blast on his horn. The Volvo was less than a yard away now, its engine revving fiercely. He glanced in his rear view mirror. There was a van right on his bumper – no room to back up. He slammed his hand down on the horn and kept it there as he braced himself for the inevitable crunch of metal as the two vehicles came together.

He saw the driver's head swivel round.

'You stupid idiot!' he screamed, releasing the horn and thumping the steering column with his closed fist.

She looked at him, aghast, through her rear window.

'Sorry!' he saw her mouth.

'Sorry?' he shouted. 'Don't you know how to do a bloody hill start?'

As she was scrambling out of the driver's seat, he took a deep breath to try to calm down. This was not the time to draw attention to himself. As he got out of his car his nostrils were filled with the acrid stench of her burnt-out clutch. He waved to the queue of traffic behind to overtake them.

'Oh, my God!' She slammed her hands to her mouth as she bent down to inspect the damage. 'I've dented your wing. I'm really, really sorry,' she said, dragging her fingers through her shoulder-length black hair as she straightened up. 'I only passed my test last week,' she explained. 'I've never done a hill start on a slope as steep as this before. I don't know what happened. It just started slipping back and I couldn't hold it. It's my father's car,' she added. 'The insurance will cover your damage, of course, though he'll kill me for losing his no-claims bonus. I'd better give you my address,' she said, fumbling in her jacket pocket for a business card and handing it over. 'We'll need to fill out an accident report form, won't we? I've got one in the glove compartment. I'll get it.'

As she hurried to fetch the form, he studied her card, an idea forming in his mind.

'I'll admit full liability, of course,' she said, unfolding the document as she came back. 'Do you have a pen?'

'It's not worth the hassle,' he said examining the dent. Exchanging insurance details was no longer on his agenda. 'It isn't worth losing your Dad's no-claims bonus over this. I know a guy who'll repair it for me. It won't cost much.'

'Really? Oh, thank you! But you must let me pay for it. I insist. Get in touch with me when you know how much it's going to cost.'

'Okay,' he said, pocketing her card. He gave her a reassuring smile. 'I'll do that.'

Monday 20 June

'Irene! Goany stop your fuckin' dog barking!' Archie Carter stood in the doorway of his caravan and shouted at the top of his voice. 'It's doin' ma fuckin' heid in!' The barking persisted. 'Irene!' he yelled again. 'What the hell's going on over there?'

Cursing under his breath, Archie trudged down the five iron steps and made his way across the field towards Irene's caravan, his bare feet squelching in the soggy turf. Stella stopped barking and hunkered down when she saw Archie approaching.

'Easy, old girl,' Archie said, holding out his hand in a reassuring gesture. 'It's only me.'

A deep-throated growl started building at the back of Stella's throat and Archie saw the bared teeth just in time to whip his hand away as Stella's attempt to launch herself at him was thwarted by the length of rope that tied her collar to one of the caravan wheels.

Archie hastily backed off. 'What the fuck's wrong with you, you daft bitch?'

As Archie plodded up the caravan steps, Stella's barking resumed, louder now, more insistent. He knocked tentatively on the door. 'Irene?' No response. He tried the handle. The door wasn't locked. He eased it open. 'Irene?' He raised his voice to try to make himself heard above the racket Stella was making.

He saw the figure lying face down on the single bed. 'Irene? Are you okay?' He blinked several times as his eyes slowly adjusted to the dim light.

Archie's jaw sagged as his gaze was drawn to the arm dangling down the side of the bed. The caravan started rocking from side to side as Stella went berserk, leaping forward again and again, straining at her leash. Archie spun on his heel to get out, but threw up before he got as far as the door.

Superintendent Nigel Hamilton surveyed the assembled journalists as he walked into the room and took his customary seat behind the long table for his weekly press conference. Pulling a manila folder from his briefcase, he straightened his tie before spreading his notes out on the table in front of him. He switched on the microphone.

'We're ready to begin,' he announced tapping the mike with his fingertips to check it was live. The buzz of conversation died away. 'At this week's meeting,' Hamilton's high-pitched voice intoned, 'I will provide you with a summary of the crime statistics for the first half of this year in my division and I will then brief you on the new reporting procedures I intend to implement over the coming months, which will significantly improve the accuracy of crime reporting for the city.' Hamilton was oblivious to the collective low groan that ran round the room.

Having summarised the stats, Hamilton launched himself into a twenty minute Power Point presentation on his new reporting methodology. When he'd concluded, he invited questions.

The first one came from a reporter on the Record, who wanted to know what progress had been made on the Keppochill rape investigation.

'We are following up several lines of enquiry,' Hamilton stated.

'Is an arrest imminent?'

'Not at this point,' Hamilton said, acknowledging the raised hand in the front row.

'Fran Gibbons, BBC Scotland. You've told us what you intend to do with regard to changing the way crimes are reported, Superintendent Hamilton,' the lilting voice said. 'However, while you might consider this to be an improvement, it appears to me that all you're doing is manipulating the statistics, which will contribute nothing towards solving or preventing crime in the city.'

The room waited in anticipation as Fran continued. 'Do you think the fifteen year-old girl who was gang-raped in Keppochhill last weekend will appreciate the fact that, statistically, there's been a three point seven percent reduction in violent crime in Glasgow during the past six months?'

Sitting at the back of the room, DCI Charlie Anderson was struggling to keep his face straight as he nudged DI Barry Crawford in the ribs.

Hamilton's face was flushed as he responded. 'You're missing the point,' he blustered, waving in the direction of a reporter from the Herald who had raised his hand. 'What is your question, Tom?'

'I don't think I am missing the point,' Fran persisted. 'You appear to be a great believer in statistics, Superintendent. My point is this. If the officers who spent their time compiling those stats had been out on the beat, how many more man hours could have been allocated to patrolling the streets in Keppochhill – and what effect might that have had on reducing the incidence of violent crime?'

'We have time for only a few questions today,' Hamilton snapped, fixing Fran with a glare. 'Everyone must get their turn,' he said, breaking eye contact. 'What was your question, Tom?'

Tuesday 21 June

Detective Chief Inspector Charlie Anderson was one of the longest serving officers in the Glasgow Division of the CID. Over six feet tall, he had broad, hunched shoulders and a permanent stoop, the legacy of acute arthritis, exacerbated by too many years huddled over an office desk. Puffy eyelids hooded his rheumy eyes and the greyness of the pouches beneath bore witness to several weeks of inadequate sleep.

As he stripped off his jacket and hung it over the back of his swivel chair, Charlie noticed that there was a brown-paper parcel on top on the habitual pile of mail in his inbox. Picking it up, he weighed it in his hand. The size of a shoe box, but too light to be a pair of shoes. He studied the address label. In bold typeface: **C.I.D. Headquarters, Pitt Street, Glasgow.** Beneath the address, in smaller, italic characters: *For the personal attention of Detective Chief Inspector Charles Anderson*, the franking on the package indicating it had been handed in to the main Glasgow post office in St Vincent Street at half past nine the previous morning.

Charlie puzzled as to what it could be. He hadn't ordered anything. Perhaps Kay had ordered something – maybe a present for Sue or Jamie? But why would she have had it delivered here?

Sitting down behind his desk, he used his paper knife to slice through the sellotape that was looped several times around the package. Stripping the paper away, he saw that it was indeed a shoe box. A playing card, the nine of diamonds, was stapled to the side of the box and a bright-yellow emoticon of a smiling face had been stuck to the centre of the card. Intrigued, Charlie removed the lid and saw the dark-stained cotton wool. When he lifted the cotton wool away, the bile rose in his stomach. His eyes narrowed as he focussed on the contents: a grey, amputated human hand, palm down, fingers slightly curled, perched on another wad of blood-saturated cotton wool. Fighting back the queasy feeling in the pit of his stomach, Charlie forced himself to examine every detail of the hand; the ingrained dirt embedded beneath the badly-bitten fingernails, the two buckled pewter rings on the scrawny middle finger, the mass of brown liver spots speckling the weather-beaten skin, the gristle and jagged bone protruding from the severed wrist.

Replacing the lid, he depressed his intercom.

'Pauline, I want a copy of the forensic report on yesterday's murder in Port Glasgow.'

Ryan Ferrie was roused from his sleep by the ring of his door bell. When he peered, bleary-eyed, at the alarm clock on his bedside table, he saw it was ten past eight. 'Who the fuck?' he muttered under his breath. The ringing became insistent, the caller holding his finger on the bell push. Ferrie clambered out of bed and shrugged on his dressing gown, yawning and running his fingers through his spiky, gelled hair as he made his way along the hall.

'Who is it?' he called out as he was unlocking the apartment door. 'What do you want at this time – ?' He broke off when he saw the tall figure standing in the doorway, a black balaclava covering his head completely, apart from narrow slits for his eyes and his mouth. Ferrie's jaw fell slack. 'What's going on?'

'Shut the fuck up!' the man snapped. Stepping across the threshold, he bundled Ferrie down the hall and pulled the front door closed behind him.

'What do you think you're playing at?' The words died on Ferrie's lips as a vicious rabbit punch crunched into the side of his neck

*

Charlie Anderson rocked back in his chair and swung his feet up onto his desk, his stubby fingers fumbling under his shirt collar to loosen his tie knot. As he stretched across his desk for the forensic report he felt a sharp, stabbing pain shoot up from the base of his spine. Wincing, he remained frozen in the outstretched position until the spasm had subsided before picking up the document between thumb and forefinger and easing himself back into his seat.

Charlie scanned the report, then his gaze flicked back to the shoe box. It was amazing, Charlie thought, how much could be deduced from just a hand. He reckoned he could have made a reasonably accurate guess as to the sex, age and lifestyle of the appendage's erstwhile owner. However, he had no need to surmise. The report in his hand said it all. He referred to the document.

'Irene McGowan,' he read. 'Age seventy-eight. Resided in a travellers' encampment on the outskirts of Port Glasgow. Body discovered by Archie Carter, who lives in the adjacent caravan. Time of death was between eight and nine o'clock on the morning of Monday the twentieth of June. The cause of death was strangulation. The left hand of the victim had been severed at the wrist. The amputated limb was not found in the caravan or in the immediate vicinity.'

Charlie dropped his feet to the floor with a thud and picked up the brown wrapping paper in which the parcel had arrived. The address label left no doubt as to the intended recipient, but there was no note of any kind enclosed, only the incongruous playing card with the smiley face attached, stapled to the side of the box.

Charlie pulled off his half-moon reading glasses and folded them carefully before slipping them into the case in the breast pocket of his shirt. He rubbed the tiredness from his eyes with the heels of both his hands, his gaze inexorably drawn back to the shoe box. 'Why you, Irene McGowan?' he mused. 'And why the hell me?'

Charlie's train of thought was interrupted by a sharp rap on his office door.

'Come in!'

'I heard what happened this morning, sir.' Detective Sergeant Tony O'Sullivan caught sight of the shoe box lying on the desk. 'Is that it?' he asked, pointing.

'Unless there's been a spate of them delivered today,' Charlie grunted.

O'Sullivan's freckles flared up. Screwing up his eyes, he lifted the lid from the box and squinted at the amputated hand. 'What do we know about her?'

'Only what's in the forensic report,' Charlie said sliding the document across the desk.

Tony flicked through the report. 'Did you have any connection with her, sir?' he asked.

'I'd never heard of her before this morning.'

'Why would the killer chop off her hand and send it to you?'

'I haven't the remotest idea.'

'And why the nine of diamonds?' O'Sullivan queried as he studied the playing card. 'What's that all about?'

'It's known as "The Curse of Scotland",' Charlie said.

'Why?'

'Did they not teach you any history at school?'

'My history teacher was rubbish. And the only history that ever got talked about at home,' he added, 'was Irish.'

'The nine of diamonds is associated with the Glencoe Massacre in the seventeenth century,' Charlie explained, 'when the McDonalds murdered the Campbells in their beds. There are several theories about the role the nine of diamonds played, the popular one being that the order to carry out the massacre was written on a nine of diamonds playing card.'

'What about the smiley?' Tony asked.

'As far as I'm aware,' Charlie said, 'emoticons weren't around in the seventeenth century.'

'This is weird,' Tony said, replacing the lid on the box.

Charlie eased himself to his feet.

'Arrange for the hand to be packed in ice, Tony, then have it sent across to the mortuary so it can be matched up with the corpse.'

When Ryan Ferrie came round he found himself bound hand and foot to a wooden chair. He opened his eyes slowly and saw his assailant sitting on the opposite side of the kitchen table, flicking through the Sunday Times sports section. The intruder folded the newspaper and put it down when he saw Ferrie stir.

'Who are you?' Ferrie grunted. 'What the hell are you playing at?'

'Are you Zoe Taylor's boyfriend?'

'That's none of your fucking business.'

'I'm making it my business. Answer the question.'

Ferrie licked hard at his lips. 'What if I am?' he mumbled. 'What is it to you?'

'Where is Zoe?' Ferrie didn't reply. 'I asked you a question,' he snarled, springing to his feet. 'Where the hell is Zoe?'

Ferrie hesitated. 'At her work.'

'This early?'

'She leaves here at eight o'clock.'

'You're going to make a phone call.'

'What are you talking about?'

'You're going to phone Zoe.'

'What?'

'You're going to call her and arrange to meet her at half-past twelve.'

Ferrie shrivelled his brow. 'The fuck I am!'

The intruder walked slowly round the kitchen table and stopped directly in front of Ferrie. Producing a set of knuckle-dusters from his jacket pocket, he slipped them over the fingers of his right hand, then he drew back his fist and smashed it into the side of Ferrie's face. 'There's an easy way to do this,' he said, holding his fist poised for a moment before hammering it into the bridge of Ferrie's nose, the crack of breaking bone resounding around the kitchen. 'And there's a hard way.'

'Stop it! For fuck's sake!' Ferrie screamed, blood spurting from his burst nose and splattering down the front of his dressing gown.

'Like I said, you're going to call Zoe and arrange to meet her at half-past twelve. You'll tell her to come to a remote spot – think of somewhere she'll know well. When you phone her, you're going to say you're in big trouble and that she has to come to see you – it's a matter of life and death. Which, in your case,' he added, flexing his fingers, 'isn't all that far from the truth. Where's your phone?' he demanded.

'In the bedroom,' Ferrie gulped, swallowing a mouthful of blood. 'On the bedside table.'

The intruder went to the bedroom and returned with Ferrie's mobile. 'Have you thought of a remote place to meet her?' Ferrie stared at him wide-eyed. 'I asked you if you've thought of a good place to meet her?' He raised the knuckle-dusters and held them poised, inches from Ferrie's eyes. Ferrie nodded slowly. Flicking open the phone, he paged through the contacts' list until he came to 'Zoe.'

When he clicked onto the number, the phone switched directly to the messaging service. 'Why is her phone switched off?'

'She always turns it off while she's at her work.'

Checking the phone, he saw the next entry on the list was 'Zoe – Work.'

Having clicked onto that number, he held the phone close to Ferrie's right ear as it rang out, the knuckle-dusters pressed hard against his left temple.

'Is that you, Emma?' Ferrie asked when he heard the familiar voice.

'Yes.'

'It's Ryan. Can I speak to Zoe?'

'Not right now, Ryan. She's in a meeting with Mr Tracy.'

'When will she be out?'

'She's just gone in, so probably in about half an hour.'

'She's in a meeting,' Ferrie mouthed to the intruder.

'Leave a message for her to meet you,' he whispered, grinding the knuckle-dusters into the side of Ferrie's head.

'Could you do me a favour, Emma,' Ferrie said, swallowing blood.

'Is there something wrong, Ryan? You sound funny.'

'I'm fine. As soon as Zoe comes out of her meeting, tell her she has to come to the boathouse in Glasgow Green at half past twelve. She knows where it is. Tell her I'll meet here there.'

'Can I tell her why?'

'For Christ's sake, Emma! Would you just give her the bloody message!'

'Okay, okay! No need to bite my head off!'

The assailant moved the knuckle-dusters down under Ferrie's chin and used them to prise up his jaw. 'Make sure she knows how important it is,' he mouthed.

'This is really important, Emma. I'm in a lot of trouble. Make sure Zoe gets this message as soon as she comes out of her meeting. Tell her she has to come to the boathouse.'

'Okay, I'll tell her, Ryan.' Emma hesitated. 'Are you sure you're all right?'

The assailant terminated the call.

The office wall-clock flicked across to twelve o'clock. Zoe Taylor exchanged an anxious glance with Emma as she gazed in the direction of Keith Tracy's open office door. Her lunch hour was from twelve-thirty to one-thirty and she knew Tracy would be furious if he caught her trying to slip out early.

Zoe was totally bemused by the cryptic message Ryan had left with Emma. It was completely out of character. She'd tried phoning the flat half a dozen times, but there was no reply, and he wasn't answering his mobile. She'd agonised all morning about his call, unable to make any sense of it, unable to concentrate on her work.

What sort of mess was he in this time?

Zoe had prepared her escape, sneaking her coat and umbrella into the toilets during the morning coffee break. Using both hands to drag her shoulder-length, black hair behind her ears, she winked at Emma as she stood up. Smoothing down her tight miniskirt, she picked up her handbag and strode confidently past Tracy's office door, making no attempt to disguise the rat-a-tat of her steel-tipped stiletto heels as they clicked loudly on the tiled surface.

Hurrying into the toilets, she snatched up her coat and umbrella before sidling out the door and trotting down the wide, marble staircase. When she stepped outside the building she saw her bus trundling along West Regent Street. Although it was raining steadily, she didn't stop to unfurl her umbrella as she ran towards the bus stop in short, titupping steps, moving as fast as her constricting skirt would allow, dodging around the puddles and pulling on her coat as she went.

As the bus drew up at the stop ahead she put on a final spurt and jumped on board, her lank hair plastered against her flushed cheeks. She was gasping for breath. 'The bottom of Stockwell Street,' she panted, scrabbling in her purse for change.

Dropping the correct money into the slot, she took her ticket and flopped down on the seat nearest to the door as the bus pulled away from the stop.

Charlie Anderson checked his watch as he climbed the flight of stairs at the far end of the corridor and on the stroke of twelve thirty he rapped on Superintendent Nigel Hamilton's half-open door and walked in. Hamilton had his back to him, working at his terminal. Charlie sat down on the leather chair facing the desk while Hamilton continued typing without acknowledging Charlie's presence. When he'd finished what he was doing, Hamilton transmitted his email and spun round in his swivel chair.

Charlie was only half listening as Hamilton droned on in his habitual, irritatingly slow manner about the importance of getting this murder solved as quickly as possible for the credibility of the Glasgow Division. Charlie knew only too well that Hamilton's primary concern was for his own reputation, the statistics of murder convictions in the division having deteriorated significantly since he'd been at the helm. Charlie thoroughly disliked his boss' humourless smile, his round, blotchy face, his thin, permanently-pursed lips and his sing-song delivery. Whenever Hamilton discussed a subject he seemed to be detached from the conversation, leaving Charlie with the impression that there was always a hidden agenda.

Charlie was gazing out of the window, intrigued by the intricate pattern the drizzle was making on the outside of the pane, when he was alerted by the sudden change in Hamilton's tone.

'Well, Anderson?' the squeaky voice piped up. 'Do you or don't you?'

Charlie had no idea what he was referring to. Pulling himself up straight in his chair, he tugged his handkerchief from his trouser pocket and blew into it noisily. 'I'm not sure,' he mumbled, wiping his nose.

'What kind of an answer is that, man? Do you, or do you not, have any idea who could have sent you that sick package? Who could be bearing a grudge against you?'

'I think, "Who could be bearing a grudge against Irene McGowan?" would be a more relevant question,' Charlie suggested, refolding his handkerchief neatly and slipping it back into his pocket. 'By my way of thinking, being strangled and having your hand chopped off rates higher up the scale of grudges than being on the receiving end of an amputated limb.'

'I can do without the homespun philosophy,' Hamilton snapped. 'Start compiling a dossier straight away. Everyone who might have a score to settle with you. Anyone who's sadistic and warped enough to commit this type of crime. We're dealing with a right weirdo here and once sick bastards like him start killing, they've got an annoying habit of doing it again. I want this chancer nailed before he gets into his stride.'

'Do I gather you want me to take charge of the murder investigation?' There was resignation in Charlie's voice.

'I most certainly do! There has to be some connection between you and this gypsy woman. You need to find out what that is.'

'I'll have to pull a team together.' Charlie stopped to consider. 'O'Sullivan can be made available, but apart from that we're really stretched.'

'Use Stuart.'

Charlie raised a questioning eyebrow. 'Who's Stuart?'

'Malcolm Stuart. He's a graduate high-flier who's been seconded to us from the Met for six months to get hands-on experience. He arrived this morning. He's been with the Merseyside Division for the past six months. He told me he'd spent most of his time in Liverpool pushing paper and he's hoping for front line activity during his time with us. This is an ideal opportunity to see what he's made of. Get him involved.'

'Is that really necessary?' Charlie protested. 'It would be better if I work with guys who know the territory. This is going to be a difficult enough nut to crack without having to wet-nurse a trainee.'

'I don't like having to repeat myself, Anderson,' Hamilton snapped. 'I told you to use Stuart,' he said, waving his hand in front of his face as if dismissing an irritating child. 'The press are going to have a field day with this when they find out the victim's severed hand was sent to CID headquarters. I'm going to have to deal with their questions, so I need to be kept up to speed with all developments.'

The rain had turned into a soaking mizzle by the time Zoe Taylor alighted from the bus and hurried along Clyde Street towards Glasgow Green. She knew the boathouse well, she and Ryan having often sneaked in there after an evening in the pub during the early days of their relationship. She glanced at her watch as she hurried into the park and saw she was already ten minutes late. Putting up her umbrella, she gathered up her coat and started to trot across the wet grass towards the isolated building on the north bank of the river. Suddenly, one of her stiletto heels skidded on a concealed stone and her legs went from under her, sending her crashing full-length on her back. She pulled herself up into a sitting position on the sodden turf and slipped off her shoe to massage her throbbing ankle, trying to feel if anything was broken. Struggling to her feet, she hobbled the last twenty yards to the boathouse with her shoe in her hand.

A typed notice, pinned to the door, announced that clubhouse would be closed on Tuesday 21st June for essential repairs. Zoe saw that the door was ajar. Puzzled, she pushed it open and limped inside.

'Ryan? Are you there?' Her hoarse whisper came echoing back from the low ceiling of the windowless room. She blinked several times to try to adjust her eyes to the gloom, the murky light coming in over her shoulder throwing elongated shadows of the fibre glass boats and the stacked oars onto the far wall. 'Ryan?' she repeated anxiously. 'Where the hell are you?'

There was a grating squeal behind her, the door screeching on its hinges as it was slammed shut. Zoe spun round, momentarily dazzled as the neon lights exploded into life. A pair of gloved hands shot forward and locked themselves in a vice-like grip around her throat, the strong thumbs driving into her windpipe and throttling the breath from her body.

Zoe's shoe fell from her grasp. She dropped her umbrella and handbag and clawed at the hands, trying desperately to prise away the choking fingers, but she was powerless to stop the muscular arms lifting her clean off her feet. Her cheeks turned scarlet and her bulging eyes stared helplessly at the wrap-round, mirrored sunglasses of her attacker. She could see the reflection of her face in the impenetrable, steel-blue, plastic strip, her tongue jutting gro-tesquely from the corner of her gaping mouth. She could make out that he was wearing a baseball cap, on backwards, but her blurred vision couldn't focus on his features.

Zoe dangled like a rag doll at the end of his fully extended arms, her legs flailing, her painted fingernails splintering as she clawed frantically at the unyielding leather gloves encircling her throat. The remorseless pressure from his thumbs was increasing all the time. Her eyes stood out on stalks and her swollen tongue filled her mouth. In less than a minute she had blacked out.

The assailant lowered Zoe's body to the ground. He dropped down onto his knees and slipped off a glove to check the pulse on the side of her neck, confirming she was still alive. Tugging his glove back on, he pushed his sunglasses onto the top of his head.

After a few moments, he saw Zoe's long, false eyelashes start to flutter erratically, like the wings of a startled butterfly. Small, gurgling noises emanated from the back of her throat as her lungs struggled for oxygen. He watched her eyelids jerk open.

'Hello, Zoe,' he said in a hoarse whisper. 'The repair cost fifty quid.'

He leered down at her panic, as a wave of recognition pulsed through her brain.

He blew her an exaggerated air kiss and their eyes were locked together when, with one sharp twist, he snapped her spinal cord. Zoe's eyes remained wide and staring and her throat issued a single low gurgle as the air whooshed down her nostrils from her collapsing lungs.

Getting to his feet, he produced a slim hacksaw blade from his jacket pocket.

CHAPTER 2

A watery sunshine was filtering through the clouds when Terry McKay and Alec Hunter came out of the fish and chip shop in Woodlands Road just before one o'clock. Both men were over six feet tall, but the similarity ended there. McKay was wearing a dark suit, a cream shirt and a silk tie. His cancer was in remission, but the chemotherapy had taken its toll. His skin was sallow and drawn, his eyes sunken and red-rimmed, his hair thin and grey. His jacket, which had been made to measure less than a year ago, hung loosely from his shrunken shoulders.

Alec Hunter ate his fish supper with his fingers as he walked alongside McKay. Less than half McKay's age, he was thick-set, with spiky, black stubble covering his head. He was wearing faded blue jeans and his tight-fitting, black T-shirt was stretched taut by his muscular upper body.

Harry Brady was opening up for business after lunch when McKay and Hunter arrived outside his hardware store. Hunter followed McKay into the shop and closed the door behind him.

When he saw who it was, Brady backed away towards the counter. 'I haven't got it...' he stammered.

McKay shook his head. 'You know I don't like excuses, Brady.'

'I didn't take two hundred and fifty quid all last week.' Brady's anxious gaze flicked from McKay to Hunter, then back again. 'I can't pay you.'

Hunter scrunched his fish supper paper into a ball and drop-kicked it across the floor. Licking the vinegar from his fingertips, he produced a cosh from his hip pocket and fondled it lovingly. Fixing his stare on Brady, he started slapping the cosh rhythmically against the open palm of his left hand.

'You're not thinking straight,' McKay said, tugging his asthma inhaler from the inside pocket of his jacket and putting it to his mouth. Depressing the plunger, he breathed in deeply. 'You know you can't afford not to have insurance,' he wheezed. 'Jim McHugh thought he could do without insurance – and look what happened.'

'For Christ's sake, McKay! I'm telling you. I don't have the money.'

'This is false economy, Brady. Without insurance, you can lose two hundred and fifty quid's worth of stock,' McKay said, grabbing at the top of a glass-fronted display cabinet on the counter and sending it crashing to the ground. 'Just like that!' The cabinet splintered on impact, shards of broken glass skittering across the tiled floor.

'How many times do I have to tell you? I can't fucking-well pay!'

'You're beginning to sound boringly like McHugh.' On McKay's nod, Hunter took a step forward and jerked his cosh up violently between Brady's legs, causing him to crumple to the floor, whimpering with pain. 'Don't ever use the word 'can't' in my presence,' McKay said. 'You know how much it upsets me.'

Brady let out a low moan as he rolled around the floor, clutching at his groin with both hands.

Picking up the Stanley knife that was lying at his feet, McKay gripped it between thumb and forefinger and held it dangling over the writhing figure. 'But because I happen to be in a good mood, and because you've been a regular payer over the years, I'm going to give you one more chance. We'll be back on Saturday – and if you know what's good for you, you'll have the two hundred and fifty quid you owe me for last week – and the same for this week.'

Releasing the knife, McKay burst out laughing as the tip of blade sliced into the top of Brady's right leg, the knife quivering in his thigh.

Dust particles were dancing in the shaft of afternoon sunlight angling through the half-open window and reflecting rainbow patterns onto the far wall from the pile of grease-stained plates stacked high in the sink. Pete Johnston trudged across the room to close the ill-fitting sash window, this doing little to muffle the incessant drone of traffic filtering up from Kilburn High Road. He rummaged through the unwashed dishes in the sink until he came across a tumbler. Giving it a cursory wipe on his shirt sleeve, he reached for the whisky bottle on the draining board and poured himself a generous measure.

Stockily built, Johnston's erstwhile taut stomach muscles had prematurely turned to fat. His complexion was grey and his cheeks were sunken. Broken, purple veins lined his bulbous nose and his chin carried several days' stubble.

As he turned on the cold tap to add a splash of water to his drink, he heard a loud knock on his apartment door. Checking his watch, he padded over in his stocking soles to answer it.

'You were expecting me?' Hassan Salman asked as he stepped across the threshold. Johnston nodded. Tall and slim-faced, Salman was wearing a white, linen suit and a blue, open-necked shirt. His flared nostrils twitched when they were assailed by the dank smell of the apartment. He crossed to the settee and flicked at the cushion with his fingertips before propping himself on the edge of the seat.

'Do you want a drink?' Johnston asked, holding up his glass.

'I don't drink.'

'Suit yourself.' Johnston shrugged.

Salman placed the bulky brown-paper parcel he was carrying on the coffee table, then produced a sealed envelope from his inside jacket pocket. 'There is an anorak and a torch in the parcel – your instructions and tickets are in this envelope.'

'What about my money?'

'You'll get paid on delivery.'

'I usually get half up front,' Johnston complained, gulping down a slug of whisky.

'Do you want this job or don't you?'

'I was just saying. I usually get half up front.'

'Don't quibble,' Salman snapped. 'You're getting paid more for this assignment than you could earn in a year as a mercenary – even working for the Israelis.'

'Don't talk to me about the Jew boys,' Johnston grunted. 'Burma and Sierra Leone pay better than that lot. I'm telling you, I made more as a squaddie during the Gulf War than in two years slogging my guts out defending their Golan Heights.'

Salman picked at his front teeth with a manicured fingernail. 'You fought in the Gulf?'

'I've got the syndrome to prove it.' There was a glint in Johnston's eye. 'I might even have run into some of your pals along the way.'

Salman raised his eyebrows. 'Do not deviate from your instructions, or the schedule, for any reason whatsoever,' he stated, getting to his feet. 'We will have no further contact until you have completed your assignment.' Striding from the apartment, he pulled the door closed behind him.

Salman's footsteps were still ringing out on the stone staircase as Johnston slumped down on the settee to rip open the envelope. He tipped the contents out onto the cushion beside him. Rail tickets, ferry tickets and a single sheet of paper. His shaky fingers unfolded the note and his eye caught the heading at the top of the page: **Consignment To Be Collected In Mull**, printed in bold type.

'Where the fuck's Mull?' he muttered.

He read the instructions.

Take the 11h30 train tomorrow morning from Euston to Glasgow Central. From there, go to Queen Street Station and catch the 18h21 train to Oban. Take the 22h30 ferry from Oban to Craignure on the island of Mull and from there walk north on the coast road in the direction of Salen. After two miles you will come across a dirt track heading inland, signposted for Drumairgh Cottage. Follow this track for half a mile until you come to an isolated barn. Wait inside the barn until someone comes to give you a package, which you will then bring back to London, retracing the same route. When you get back, remain in your apartment until we make contact. For the journey, wear the anorak you'll find in the parcel. When you have memorised these instructions, destroy this note.

Johnston picked up the syringe lying on his coffee table and primed the plunger. Holding his breath, he clenched his left fist and selected a vein in his forearm. Having injected a fix, he stretched out on the settee and breathed in and out deeply, wallowing in the comforting sensation of the heroin being absorbed into his bloodstream. When he closed his eyes, his mind filled with confused, kaleidoscopic images.

Charlie Anderson was sitting in his office, in conversation with Tony O'Sullivan, when his intercom buzzed. He flicked across the switch.

'Renton here, sir. There's a guy called Harry Brady at reception. He insists that he has to speak to you. He says it's urgent, but he won't tell me what it's about – and he won't talk to anyone else.'

'Okay, Colin, I know him. Wheel him along to an interview room. Tell him I'll be down in a few minutes.'

'Who's Brady?' O'Sullivan asked as Charlie disconnected.

'He has a hardware shop in Woodlands Road. I used to play golf with his father – in the good old days, when I could still manage to grip a club,' Charlie said, pulling himself stiffly to his feet and flexing his arthritic fingers.

'Do you need me for anything else today, sir?'

Charlie raised a bushy eyebrow. 'A hot date, is it?'

'Chance would be a fine thing! I was thinking of going down to Saltcoats to see my folks.'

'On you go. There's nothing more we can do here tonight.'

When Charlie walked down the stairs and into the interview room, he saw DC Colin Renton sitting beside the door. Renton was in his late fifties, a colleague of Charlie's since their time together in the uniformed division in Paisley. On Charlie's instigation, he had transferred to the CID late in his career. Acknowledging Renton's presence with a wave, Charlie went across to the desk in the middle of the room where Harry Brady, a slight man in his forties, was sitting on an upright chair. Charlie took the seat on the opposite side of the desk.

'What can I do for you, Harry?'

'I need to talk to you, Charlie.'

'Fire away.'

'It has to be on your own,' he said, glancing nervously in Renton's direction.

'Okay, Colin. You can leave us.'

Brady waited until Renton had gone out of the room and closed the door behind him. 'Do you know Terry McKay?'

'I ought to. I sent him down for ten years.'

'I want him sent down for another ten.'

'Nothing would give me greater pleasure.'

Brady hesitated. 'I've been paying him protection money, Charlie. Two hundred and fifty quid a week.'

Charlie's brow furrowed. 'How long has that been going on?'

'Best part of five years – ever since he got out of Barlinnie. It's not just me. He's putting the squeeze on half the shopkeepers in Woodlands Road. You remember the chemist's that went up in flames last month? Where Jim McHugh and his wife died in the upstairs flat?'

'What about it?'

'McKay and his sidekick, Alec Hunter, started that fire.'

'We suspected it was started deliberately, but there wasn't any proof.'

'It was arson and it was McKay – you can take my word for that.'

'Can you prove it?' Harry bit into his bottom lip and shook his head. 'Why did you decide to come to me now?' Charlie asked.

'I'm at my wits' end. Business is terrible. I'm hardly able to make ends meet as it is, without having to stump up two hundred and fifty quid a week for the likes of McKay. I can't go on like that.'

'Before we could prosecute him, Harry, we'd need proof – and we'd need witnesses. Would you be prepared to take the stand and testify?' Brady nodded nervously. 'We'll need more than that to secure a conviction. If it comes down to your word against his, he'll walk. Do you know who else he's putting the squeeze on?'

'McKay and Hunter do their round on Tuesday afternoons. One day last month, after they'd been to my place, I followed them along Woodlands Road and I made a note of all the shops they went into.'

'In order to secure a conviction, we'd need at least one of those guys to take the stand and testify.'

'None of them will do it. I've tried talking to all of them. I did my level best to convince them that, if we all stick together, we could have McKay and Hunter put away. But they just clam up. They're scared shitless. Most of them won't even admit to having a problem with McKay. They claim not to know what I'm talking about. They're terrified because of Jack Williams.'

'What happened there?'

'Jack has the grocer's shop along the street from me. A couple of years back he decided he'd had enough of their demands, so he went to the local nick and filed a complaint. The cops pulled McKay and Hunter in for questioning and, while they were being interviewed, one of McKay's pals went round to Jack's place and slashed his face. Nice timing, eh? McKay and Hunter had the perfect alibi because Jack was cut up when they were being interviewed by the polis. The slasher warned Jack his wife would be next in line for the razor treatment, so he withdrew his complaint.'

'Is there any chance Williams could be persuaded to file a complaint against them again, if I put in place protection for him and his family?'

'I don't know, Charlie. He might go along with it if he was a hundred per cent sure they'd be put away. I'll sound him out, if you like?'

'Do that. If you and Williams are both willing to take the stand, I'll ask the Procurator Fiscal if he'd be prepared to prosecute on that basis. Once you've spoken to Williams, give me a bell and let me know what the score is. That number will get you straight through to me,' Charlie said, taking a card from the breast pocket of his jacket and handing it across.

'Okay, Charlie,' Brady said, getting to his feet.

'And don't worry, Harry,' Charlie said, standing up. 'If Williams won't play ball, we'll find some other way to deal with them.'

Light rain was falling when Charlie drove up the ramp out of Pitt Street's underground car park. Flicking his windscreen wipers on to an intermittent wipe, he turned into West George Street, then made his way down the hill to Waterloo Street to join the Clydeside Expressway. The early-evening commuter traffic was heavy when he joined the M8 and progress was slow all the way to the Renfrew exit. Taking the slip road, he drove towards the town centre, then turned left in front of the town hall into Hairst Street. He spotted a vacant parking bay outside Auld's the bakers and pulled into it. Turning his jacket collar up to protect his neck from the drizzle, he hurried the short distance to James Davidson's. When he went inside he saw Bert Pollock leaning against the bar, chatting to the barman. The pub was quiet, the only other customers being two men playing darts and four students sitting at a corner table, arguing heatedly about football.

Bert was bemoaning the latest tax increase on cigarettes when his flow was interrupted by the sound of the pub door being pushed open.

'Not too bad, I suppose,' he said, glancing at his watch. 'I was just about to give you up. When I heard on the news that there'd been a murder in Port Glasgow yesterday, I wasn't sure if you'd manage to get away.'

'That makes two of us,' Charlie said, turning down his jacket collar.

'Glad you managed to make it, you old bugger,' Bert said. 'Would that be a hauf an' a hauf-pint, by any chance?'

'Good guess.'

'Two haufs and two hauf-pints of heavy, Tommy,' Bert said, taking a twenty pound note from his wallet and placing it on the bar. 'Okay if we sit over by the door?'

'If you can find room.'

Having poured the drinks, Tommy carried them across to the table where Charlie and Bert had installed themselves. He handed Bert his change.

'How's life treating you?' Charlie asked, picking up his beer and taking a sip.

'Business isn't great. I was saying to Tommy just before you got here that the latest tax increase on cigarettes has dented sales badly – and now there's talk about us having to keep the fags out of sight of the customers! What with that and newspaper sales being right down, it looks like I'll have to rely on selling sweeties to school kids in order to scrape a living.'

'You can put me down for a couple of packets of strong mints.'

'If I'd have known that, I'd have bought you a large one.' Bert picked up his whisky glass and chinked it against Charlie's.

Charlie raised his glass to eye level. 'Cheers!'

'Things going any better with Niggle these days?' Bert asked.

'What a poser!' Charlie shook his head. 'Yesterday was a case in point. The great and the good of Glasgow's media circus turned up for the weekly press conference and Niggle subjects them to a twenty minute monologue on the new procedures he's planning to introduce to improve crime reporting – which in essence boils down to: "take care of the stats and let the facts take care of themselves". And I had to sit through it all. After he'd succeeded in boring the arse off everyone, he opened the session up for questions and he was having a bit of back chat with a reporter from the Record when Fran Gibbons piped up.'

'The bit of stuff who fronts Newsnight?'

'I wouldn't recommend you to refer to her like that in her presence.'

'My brother calls her the Drinking Man's tottie.'

'Good to know political correctness is alive and well and living in Renfrew.' Charlie grinned. 'Anyway, Gibbons slips the knife in and more or less accuses Niggle of fiddling the sats. You should have seen his podgy kisser. It turned scarlet. He looked like a beetroot with a bad case of acne.'

'I can see why you can't stand him.'

'I'm sure the feeling's mutual.' Charlie threw back his whisky. 'I can't wait to pack it all in.'

'How much longer do you have?'

'Still the best part of a year. But at least I'll be on my bike before the big reorganisation takes place. That has the potential to be a complete shambles.'

'What's happening?'

'The current plan is to move the Glasgow CID headquarters from Pitt Street to a new building in the east end, in South Dalmarnock, but that's all up in the air because they're now talking about reorganising all the divisions into one unified Scottish police authority. The plan still needs parliamentary approval, but if it goes ahead there will be a lot fewer senior positions in the force in a couple of years' time – and that'll mean a real dogfight over who gets what.'

'You're well out of that,' Bert said, draining his beer.

'I'm sorry now I didn't take early retirement last year when it was on offer, but that's water under the bridge. Kay told me at the time I should jump ship, but, of course, I didn't listen to her.'

'How is Kay?'

'Couldn't be better. But that's because Sue and Jamie are coming back from Brussels tomorrow.'

'What were they doing over there?'

'Sue's best friend, Linda, is out there teaching. She broke her hip skiing in February, and she had no family to help her with her kids, so Sue took leave of absence for the spring term and got a job out there, teaching part-time, in the International School.'

'How did Jamie cope with that?'

'He took it in his stride, as you do when you're seven. It was all a big adventure for him. And he seems to have picked up a fair bit of French, which can't be bad.' Charlie finished his beer. 'Same again?' he asked, pointing at their empty glasses.

'I thought you'd never ask.'

Charlie carried the glasses over to the bar and ordered another round. 'So you heard about the murder?' he said as he came back to the table and sat down.

'It was on the news. Are you involved?'

Charlie lowered his voice to a whisper. 'A lot more than I'd like to be.'

'How come?'

Charlie kept his voice down. 'Did they mention on the news that the victim's hand had been chopped off?'

'Aye. Weird that.'

Charlie broke off as the barman brought across their drinks on a tray. 'Thanks, Tommy.' He waited until Tommy was out of earshot before continuing. 'What's even weirder is that the hand was sent to me.'

Bert froze with his beer glass halfway to his lips. 'What!'

'It was posted from St Vincent Street post office yesterday morning. Sent to CID headquarters in Pitt Street, addressed to me personally.'

Bert sucked in his breath. 'That must've pleased Niggle no end.'

'He was chuffed to buggery – as you might imagine.'

'What kind of weirdo would murder a harmless old woman? And why chop off her hand and send it to you?'

'Believe you me,' Charlie said, his fingers travelling over his bald skull. 'Those questions have been uppermost in my mind all day.' Picking up his whisky, he downed it in one.

*

Tony O'Sullivan pulled up outside the terraced row of council houses on the outskirts of Saltcoats. Getting out of his car, he walked up the overgrown path to number twenty-eight and rang the doorbell. His mother came to answer it.

'What a lovely surprise!' Dympna said, blessing herself quickly before standing on tiptoe to give Tony a big hug. 'Come on in, son.'

'Sorry I haven't been down for a while, Mum,' Tony said as he stepped across the threshold. 'I've been working a lot of overtime recently.'

'Will you be able to stay over?'

'I'm afraid not. It's just a flying visit. There's a lot going on and I have to get back to Glasgow tonight.'

'I understand. Can I get you something to eat?'

'No thanks, I'm fine.'

'How about a cup of tea?'

'That would be good.'

'Go on through and see your Dad while I put on the kettle. He's in the front room with his head buried in the paper, as usual. I don't know what he finds to read in it,' she added with a smile.

Tony walked along the narrow corridor under the intense scrutiny of St Anthony of Padua, staring down on him from the elevated shelf.

Rory O'Sullivan folded the Ardrossan and Saltcoats Herald and got to his feet when he heard Tony's voice. 'Good to see you, son,' he said as Tony came into the lounge.

Religious statues covered every available surface in the cramped living room, while framed photographs of Celtic's heroes over the years adorned the walls. In pride of place, above the mantelpiece, hung an autographed photograph of Jimmy Johnstone in full flight, nutmegging the Rangers' full back.

'You're looking well, Dad,' Tony said, sitting down on an armchair.

'Mustn't grumble,' Rory said, smoothing back his thinning, red hair as he settled back down on the settee. 'How are things in Glasgow?'

'Hell of a busy. We had another murder yesterday.'

'Who was it this time?' Rory asked.

'An old gypsy woman.'

'The world's going to hell in a handcart,' Rory said with a quick shake of the head. 'Are you involved in the case?'

'It looks like it.'

'Still working for that old curmudgeon, Anderson?'

'Most of the time.'

'At least it's better having him in charge, rather than one of the other lot.'

'That's true. Talking of the other lot, Matt Buller got promoted to DI last week.'

Rory snorted. 'I told you when you joined the Glasgow Division things like that would happen. Why don't you put in for a transfer?'

'I like living in Glasgow – and I'd hate to get transferred to Edinburgh.'

'You mark my words. As long as you stay in Glasgow, you'll have to suffer a succession of useless pillocks getting promoted ahead of you, just because their faithers are high up in the Lodge.'

'What are you two blethering about?' Dympna asked as she came into the living room carrying a tray stacked high with salmon sandwiches, fairy cakes and chocolate biscuits.

Charlie Anderson turned the key in his front door. 'It's just me, love!' he called up the stairs. 'Sorry I'm late.'

Kay appeared at the top of the staircase in her dressing gown and slippers; a petite figure with fine, chiselled features, the narrowness of her face giving emphasis to her large, turquoise eyes and long eyelashes. She walked down the stairs and, even standing on the bottom step, she had to stand on tiptoe to give Charlie a peck on the cheek. 'As I knew you were meeting Bert, I made stovies. I left yours in the oven. Are you hungry?'

'Famished.'

'I'm off to bed. Mind you don't burn yourself – and don't forget to turn the oven off.'

Charlie put on the kettle and made himself a pot of strong tea, which he used to wash down a large helping of stovies. When he'd finished eating, he went through to the lounge and switched on the top light. He crossed to the drinks cabinet to pour himself a hefty belt of Glenmorangie and carried his drink across to his favourite armchair in front of the unlit fire.

Blakey stirred in his basket. Standing up and stretching out all four paws, he padded across the room and jumped up onto the arm of the chair. From there, he stepped delicately onto Charlie's knees and turned in a full circle before curling up in Charlie's lap. Charlie took a sip of whisky as he scratched gently at the top of the cat's jet-black head. When he closed his eyes, Charlie's mind filled with the image of the amputated hand. He tried to think of all the people, over the years, who could be bearing a grudge against him. After a few minutes his tired brain gave up – there were too many possibilities.

When he'd finished his drink, he put his glass down on the coffee table and struggled to his feet, cradling Blakey in both arms. He carried the limp cat across the room and placed him down gently in his basket. Switching off the light, he tiptoed up the staircase and went to the bathroom to brush his teeth. When he eased open the bedroom door, he saw his bedside lamp was on. 'Are you still awake?' His whispered question was louder than he'd intended.

'Mmm…' the drowsy voice drawled.

Charlie stripped off his clothes and draped them over the chair at the bottom of the bed. Feeling under the pillow for his pyjamas, he pulled them on and got into bed. 'How was your day?' he asked quietly.

Kay rolled over onto her back and peered through half-open slits. 'I went across to Sue's place this afternoon and stocked up her fridge.'

'That was a nice idea.'

'I had a long chat with her on the phone this evening. Her flight's due in at four o'clock tomorrow afternoon. I offered to meet her and Jamie off the plane, but she insisted on getting a taxi to go home and drop off their cases, then she and Jamie are coming across here for dinner, so do try to get home at a respectable hour tomorrow, Charlie.'

'Nothing will get in the way of that.'

'How was work today?'

Charlie hesitated. 'So-so.'

'Did you manage to avoid getting involved in the Port Glasgow murder?' Charlie was on the point of responding, but the words died on his lips. He had never held back anything from Kay with regard to his work, but for some reason he couldn't bring himself to tell her about the amputated hand sent to him. 'Did you?' Kay said, yawning as she rolled over on her side to face the window.

'Not exactly, love. I'll tell you about it in the morning.' Charlie leaned across to switch off his bedside lamp. As soon as he closed his eyes, the image of an amputated hand filled his consciousness. It was floating in mid-air, blood spurting in all directions from the severed wrist. A nine of diamonds, attached to a blood-stained shoe box, was pulsing like a living organ in the background – and the bright-yellow smiley attached to the card was laughing its head off.

CHAPTER 3

In his heroin-induced dream, Pete Johnston was lying face down in the jungle, just beyond a clearing, his eyes tightly closed, his cheek pressing into the stinging, dank vegetation. His arms were stretched out above his head, his sweaty left palm grasping the barrel of a semi-automatic rifle while the index finger of his right hand twitched against the trigger. Excited, high-pitched voices were getting closer and he could hear what he assumed to be instructions being called out, although he couldn't understand the language. The perspiration of raw fear was streaming down his face. He bit hard into his bottom lip, trying to hold back the tears welling up in his eyes. The rhythmic slashing of the undergrowth being hacked away was pounding in his eardrums, getting louder and louder, closer and closer. When a swinging machete blade sliced through his left leg he let out an agonised scream. His bloodshot eyes jerked wide open. The room was in pitch darkness. He sat bolt upright on the settee, his head spinning, his heart thumping crazily against his rib cage.

It took Johnston a few moments to orient himself. He got to his feet slowly and limped to the bathroom to splash cold water onto his face. When he came back to the lounge, he switched on the top light and struck a match to light a cigarette. He picked the sheet of paper up from the floor and forced himself to concentrate on committing the information to memory. Sucking hard on the cigarette, he read the instructions three times, then closed his eyes and repeated them out loud. He struck another match and set the sheet of paper alight, holding it by the corner between thumb and forefinger until he felt the flames licking at his knuckles. He dropped the charred remnants into an ashtray and watched as the paper slowly curled and disintegrated.

Johnston stubbed his cigarette out among the black ashes and slapped his face hard with the palm of his hand. Tugging at the string on the brown-paper parcel, he burst the package open. Inside he found a thin, red anorak and a torch. He tried on the anorak. It fitted adequately, although the sleeves were too long, coming down almost to his fingertips. He bunched the sleeves up his arms and picked up the rail and ferry tickets from the settee, examining them to confirm they matched the instructions. He flicked on the flashlight to check it was working, the powerful beam reflecting glaringly from the low ceiling. Switching off the torch, he thrust it into the side pocket of the anorak.

Wednesday 22 June

Harry Brady pushed open his shop door and looked around the store disconsolately. The discussion with Jack Williams last night hadn't gone well. There was no way Jack was going to go to the police – and several whiskies in the The Halt Bar had done nothing to change his mind.

McKay and Hunter would be here on Saturday, demanding their five hundred quid – and the sum total of his takings so far this week was less than a hundred. Remembering what had happened to Jim McHugh, he knew he would have to do something.

As he was hanging up his jacket in the back shop, his eye caught the old cassette recorder on the top shelf. An idea suddenly came to him. He hadn't used the recorder in years. Was it still working? He lifted it down and checked that there was a cassette inside. When he pressed 'play', the tape didn't move. He flipped it over and opened the battery case. It was empty. He hurried through to the shop to get a pack of batteries. When he inserted them and pressed 'play', he heard the sounds of drunken singing at a long-forgotten party. He quickly rewound the cassette and depressed 'record', then counted from one to ten into the microphone. When he rewound the tape it played back perfectly. He took the cassette player across to the counter and placed it under the shelf. Depressing 'record', he walked to the other side of the shop and counted from eleven to twenty. That also played back clearly.

Harry broke out in a cold sweat at the thought of what McKay and Hunter would do to him if they sussed what he was up to. But he was going to get a kicking in any case when he didn't pay up, and if he managed to record what they said to him, it could be used in evidence. He realised he would be taking a hell of a risk, but if it resulted in those two bastards getting sent down, it would be worth it.

The tall, loose-limbed figure, dressed from head to toe in black – cord jacket, polo-neck sweater, cavalry twill trousers and casual shoes – slouched in the shop doorway opposite Pete Johnston's apartment block, his eyes fixed on the main entrance. A spent matchstick was in permanent motion as his tongue flicked it continuously from one side of his mouth to the other. The matchstick froze when he saw Johnston emerge from the building. He remained in the shadow of the doorway for a few moments before moving off in the same direction, on the opposite side of the street. The matchstick started flicking back and forth again rhythmically. He rarely glanced across, but he appreciated Johnston's red anorak – it made the task of following him a whole lot easier.

The morning rush hour had slackened off and the tube station was relatively quiet by the time Johnston descended to the platform. He boarded the train when it arrived, then changed to the Metropolitan line at Finchley Road. Alighting at Euston Square, he walked briskly to the main-line railway station. When he looked up at the station clock he saw he had fifteen minutes to spare before the Glasgow train was due to leave. He went across to a kiosk and bought a newspaper and a packet of cigarettes. Scanning the departures board, he found his platform number. He checked his ticket for his carriage number before climbing on board the train and making his way up the aisle until he came to his window seat.

The figure in black stood at the end of the platform and pulled out his mobile phone, clicking onto a number in his contacts' list. His call was answered on the first ring.

'It's Farrell.' He spoke urgently. 'I followed Johnston to Euston Station and he's got on the Glasgow train. What do you want me to do?' Chewing hard on his matchstick, he tapped his foot impatiently on the ground while he waited for instructions.

'Stay with him.'

Snapping his phone closed, Farrell hurried to board the train. He sought out the ticket collector and explained he hadn't had time to go to the ticket office to buy a ticket. He paid for his fare to Glasgow in cash.

As soon as the train was clear of the station, Johnston left his seat and made his way to the buffet car where he sat down at a narrow table. He started drinking heavily, alternating between miniatures of whisky and cans of lager. The combination of the alcohol and the rocking motion of the train made him feel drowsy. After two hours in the buffet car, he returned to his seat where he closed his eyes and drifted off to sleep.

Grey, lowering clouds were scudding across the heavy sky, driven by a gusting westerly wind. Sergeant Jerry Condron gnawed at the ragged quick of his thumbnail as he waited patiently for the tug to manoeuvre the stricken fishing boat onto its moorings.

The policeman glanced up when heard the Tobermory town hall clock chime noon. He used the back of his hand to wipe the stinging salt spray from his lips, then pulled his raincoat belt tight around his waist. Turning up his jacket collar to shield his neck from the wind, he watched while two coiled ropes were thrown ashore and lashed securely around the capstans. Condron tried, without success, to decipher the washed-out, Cyrillic script on the bow of the vessel bobbing low in the water.

As soon as the boat had been tied fast, a gangplank was swung into position and Condron weaved his way across, steadying himself on the rope handrail. A tall figure in green oilskins and wearing a black sou'wester was waiting to meet him.

Condron spoke slowly and deliberately. 'Do you speak English?'

'Speaking English – just a little.'

Condron took out his notebook. 'Are you the captain?'

He nodded. 'Captain?' he said, pointing to his chest. 'Yes. Me Captain.'

'What is your nationality?' The question was met with a puzzled frown. 'What country are you from?'

The captain gave a toothy grin. 'Russia,' he proclaimed proudly, indicating the shredded flag wrapped tightly round the flagpole.

'What's your name?'

'Bespalov – Roman Timofeivitch Bespalov.'

Not a lot of point in asking him to spell it, Condron thought to himself as he jotted down a rough approximation in his notebook. 'What brought you to these waters?'

Bespalov looked perplexed. 'Please?'

'Why are you here?' Condron spoke louder, pausing between words and directing each syllable directly at the captain's face, hoping volume and lip reading might aid comprehension. 'Why are you in Mull?' he mouthed slowly.

Bespalov nodded his understanding. 'Problem – engine.' To amplify his statement he pointed towards the hold with his left hand while drawing the horizontal fingers of his right hand sharply across his throat. 'Engine kaput!' he shouted dramatically. 'Mayday – yesterday night.'

'How many people on board?' Bespalov hesitated again. 'The crew? How many men?' Condron pointed towards a sailor and held up a hand as he counted out on his fingers. 'One... two... three... four...?'

Bespalov held up six fingers. 'Me – and five men,' he said. He waved towards the four sailors standing sullenly in line along the far side of the boat, then jabbed his thumb in the direction of the solitary figure leaning against the bulkhead.

'Papers? Do you have papers?'

'Papers, yes. Have papers.'

Condron waved towards the crew. 'Do any of them speak English?'

Bespalov shook his head and grinned, sticking out his chest proudly. 'Speak English – only me.'

'Okay. Now listen to me very carefully, captain. Everyone stays on board and I'll send someone to check your engines. Do you understand what I'm saying? No one's allowed to go ashore.'

'Stay here – fix engine – yes?'

Condron nodded. 'That's the ticket. I'll come back and see you later on when we know how serious the problem is.'

'Stay here – fix engine,' Bespalov repeated. 'I understand.'

As Condron turned to make his way back across the gangplank an animated babble of Russian broke out behind him.

Tony O'Sullivan was sitting at his desk, writing out a cheque, when Charlie Anderson wandered across.

'What are you doing for lunch?' Charlie asked.

'I'm going out,' Tony said, putting the cheque into a white envelope and sealing it before slipping it into his inside jacket pocket.

'Anywhere in particular?'

Tony hesitated. 'I was thinking of nipping across to Òran Mór.'

'I've never been there. I hear it's good. Okay if I join you?'

'Er... fine...'

'We can take my car.'

Charlie found a parking place in the middle of Dowanside Road and they walked from there, along Byres Road, past the multitude of coffee shops and delicatessens, to the junction with Great Western Road. Òran Mór stood on the corner, a modern pub occupying the building that had once been Kelvinside Parish Church

'They've done a nice job with the conversion,' Charlie commented as they climbed the stone steps and walked through the pub door.

'Probably not the kind of conversion the Church of Scotland had in mind when they had the place built,' Tony said. 'Do you think there's any chance the idea might catch on?'

'What do you mean?'

'How many churches do you reckon there are in Glasgow?'

'I haven't a clue.' Charlie scratched at the back of his bald head. 'There must be dozens of them.'

'Just imagine it – dozens of new pubs. All spacious – with plenty of room for discos. What is there not to like about that? I must remember to mention the idea to the Glasgow tourist board.'

'I'm looking forward to you selling the concept to the Wee Frees.'

Tony crossed to the bar while Charlie wandered across to look at the stained glass windows in one of the alcoves. Tony waved to the red-headed barmaid at the far end of the long counter. 'Hi, Kylie.'

Kylie came hurrying down, greeting Tony with a beaming smile. 'What will it be, Tony?'

'Before we order, would it be okay if we go upstairs for a minute? I'm with my boss', Tony said, indicating Charlie, who was still studying the stained glass windows. 'This is the first time he's been in and I'd like him to see the ceiling.'

'Go ahead. There's nothing going on upstairs right now.'

Tony waved Charlie across and led the way up the spiral staircase to the Auditorium. 'What do you think of that?' he asked, stepping aside to give Charlie a clear view of the roof.

'I've heard about this,' Charlie said, gazing up at the stunning depiction of the night sky. 'I've seen photographs of it in magazines, but they don't begin to do it justice. It's by Alasdair Gray, isn't it?'

Tony nodded. Charlie gazed up at the questions and statements interwoven into the design.

Where Are We From?
Rooted in Death's Republic.
What Are We?
Animals Who Want More Than We Need.
Where Are We Going?
Our Seed returns To Death.

'The man has an incredible talent,' Charlie said. 'They say *Lanark* is a classic. Apparently it took him more than thirty years to write it. I reckon it would take me at least that long to read it. I tried it a couple of times, but I could never get into it.'

'I started it a few years back, but I soon gave up,' Tony said. 'It was way beyond me.'

Tony led the way back down the staircase to the bar. 'I'll get them in,' he said. 'What are you for?'

'I always judge a pub by its Guinness.'

'The bar menus are on the tables,' Tony said, indicating an empty alcove.

Charlie sat down on the circular bench seat and studied the menu while Tony went over to the bar. Charlie noticed that Kylie again hurried the length of the bar to serve him. He wasn't close enough to pick up any of the conversation, but he recognized the tell-tale signals as Kylie was giggling away and Tony had a fixed grin on his face as she poured two pints of Guinness. While Tony was waiting for the drinks to settle, Charlie saw him take something from his inside jacket pocket and slide it across the bar. Kylie blew him an air kiss as she slipped the envelope into the hip pocket of her jeans.

'What do you fancy?' Tony asked, placing the drinks down on the table in front of Charlie and picking up a menu card.

'It doesn't take a genius to figure out what you fancy,' Charlie said. 'I'd hazard a guess at – mid-twenties, five feet six, cracking figure, shoulder-length red hair.'

Tony felt his freckles redden. 'This is my local. Kylie's just a friend.'

'I'm not cramping your style, am I?'

'I told you – she's just a friend. More the wife of a friend, actually. She's married to one of my old schoolpals, Patrick O'Connor.'

Charlie frowned. 'Would that be the Patrick O'Connor who was up in front of the beak last month for disrupting the Orange Order march in George Square?'

'He was demonstrating peacefully,' Tony said defensively.

'That wasn't how the judge saw it.'

'No suprise there.' Tony gave a shrug. 'What do you want to eat?' he asked.

'I can't remember the last time I had cullen skink,' Charlie said, closing the menu card. 'I think I'll give it a try. How about you?'

'I'll have the same.'

'Let me get these,' Charlie said, heaving himself to his feet. 'I wouldn't want your reputation ruined by being seen chatting up a married woman.'

Charlie crossed over to the bar where a barman took his order. Having paid for the food, he came back to the table.

'I didn't notice Mrs O'Connor sprinting half the length of the bar to serve me,' Charlie commented as he sat back down.

'Give it a break.'

'Well you might as well let Kylie know she won't be seeing a lot of you for the foreseeable future,' Charlie said. 'I've been lumbered with the SIO role for the gypsy's murder, so you can expect to be working all the hours God sends for however long it takes us to nail the bastard.'

Charlie broke off as the barman arrived with two bowls of cullen skink and two bread rolls on a tray. Placing the food down on the table in front of them, he handed them their cutlery, wrapped in paper napkins.

'I'm going to need you full-time on this case,' Charlie said as they were sipping at their hot soup, 'so hand over everything else you've got on your plate to McLaren and Dawson.'

'They won't be happy bunnies. They're both snowed under.'

'They're not paid to be happy. By the way,' Charlie added, 'Niggle's lumbered us with some wet behind the ears kid called Malcolm Stuart. Apparently he's been assigned to Glasgow from the Met for six months training. Niggle says he's a sharp cookie, but I'll be the judge of that. He's coming to see me at three o'clock this afternoon. If I don't like the look of him, I'll try to get shot of him. We can't afford to carry any passengers. But if we do get saddled, I want you to keep an eye on him. There may be nothing in it, but I suspect he might be Niggle's mole.'

When he got back to his office, Charlie stripped off his jacket and draped it over the back of his chair before rolling up his shirt sleeves and settling down to work his way through the pile of mail in his in-tray.

When he'd moved the last item to his out-basket, he slowly screwed the top back onto his fountain pen, his thoughts drifting back to Kay. Over breakfast, he'd been on the point of telling her about the amputated hand being sent to him, but he'd backed off at the last minute – he didn't really know why. Of course, he didn't want to worry her unduly, but this was the first time in his life he'd ever held anything back from her about his work.

A knock on the office door jolted Charlie out of his reverie. Glancing up at his wall clock, he saw it was exactly three o'clock. 'Come in!' he barked.

Charlie had been predisposed to dislike Malcolm Stuart, however, as he now eyed him up and down, he had to admit that first impressions were favourable. In his early twenties, Stuart was tall, slim and muscular, with high cheek bones and intelligent grey eyes, set wide apart. Clean-shaven, he had a square jaw and a deep dimple indented the point of his chin. His short hair was a mass of natural, tight blond curls. Although more casually dressed than Charlie would have advocated, his open-necked shirt was restrained, his jacket was fashionable, his trousers well cut and his brown shoes were highly polished. Most important of all, he'd arrived for his briefing on time.

Stuart crossed towards Charlie's desk. 'DC Malcolm Stuart,' he announced, proffering his hand. The voice was deep and resonant, the accent Home Counties. 'I've heard a lot about you, sir. It's a pleasure to get the opportunity to work with you.'

Charlie half stood up and leaned across the desk to take Stuart's hand. 'I'd hold back on the pleasure for the time being,' he said gruffly. 'Before too long you might be wishing our paths had never crossed.'

'Pleasure on hold, sir.' Stuart grinned fleetingly.

'Sergeant O'Sullivan will be joining us in a few minutes. He's handing over his current work assignments to his colleagues so we can focus full-time on the murder enquiry. By the way,' Charlie added, 'full-time means exactly what it says. Don't be making any plans to sample the local night life in the foreseeable future.'

'I've heard you drive hard, sir. Night life also on hold,' Stuart said with a disarming smile.

Charlie couldn't help but return the smile. 'Take a seat, son. Tell me a bit about yourself.' Charlie leaned back in his chair and swung his legs up onto his desk.

Stuart sat upright on the edge of the chair opposite. 'Originally from Sussex, sir. Twenty-four years old. I got a first in sociology and politics at LSE. I applied to join the Met last year. I went through basic training in London, graduated top of the class. I was assigned to Liverpool for the past six months for hands-on experience. A further six months is planned here, then back to London. My main outside interest is playing rugby. I had a couple of games last year for Harlequins' reserves, but my posting to Liverpool put paid to any prospects for this season.'

Charlie nodded his approval – confident, clear, factual, succinct. No arrogance or boastfulness in the tone, but no false modesty either. Despite his initial misgivings, Charlie was starting to warm to him.

'What position do you play?'

'Open side flanker.'

'That's a good Highland name you've got. Is there any Scottish blood in your family?'

'Though you'd never guess it from my accent, yes, sir. My mother's from Ayr. She moved south when she was pregnant with me.'

'And your father?'

Malcolm cast his eyes down. 'I never knew my Dad,' he said quietly. 'He died before I was born.'

'I'm sorry to hear that.'

'These things happen,' Malcolm said, looking back up.

'Does the SRU know about you?' Charlie asked. 'Scottish rugby needs all the help it can get.'

'That would be good,' Malcolm said with a wry smile. 'But I'm afraid I'm nowhere near international standard.'

Charlie swung his legs down and picked up a sheaf of papers from his desk. 'I'm going for a leak,' he said as he handed the papers across. 'Have a look through that lot while I'm away. It's the initial forensic report on Irene McGowan's murder. We'll get the full chapter and verse from the post mortem later today.'

Stuart was still studying the report when Charlie returned to the office a few minutes later. 'Sorry about that,' he said with a grunt as he sat down. 'When you get to my age, you'll know all about the joys of an enlarged prostate.'

When Tony O'Sullivan joined them, Charlie did the introductions.

'Malcolm's been assigned to us from the Met for six months, Tony. He's going to be working with us on the McGowan case.'

O'Sullivan took Stuart's hand in a firm grip. 'Good to have you on board, Malcolm. By the way, sir, here's the post mortem on Irene McGowan,' O'Sullivan said, placing a document on Charlie's desk. 'Hot off the press.'

'You'll get used to my style soon enough, Malcolm,' Charlie said. 'It involves interviewing, taking notes, fact-finding and data analysis. Tony'll tell you about it. It might drive you round the twist at times, but it gets results. Doesn't it, Tony?'

'Quite often – though it didn't get us very far with the Possilpark murder enquiry last month.'

'And Sergeant O'Sullivan's getting far too big for his boots because he knows he's only got to suffer me for a few more months. He wouldn't have dared make a crack like that a few years back. Have you heard of brainstorming, Malcolm?' Charlie asked.

'Basic training, sir. Day two.'

'Good. Let's summarise what we've got. Have you had a look at the post mortem, Tony?'

'I had a quick flick through.'

'What does it tell us?'

'Not a lot we don't know already. Irene McGowan was strangled in her caravan on Monday morning. There were no marks on her body to indicate that any kind of struggle took place before she was killed. Thumbs were driven into her windpipe by a powerful person, but there were no fingerprints on her neck or her throat – her attacker was almost certainly wearing gloves. There was no sexual assault involved. As you know, her left hand was amputated at the wrist – apparently sawn off using some kind of serrated blade.

'The victim's hand was sent here in a shoe box, Malcolm,' Tony explained. 'Addressed to Inspector Anderson.'

'Really?'

'If you want to see the evidence,' Charlie said, 'It's across in the mortuary. But I warn you, you'll need a strong stomach. What about Irene McGowan, Tony? What do we know about her?'

Tony referred to the report. 'Aged seventy-eight, gypsy lifestyle, never married. Her origins are obscure, but she's been travelling in caravans and vans for most of her life. She was shacked up with a bloke in a campsite near Perth for a long time, but she left him about twenty years ago. According to one of the old timers on the site, it was because of the repeated beatings he was dishing out. She has a son in his mid-forties. He lives somewhere in the Glasgow area, but the uniformed boys haven't managed to track him down yet. That's about it.'

'The sawn off hand – any ideas?' Charlie asked.

'Isn't cutting off a hand an Islamic punishment?' Tony suggested. 'For theft, or adultery, or something like that?'

Charlie raised a questioning eyebrow in Malcolm's direction. 'Any thoughts?'

'Chopping off a hand is certainly a method of Islamic punishment. But as far as I'm aware, it's used primarily as a deterrent. Seems pretty pointless trying to deter someone after you've strangled them.'

'Good point,' Charlie said, turning back to Tony. 'Love-fifteen, Tony. Still your service.'

'Are you not playing today, sir?'

'I thought I'd try my hand at umpiring for a change. You never know, I might get to like it.'

'Well, if ritual punishment's a non-starter,' Tony said, 'let's look at it from another angle. The murderer was taking a big risk going into the post office in St Vincent Street to send the parcel to you. One of the counter clerks might remember him – might be able to give us a description. To justify sticking his neck out that far, he must've been awfully keen for you to receive the dismembered hand. So what does he stand to gain?'

Charlie scratched at the tufts of hair on the nape of his neck. 'I have no idea.' He looked at Stuart. 'Malcolm?'

Malcolm sucked hard on his bottom lip and shook his head.

'And why the nine of diamonds and the smiley?' Tony asked. Malcolm looked puzzled. 'A playing card – the nine of diamonds, with a smiley emoticon attached, was stapled to the side of the shoe box,' Tony explained.

'Is there some significance?' Malcolm asked.

'The nine of diamonds is known as the Curse of Scotland,' Charlie stated.

'I've heard of that,' Malcolm said. 'If I remember right, the order to start the Glencoe Massacre was written on the playing card, wasn't it?'

'Good to know someone was paying attention in school,' Charlie said, looking pointedly at Tony. Tony raised his eyebrows. 'Okay,' Charlie continued. 'There's nothing to be gained by speculating at this stage. We need facts to work on. Let's pull together a plan of action. Tony, you and Malcolm go to St Vincent Street post office first thing tomorrow morning. I've checked – it's the same shift who were on duty on Monday. Talk to everyone. See if anyone can remember who handed in that parcel. Take the wrapping paper and the address label with you as a memory jogger.'

'I've a bit of a problem there, sir.' Malcolm spoke hesitantly.

'What kind of problem?'

'I'm supposed to be at an estate agent's in Byres Road at ten o'clock tomorrow morning to sign the lease for my apartment. Should I change the appointment?'

'No, there's no point postponing that. Life won't get any quieter around here over the next few days. You go ahead and get your flat sorted out. I'll get Colin Renton to go to the post office with Tony.'

Charlie stabbed at his intercom button. 'Pauline, try to find Renton and ask him to come to my office.' Charlie released the button. 'Check if the forensic boys managed to lift any prints from the shoe box, Tony, and see if they were able to identify where it came from. They should have established the make of the playing card by now, so find out who sells them. When you've done that, set up an incident room downstairs. I'll go down to the campsite in Port Glasgow this afternoon and see if I can dig up anything about Irene McGowan's background.'

DC Colin Renton stuck his head round the door. 'Pauline said you wanted to see me, sir?'

'I want you to go to the St Vincent Street post office with Tony tomorrow morning and help him interview the staff,' Charlie said.

Renton hesitated. 'I'm supposed to be doing a door-to-door on the Keppochhill rape tomorrow, sir.'

'Any point to it?' Charlie asked.

Renton shook his head. 'We're just going through the motions.'

'Then forget it and give Tony a hand.'

Renton looked doubtful. 'Inspector Crawford won't be happy.'

'I'll square it with Barry. Any questions?' Charlie asked, pulling himself to his feet and stretching his spine. They all shook their heads. 'In which case, we'll meet back here at two o'clock tomorrow afternoon and pool what we've got.'

Pete Johnston was jolted awake by the shudder of the train rumbling to a halt in Glasgow Central station. He recalled little of the trip from London, having spent most of the journey semi-comatose. Although they'd arrived ten minutes behind schedule, he still had more than two hours to kill before his connection for Oban.

Johnston walked across the station concourse and out through the main entrance into Gordon Street. He bought an early edition of the Evening Times from a street vendor. 'How long does it take to walk to Queen Street Station?' he asked as he was being given his change.

'Ten minutes – max.'

'Will I pass any pubs on the way?'

'You'll see quite a few. Whether or not you pass them is up to you, pal.'

Johnston pushed open the door of The Drum and Monkey and looked around. The first thing that caught his eye was the motto printed in large gold letters on the wooden rail above the horseshoe-shaped bar: "*Beer is the looking glass of the mind*".

There were only a few early-evening customers, all clustered around the bar. He ordered a pint of lager and, while his drink was being poured, he made his way to the toilets. He went into a booth, locked the door, took off his anorak and sat down on the toilet seat. Rolling up the sleeve of his sweater, he took a syringe from his anorak

47

pocket and primed the plunger. Selecting a vein, he injected a fix.

When he went back to the bar he paid for his drink and carried it across to a table by the window. He flicked through the Evening Times as he sipped at his pint.

The man in black, sitting in the raised area at the other side of the bar, swallowed a mouthful of tonic water before replacing his well-chewed matchstick with a fresh one.

When Constable Glancy walked into Sergeant Condron's office at five o'clock, he found him putting the finishing touches to his report.

'What's the score on the boat's engines, Tosh?' Condron asked.

'It's nothing too serious, sir. Just a fractured fuel pipe. We might need to get a few bits and pieces from the mainland to fix it properly, but we should have it repaired by the morning. It's not clear what caused the problem – and it's a waste of time trying to get anything out of the crew, although apparently one of them speaks a bit of Spanish, if that's any help?'

Condron snorted. 'My Spanish is every bit as fluent as my Russian. Anyway,' he added, 'I don't think they're in the business of communicating. There's something fishy about that lot – and I'm not talking about the contents of their hold.'

'Sir?'

'Are you trying to tell me six professional fishermen couldn't diagnose a broken fuel pipe and patch it up at sea? Pull the other one. They're here for a reason.'

'Do you think they might be running drugs?'

'The recent glut of cocaine has to be coming from somewhere.' Condron shook his head. 'But they'd be taking a hell of a risk trying to smuggle anything in this way. They must realise we'll crawl all over their vessel. And there's not a lot of room to hide stuff on a boat that size. Have you checked their papers?'

'Everything seems to be in order. They were fishing in the North

Atlantic, in international waters, when their engines packed in. The north-westerly drove them down here and the coastguards sent out a tug when they picked up their Mayday.'

Condron got to his feet. 'Okay, Tosh. Organise a search of their boat. Give it a good going-over. Then get their fuel pipe patched up and send them packing as quickly as you can. I want twenty-four hour surveillance while they're in harbour, mind. I don't want any of that lot putting a foot ashore without me knowing about it.'

'Yes, sir.'

Charlie Anderson pulled up at the end of the rutted track and got out of his car. Turning up his jacket collar to protect his neck from the drizzle, he made his way across the muddy surface. As he approached the encampment, he noticed that the caravan nearest to the road was encircled in yellow, scene-of-crime tape.

A young girl was kneeling by the stream, washing up plates and cutlery. She got to her feet quickly when she saw Charlie. 'Dad!' she called out loudly before hurrying away.

An unshaven figure with a bushy, salt-and-pepper beard appeared in the doorway of the adjacent caravan. He clenched his pipe between his uneven teeth and sucked on it hard as he stood at the top of the steps, watching Charlie walk towards him. Taking the pipe from his mouth, he tapped it out against the side of the caravan, then folded his thick, tattooed arms across his chest.

'Who are you, and what do you want?'

Charlie produced his warrant card and held it up high as he picked his steps carefully across the sodden turf. 'DCI Anderson,' he called out. 'Glasgow CID. I'd like a word.'

The man waited until Charlie had reached the foot of his caravan steps before responding. 'I don't have any truck with the polis.'

'I'm investigating Irene McGowan's murder.'

'Your lot have been here all day – crawling all over Irene's caravan.'

'I know.'

'I've already given them a statement.'

'I realise that.'

'Why are you here pestering me? Do you think I killed Irene?'

'No. But I'm hoping you might be able to help me find out who did.'

'I don't know any more than what's in my statement.'

Charlie huddled into his jacket. 'All the same, I would like to talk to you.'

The man held eye contact with Charlie for a few seconds, then nodded. Unfolding his arms, he stepped back into the caravan.

Charlie slipped his warrant card into his pocket and climbed up the iron steps. Standing inside the door, he shook the dampness from his jacket as he took out his notebook and pen. 'Your name is – ?' he asked.

'Carter. Archie Carter,' he said, indicating a seat for Charlie beside the single bed.

Charlie eased himself down onto the rickety chair. 'It was you who found Irene McGowan's body?'

'That's right.'

'Is your caravan the nearest one to hers?'

Carter gave a dismissive shake of the head. 'Was it your razor sharp powers of observation that got you to the rank of DCI?'

The pen slacked in Charlie's grip. He fixed Carter with a glare. 'How long had you known Irene McGowan?' he asked, gripping his pen tightly again and casting his eyes down to his notebook.

'Since she first came here.'

'Which was?'

'Must be the best part of twenty years ago.'

'Where was she before that?'

'No idea. Unlike the polis, I don't ask a lot of nosy questions.'

Charlie looked up again quickly. 'I can do without the smart-alec crap. Just answer the questions. When did you last see Irene McGowan alive?'

'On Sunday night. I saw her round the back of her caravan about nine o'clock. She was feeding her dog, but I didn't speak to her.'

'Tell me what happened on Monday morning.'

'I was making porridge when I heard a car pull up on the road, on the other side of Irene's caravan.'

'What make of car was it?'

Carter shrugged. 'I didn't get a good look at it. Anyway, I know bugger all about cars.'

'Did you see what colour it was?'

'A dark colour – it might've been black.'

'What time was that?'

'About eight o'clock.'

'Did you not think it strange that someone would come to visit Irene that early?'

'Her boy dropped in to see her from time to time and when he did, it was usually early in the morning, so I didn't think anything of it.'

'Did you see who got out of the car?'

'I looked out of the window and saw a man going over to Irene's caravan.'

'Did you recognise him?'

Carter shook his head. 'My eyesight isn't that great. I don't know her son that well. I only met him a couple of times. It could've been him, or it might've been somebody else.'

'Have you met the boy's father?'

'I don't even know who he is.'

'Did Irene ever talk about him?'

'Not to me.'

'So, it could've been him who came to see her?'

'It could've been. Or it could've been the Moderator of the General Assembly, for all I know.'

'How long did he stay?'

'Couldn't have been more than ten minutes. I heard the car driving off as I was putting on the kettle.'

'When did you first think something might be wrong?'

'About ten o'clock. Irene keeps her dog tied up outside at night during the summer months. Round about ten o'clock, Stella started barking – and she didn't stop. That was unusual, because she hardly ever barked. At first I thought Irene might've forgotten to feed her, but that didn't stack up because she doted on that dog. I thought she might be sick, or something, so I went across to check. I chapped on her door, but there was no answer. I tried the handle and it wasn't locked. When I went inside, I found her there – lying face down on her bed. There was blood everywhere.' Carter rubbed hard at his beard as he stared out of the window in the direction of Irene's caravan. 'Her hand had been chopped off,' he said in little more than a whisper.

'Can you tell me anything at all about the man who came to see her?'

'Not really, except he was quite tall. One thing I did notice,' Carter added, 'was he had a cap on with the peak at the back.'

The rain started coming down in large, steady droplets as Charlie was driving back to Pitt Street. He got tangled in the rush hour traffic and by the time he drove down the ramp to the underground car park it was after six o'clock. Hurrying up the staircase, he headed along the corridor, picking up a coffee from the vending machine on the way. When he went into his office, he found a grim-faced Colin Renton waiting for him. A boy, who couldn't have been more than ten or eleven, was standing by the window; jeans torn above the knee, dirty trainers split along the seams, spiky hair. His face was ashen.

'Who do we have here, Colin?'

'He doesn't appear to have a name, sir.'

'What's he doing here?'

'He brought you that.' Renton nodded towards Charlie's desk.

Charlie felt the bile rise in his stomach as he gazed down on the open shoe box. An amputated hand, lying palm down, the scarlet varnish of her splintered fingernails seemingly a perfect match for the coagulated blood adhering to the back of her hand. The solitaire diamond ring on her engagement finger sparkled brightly under the office strip lighting. Stapled to the side of the box, with a yellow smiley attached, was a nine of diamonds.

CHAPTER 4

'He handed that box into the reception desk ten minutes ago, sir.' Renton nodded towards the boy. 'I happened to be there at the time and I heard him tell the duty officer it was a present for you. He tried to run off, but I held onto him while the parcel was being checked out.'

'What does he have to say for himself?'

'The cat seems to have got his tongue.'

Charlie walked across the room and towered over the cowering youngster. 'What's your name, son?' The question was greeted with a stony silence. 'Where did you get that box?' All the remaining colour drained from the boy's face and he sank his teeth into his quivering bottom lip. 'Did you have anything to do with this?'

Panic flashed in the boy's eyes. His whole body started trembling. 'It husny got anythin' tae dae wi' me, mister,' he yelped. 'I don't know nuthin' aboot it.' Tears started coursing down his cheeks.

'Where did you get the shoe box, then?' Charlie's tone was calm and conciliatory. 'Tell me where you got it and why you brought it here.'

'A man telt me tae dae it, mister,' he whimpered.

'What man?'

'I don't know. Jist a man – in Sauchiehall Street. He gave me a fiver. He telt me tae bring the box here an' say it wis fur Inspector Anderson. I didny know whit wis in it, honest.' The words were jerked out between huge sobs. 'He telt me tae say it wis a present.'

'What did the man look like?' The boy shook his head.

'Tall or short?'

'Quite big.'

'What was he wearing?'

'I don't know.'

'You must remember something about him.'

'He had sunglasses on.'

'Sunglasses? It's pissing down out there, son. Why would he be wearing sunglasses?'

'I don't know. It wis thae shiny blue wans. The kind you canny see his eyes through.'

'What was he wearing?'

'He had a cap on – a baseball cap – on backwards.'

'What else?'

The boy again bit hard into his swollen bottom lip, drawing blood. He shook his head. 'I don't know.' Burying his head in his hands, he started to wail.

Charlie spoke quietly to Renton. 'Get his name and address out of him, Colin. Arrange for someone to take him home and tell his parents what happened. We'll have him back in later to make a statement and work on an e-fit picture, once he's got over the shock.'

As Renton was leaving with the boy, Charlie pressed his intercom button. 'Pauline, find O'Sullivan and Stuart. Tell them I want to see them straight away.'

Charlie stared long and hard at the amputated hand. There was no doubt about it, the fingers had moved. The change was barely perceptible, but a lifetime of attention to detail told Charlie the fist had clenched ever so slightly in the past few minutes, probably, he surmised, due to the heat of the office drying out the blood and causing the skin to contract.

Tony was hurrying along the corridor towards Charlie's office when he met Malcolm approaching from the opposite direction. When they walked into the office together they found Charlie sitting with his feet up on the desk, his gaze locked on the shoe box.

'We've got another one, boys.' Charlie didn't deflect his stare.

Malcolm screwed up his eyes when he caught sight of the dismembered hand. 'Jesus wept!'

'Where in the name of God did that come from?' Tony asked.

'Some sick bastard paid a kid to bring it here. Told him to say it was a present for me.' Tony approached the desk tentatively to look at the contents of the box. 'When you've seen all you want to see,' Charlie said, 'cover it up.'

'The same killer?' Tony asked as he replaced the lid and sat down.

'Not much doubt about that. The same shoe box, the same nine of diamonds and the same yellow smiley,' Charlie said. 'And the same recipient for the dismembered hand,' he added grimly.

'Where do we go from here?' Malcolm asked.

'There must be a reason for the nine of diamonds', Charlie said. 'All I know about it is the standard folklore stuff. Do some digging on the Internet, Malcolm. Try and find out if it has any significance.'

'And why the smiley?' Tony asked.

'God only knows. And as it looks as if we have a serial killer on our hands, whether I like it or not, I'll have to involve Niggle's little protégé,' Charlie said with a dismissive shake of the head.

'Dr Mhairi Orr,' Tony said to Malcolm. 'She's a consultant psychologist who specialises in profiling techniques.'

'She's a wee lassie who looks to be about fifteen,' Charlie grunted, 'But apparently she's the world expert in tracking down serial killers because she got two university degrees and half a dozen letters after her name.'

'As you may gather, Malcolm,' Tony said with a grin, 'Inspector Anderson isn't completely sold on the value of criminal profiling.'

'Load of mumbo-jumbo as far as I'm concerned.'

'The Met have had a fair amount of success using profiling, sir.' Malcolm offered.

Charlie snorted. 'Catching criminals isn't some kind of psychological black art. What's required is the ability to structure data, analyse it methodically and apply a modicum of common sense. You don't need a couple of degrees and a string of letters after your name to do that. However, Niggle has mandated that his wee profiling expert has to be drafted in if there's any possibility of a serial killer operating on his patch, so we'll have to go through the motions, even though it will be a complete waste of time and money.' Charlie punched the button on his intercom. 'Pauline, I need a meeting with Doctor Orr. Try to set something up for tomorrow morning, if you can.'

'Do you want us to be there?' Tony asked.

Charlie shook his head. 'There's no point in all of us wasting our time. I'll handle little Miss Profiler while you and Malcolm – '

Charlie's flow was interrupted by the buzz of his intercom. He jabbed at the button. 'What is it?' he demanded testily.

'Duty officer here, sir. Sorry to disturb you, but news is coming in about a body being recovered from the Clyde, near the weir at Glasgow Green. Young girl – left hand amputated.'

'Do we know anything about her?' Charlie asked.

'Not so far, sir. We're trawling through the Mis Per files.'

Charlie released the intercom button without comment. He stared hard at the shoe box. It crossed his mind to call Niggle at home, but he decided against it.

Charlie's intercom buzzed again. 'Doctor Orr is free tomorrow morning, sir,' Pauline said. 'She can come to your office at nine o'clock.'

'Thanks, Pauline,' Charlie said. 'Tony, arrange for someone to take the box across to the mortuary so they can match the hand up with the young girl's corpse when it's brought in. Tell them I want the pathology report on my desk first thing in the morning. I'm going home now to see Sue and Jamie.'

Tony hesitated. 'I didn't realise they were back,' he said, trying to conceal a smile.

'They flew back today,' Charlie said. 'They're my daughter and my grandson, Malcolm,' he added, by way of explanation. 'They've been over in Brussels and I haven't seen either of them since February. I suggest both of you head off home and get some kip. For now, we'll stick to the plan for tomorrow morning. Tony will go with Colin Renton to St Vincent Street to interview the post office staff,

Malcolm will get the lease for his flat sorted out – and also see if he can find out anything more about the significance of the nine of diamonds on the Internet – and I'll have a meeting with the world expert in profiling. We'll meet back here at two o'clock and pool what we've got. Any questions?'

O'Sullivan and Stuart looked at each other and shook their heads. Scraping back their chairs, they got to their feet.

Having arranged with the duty officer to have the shoe box taken across to the mortuary, Tony walked down the steps to the car park with Malcolm.

'Where do you live, sir?' Malcolm asked.

'Wilton Street, if that means anything to you?'

'Not a lot.'

'It's not far from Great Western Road.'

'I haven't got my bearings yet. Is that anywhere near Roxburgh Street?'

'About half a mile away. Why?'

'That's where my flat is. If it's not too presumptuous, I was wondering if you might like to drop in for a nightcap? It'd have to be whisky, though – I haven't got anything else in.'

'It's never presumptuous to offer a Scotsman a whisky, Malcolm. Sounds like an excellent idea. You lead the way and I'll follow.'

'It might be better if you led the way. I'd probably get us lost.'

'No problem.'

Roman Timofeivitch Bespalov cooperated fully with the search of his vessel, instructing his men to remain on deck while Constable Glancy made a thorough search of the captain's cabin and the crew's quarters. Glancy then donned thigh-length waders and ploughed his way through the knee-deep fish sludging around in the hold, prodding and peering into every nook and cranny with the aid of a powerful flash lamp. He came across nothing untoward.

When he heard Charlie's car pull up outside, Jamie came sprinting out of the house and hurtled down the driveway. '*Bon soir, Papy! Comment allez-vous?*'

Charlie grabbed Jamie by the waist and swung him round and round until both of them were dizzy. 'We'll have none of that foreign gobbledegook around here, my lad. I want to hear you say: "It's a braw bricht, moonlicht nicht, the nicht".' Charlie put Jamie down on the path and ruffled his long, tousled hair. 'Do they not have any barbers in Brussels?'

'Come on in!' Jamie grabbed Charlie by the hand and tugged him up the path. 'Mum's dying to see you.'

As soon as Charlie walked through the front door, Sue threw her arms around him and held him close. 'What time do you call this to be coming home from your work, Detective Chief Inspector Anderson,' she whispered in his ear.

'Sorry I'm late, love,' Charlie called down the hall in the direction of the kitchen, his arms still wrapped around Sue. 'It was a right pig of a day.'

'Aren't they all?' Kay said, appearing at the kitchen door and wiping her hands on her pinafore.

'You're not wrong there. But today was even worse than usual.'

'What happened?' Sue asked.

'Don't start me! I'm not going to bore you by talking shop tonight. Is the champagne open yet?'

'I was waiting for you,' Kay said. 'But not for much longer,' she added, looking pointedly at her watch.

Charlie went through to the kitchen and took the champagne bottle from the fridge. Removing the foil from the neck of the bottle, he uncorked it with a loud bang.

'Did you miss Partick Thistle while you were away, Jamie?' Charlie asked.

'Yeah! But at least Sean sent me the programmes for all our home matches.'

'Not long now till the start of the new season,' Charlie said, lifting a flute from the drinks trolley. 'You and I must go to the first home game.' Holding the glass at an angle, he started to pour.

'It's against Dundee,' Jamie said excitedly. 'Is that all right Mum? Can I go?'

'Of course you can.' Sue smiled at Charlie.

'Could I tempt you?' Charlie asked, offering the glass to Sue.

'No, thanks, Dad. Still strictly TT.'

Charlie handed the glass to Kay.

'Would you like a tomato juice, Sue?' Kay asked.

'Yes, please.'

'I'll get it,' Kay said, heading towards for the kitchen. 'With Angostura bitters?' she called over her shoulder.

'Please.'

'How's Linda making out?' Charlie asked as he poured himself a glass.

'She's back on her feet now and she's well on the way to recovery,' Sue said.

'Do you have something to drink, Jamie?' Charlie asked.

'I've got an Irn Bru, Grandad.'

Coming back into the lounge, Kay handed Sue her tomato juice.

'Thanks, Mum.'

'Cheers!' Charlie said, raising his glass and chinking it against everyone else's in turn. 'Welcome home.'

'I'll leave you two to catch up,' Kay said, 'while I finish fixing dinner.'

When Charlie settled himself on the settee, Sue came across to sit down beside him. 'Jamie,' she said, 'Be an angel and go and see if Grandma needs any help.' She waited until Jamie had trotted out of the room. 'How are you, Dad?' she asked quietly.

'I'm fine,' Charlie said, taking a long, slow swig from his glass.

'You look tired.'

'Och, that's just old age catching up with me.'

'Mum says you've been working all the hours God sends.'

'I do have a lot on my plate right now.'

'Don't overdo it,' Sue said, leaning across and planting a tender kiss on the top of Charlie's bald head. 'You do realise Jamie will be expecting you to play football with him every day when you retire?'

'I'll be fine,' Charlie said with a smile. Gulping down a mouthful of champagne, he reached for the bottle to top up his glass.

'It's just me!' Mhairi Orr called out as she turned the key in her apartment door. Stretching up to hang her jacket on the hallstand, she kicked off her high heels.

'I'm in the kitchen!' came echoing down the hall.

When Mhairi appeared in the doorway, Rachel stopped unloading the dishwasher and came over to give her a peck on the cheek and a quick cuddle. 'How was your day?' Rachel asked.

'Everything was going fine – until a couple of hours ago.'

'What happened?'

'I got a call from DCI Anderson's secretary. He wants to see me tomorrow.'

'Oh, my God!' Rachel clasped her hands to her mouth. 'It wasn't me who shopped you for doing fifty along Great Western Road last Saturday. Honestly!'

Mhairi smiled. 'He's the one I told you about. Old Luddite Anderson.'

'Wasn't he the guy who gave you a hard time at the police seminar last year?'

'It wasn't so much a hard time. It was more a case of him rubbishing the very idea of criminal profiling, with a hefty dollop of cynicism ladled on top. The seminar was supposed to be an education session for me to bring the Glasgow CID up to speed with the improvements offered by HOLMES 2 and – '

Rachel held up a hand. 'Remind me?' she interjected.

'Home Office Large Major Enquiry System.'

'I knew that. I was just testing you.'

'HOLMES 2 is a massive leap forward. It can link information databases, cross-reference them with witness statements and pinpoint repeat offenders. After the formal session, Superintendent Hamilton asked me to give a talk on how profiling techniques could be used in conjunction with HOLMES 2. So, you know, my computer module can compare a database of photographs against CCTV footage and highlight any matches. Tell me when you're getting bored'.

'About three sentences ago,' Rachel said, lifting two wine glasses from the dishwasher and holding them up.

'Talking about getting bored,' Mhairi said. 'Anderson sat throughout my session with a face like fizz. He spent most of the time staring out of the window. I don't think he took in a word I said. As far as he's concerned, the only Holmes worth the time of day is Sherlock. By his way of thinking, everything anyone needs to know about criminal detection techniques was covered on his basic training course sometime in the latter half of the nineteenth century. In the bar afterwards, one of the officers told me the uniformed boys call him Dino, after Fred Flintstone's dinosaur. Very appropriate.'

'Do you know why he wants to see you?'

'I can only imagine it's because he doesn't have any other option. Superintendent Hamilton is a big fan of profiling – and he's open to new ideas. After I gave my talk at the seminar he instructed everyone there to consult me if there was any suspicion of a serial killer operating on their patch.'

'A serial killer? Good grief! Don't tell me we've got one of those?'

'I caught the news headlines in the car on the way home. The body of a young girl was fished out of the Clyde earlier this evening – and her hand had been chopped off. I can only imagine the police have established some kind of link with the murder of the gypsy in Port Glasgow on Monday, where the victim's hand was also cut off.'

'Sounds like you could do with a drink,' Rachel said.

'Your mind-reading gets better every day.'

'Will that be small, medium or large, madam?' Rachel asked,

flourishing the bottle of New Zealand Sauvignon Blanc she'd taken from the fridge.

'Large – and keep them coming,' Mhairi said with a sigh as she flopped down on a chair.

The traffic was light and O'Sullivan and Stuart had no difficulty staying in convoy as they drove across the city, both of them finding parking spaces in Roxburgh Street, close to Malcolm's red sandstone tenement building.

'This is real class,' Tony commented, running his fingertips along the wall as they mounted the staircase. 'It's what's known as a wally close.'

'What's that when it's at home?'

'It refers to the tiles,' Tony explained. 'Only the classiest tenements have them. 'Très snob, as they say in Germany.'

When they reached the second-floor landing, Malcolm took out his keys and unlocked the glass-panelled front door, ushering Tony in ahead of him.

Tony let out a low whistle of appreciation as he admired the high, intricately-corniced ceiling in the lounge and the tasteful, modern furniture. 'Looks like you landed on your feet with this pad all right, my boy. I assume you rented it furnished?'

'You don't think I could afford this kind of stuff? I was really lucky. I was flicking through a brochure in an estate agent's office in Byres Road on Saturday morning when I overheard a bloke describing this place to an assistant. He wanted to rent it out, but he didn't want students who might damage his precious furniture. I introduced myself and told him I was looking for somewhere to rent in the area. He brought me round and showed me the place and I snapped it up straight away. I even sweet-talked him into letting me have a six month lease when he was after a minimum of a year.'

'Not just lucky – the gift of the Blarney to go with it.'

Malcolm smiled. 'I thought that would be more in your line, with a name like O'Sullivan. Do you have Irish blood?'

'You need to ask?' Tony said, tugging at his red hair.

'It's better than this,' Malcolm said, dragging his fingers through his tight, blond curls. 'Curly Top was one of the nicer things I had to put up with at school.'

'Red hair's never been an asset in this part of the world – especially not our line of work.'

Malcolm looked perplexed. 'What's the problem?'

'Red hair equates to Southern Irish, which equates to Catholic – and the Glasgow Division of the CID might as well be a branch of the Orange lodge as far as promotion prospects are concerned.'

'You've done all right for yourself.'

'I'd have been promoted to sergeant a year earlier if I'd kicked with the other foot.'

'You really think that?'

'I know it.'

'Did your parents come across from Ireland?' Malcolm asked.

'My family's been here a lot longer than that. My great-grandfather was involved in the Easter Rising, if that means anything to you?'

'The Irish Republican Brotherhood's occupation of the Dublin Post Office in 1916,' Malcolm said. 'And if I really wanted show off,' he added with a grin, 'I could tell you the uprising started on Easter Monday, the twenty-fourth of April.'

'How come you know so much about it?'

'I studied politics at LSE, and Irish political history was a major part of the syllabus. So what happened to your great-grandfather?'

'He was put on trial, convicted, and shipped across to England where he served seven years in Reading jail. There was a lot of acrimony within his family because his brother was opposed to the uprising. Relationships broke down to such an extent that his brother refused to speak to him, even after he got out of prison, so he decided not to go back to Ireland. He wasn't going to spend any more of his life in England, obviously, so he moved to Scotland. Our family has been in Saltcoats ever since. And the Irish connection's as strong as ever it was, 'cause my Dad married a girl from Donegal.'

'Do you go to Ireland much?'

'A couple of times a year. I've got so many cousins over there I can't remember half their names.'

Malcolm produced a bottle of Balvenie and two crystal tumblers. 'That's enough politics,' he said, pouring two generous measures. 'Would you like anything in it?'

'Do you have any ice?'

'Sorry! I haven't got round to filling the ice tray.'

'No problem. It's fine as it is.' Tony took a seat on a high-backed, leather armchair and held up his glass. 'Welcome to swinging Glasgow, Malcolm.' They chinked glasses and sipped at their drinks.

'What a start!' Malcolm said, collapsing onto the settee. 'After six months of pushing paper in Liverpool, I was hoping for a bit of action. But two mutilated corpses within forty-eight hours! This isn't normal, I hope?'

'We're never short of a murder or two around here. There was a brutal rape and stabbing in Possilpark last month. Charlie was in charge of that investigation, but we didn't get a result. And there were a couple of gangland killings not so long back. Fallout from a turf war, you know, drugs and that, but I wasn't involved in the case.'

'What's Charlie Anderson like to work for?' Malcolm asked.

Tony took a swallow of whisky. 'Dino? He's a hard taskmaster, and no mistake – though his bark's a lot worse than his bite. He's very old-fashioned. As you can guess from the nickname. And you heard this afternoon what he thinks of profiling.'

'It sounded to me more like a sexist attack on the profiling expert.'

'I wouldn't call him sexist, actually – "ageist", perhaps, or maybe that should be "youngist". He puts a lot more store by experience than modern theory. And he's dead set in his ways. He still takes down all his notes in shorthand. Computers scare him shitless. We're supposed to handle our correspondence on our terminals, but Charlie refuses to even switch his on. He gets Pauline to print out his emails and he hand-writes his replies in the margins, which she then sends out from his email account. If Niggle knew what was going on he'd go ballistic. And Charlie's a real stickler for detail,' Tony added. 'He'll drive you nuts going over the same ground again and again until he uncovers *The Key Question*, as he calls it. If you haven't heard that phrase yet, you will. Charlie's theory is that if you analyse data to death, you'll find a vital clue. There's no denying he's had his successes, but there've been a few occasions recently when we've spent half the night brainstorming to no avail.'

Malcolm uncorked the whisky bottle and topped up both their glasses.

'Who are they?' Tony asked, pointing to the two framed photos that were standing side by side on the coffee table.

'The women in my life. This is my mother,' Malcolm said, lifting up one of the photos and handing it across.

'Is the other one your girlfriend?'

'My sister.'

'Even better!' Tony said, picking up the photo. 'When is she coming up to Glasgow? I'm looking forward to showing her around.'

'Too late.' Malcolm smiled. 'She's engaged.'

'You can't win 'em all,' Tony said with an exaggerated sigh. 'You got a girlfriend?'

'There've been a few over the years, nothing serious. I move around a lot.'

'First time in Glasgow?' Tony asked, taking a sip of whisky.

'No, I've been here a few times. As I was telling Charlie earlier, I'm more Scottish than English. Most of my relations live in Ayrshire.'

'But you ended up down south?'

'My Dad died before I was born.' Malcolm hesitated. 'And my mother wanted to get away from some painful memories, so she moved to Brighton to be close to her sister.'

'I'm sorry to hear that,' Tony said. 'Are you planning to visit your family while you're here?'

'The way Anderson was going on I'll be lucky to fit in a pint in the next few weeks, never mind see the relations.' Malcolm took a bigger sip of whisky than he'd intended, screwing up his face as he spluttered and choked. 'I'm not used to drinking this stuff neat,' he said with a grimace as he put his glass down on the coffee table.

Tony glanced at his watch. 'Christ, is that the time?' He got to his feet quickly and threw back the rest of his drink. 'I've got to hit the road. And by the way – a word of advice. When Charlie says we're meeting in his office at two o'clock tomorrow afternoon, he doesn't mean five past.'

'I gathered that.'

'Thanks for the drinks. You must come round to my place sometime and sample a few malts.'

'I'd like that.'

The train from Glasgow Queen Street pulled into Oban Station on schedule. Getting off the train, Pete Johnston asked a porter for directions to the Mull ferry, then walked the short distance along the quayside to board the waiting boat.

It was a clear, moonlit night with a flat calm sea, but Johnston was the only person who remained on deck throughout the crossing, all the other passengers having gone below deck to escape the chill in the evening air. Johnston lit a cigarette and leaned on the starboard rail as they headed across the Firth of Lorn. When they entered the Sound of Mull he could make out a large cluster of lights on the island, a long way to the north, but the street lights of Tobermory quickly vanished when the ferry turned in a gentle arc towards Craignure Bay, the smaller batch of twinkling lights of the town of Craignure shining ever more brightly as they approached the jetty.

Johnston's fellow passengers appeared on deck in dribs and drabs as the ferry was preparing to dock. A lot of them seemed to be acquainted; several bored, briefcase-clutching commuters returning from a late night in the office; four teenage girls giggling about the boys they'd met in the café in Oban while the attractive redhead, clearly the ringleader, was trying to get them to agree on a plausible excuse for having missed the earlier ferry; a group of boisterous youths, slightly the worse for wear from their visit to a mainland pub, arguing the merits of their respective football teams. There was a steady drone of conversation, interspersed with complaints about the so-called summer weather, while everyone waited for the ferry to tie up. Johnston avoided all eye contact. He was the first to disembark.

On leaving the harbour, Johnston saw a road sign indicating the direction for Salen. He tramped along the tarmacadamed surface and soon found himself beyond the limits of the street lighting. He reached into his anorak pocket and pulled out his torch but, when his eyes adjusted to the gloom, he realised there was no need for the flash lamp, the moon providing more than enough light to pick out the road ahead. There was only an occasional car using the road, but every time he heard an engine approaching, he stepped across the ditch at the side of the road and waited in the deep shadows of the tree-lined verge until the vehicle had passed.

Johnston made good time, coming across the sign for Drumairgh Cottage sooner than he expected. The tree-lined dirt path cut inland through the depths of the forest and, as he threaded his way along the rutted track, the dense foliage overhead soon obliterated the light of the moon.

Fishing in his pocket for his torch, he directed the beam low to illuminate the path in front of his feet. Progress was slow as he moved haltingly along the narrow, overgrown track. The path re-awakened memories of the Burmese jungle. He froze every time he heard an unexpected noise; an animal scurrying through the woods; the piercing hoot of an owl. A cold sweat broke out all over his body when he thought he heard someone approaching from behind. He spun round and the hairs on the back of his neck stood on end as the shadows danced crazily in the sweeping light of the torch.

Johnston's imagination was running riot. He heard a sharp, crackling noise. It sounded like a twig being snapped underfoot.

Convinced he was being followed, he switched off his torch, dropped to his knees, then stretched out full-length in the long, damp grass by the side of the path, his ears straining to detect the sound of footsteps. Rain started falling steadily. Large drops, not penetrating the dense tree cover, but pinging off the foliage high above his head, like the report of rifle fire. He lay prone for a long time, hardly daring to breathe, until he could stand the darkness no longer. Scrambling to his feet, he flicked on his torch. Strange shapes loomed in front of him and he heard many sounds he couldn't identify; unseen creatures shuffling and scuttling in the undergrowth.

Johnston tried to lick some moisture into his dehydrated lips while beads of clammy sweat dribbled down his cheeks. He forced himself to keep moving. The path seemed to go on forever and it was with an overwhelming sense of relief that he came across a tall, isolated barn by the side of the track. He switched off his torch and tried the handle on the door. It wasn't locked. He eased the door open and stepped inside. 'Is there anybody here?' he called out in a hoarse whisper.

There was no response. He flicked on his flash lamp and scanned the high-roofed building – completely empty apart from a stack of hay piled up against the far wall. Rain water, seeping through a corner of the roof, was running down the inside of the rusty, corrugated-iron wall. Johnston swept his torch at ground level through three hundred and sixty degrees, causing a startled rat to scurry out from a dark corner and scuttle for the sanctuary of the hay. If anything, it felt colder inside the barn than out. Johnston tugged the door closed behind him. Zipping his thin anorak up to his chin, he crossed to the pile of hay. He sat down with his back to the wall, facing the barn door. Although physically exhausted, his nerves were still jangling. His cold fingers struggled to light a cigarette. He switched off his torch and huddled, shivering, in the inky blackness, sucking hard on the cigarette cradled in both hands while staring at the barn door. He had no idea how long he would have to wait.

CHAPTER 5

Thursday 23 June

Roman Bespalov stood on deck, gazing at the lights of Tobermory while listening to the rhythmic sound of the water lapping gently against the hull. The moon appeared for a moment before disappearing again behind the high clouds drifting across the sky. He checked his watch, confirming it was two o'clock in the morning. Signalling to one of his crew, they descended together to the captain's cabin.

'*Ti uhodish, Roman*?'

'Speak in English, Dimitri. I want to practise for tonight.'

'Whatever you say.' Both of them spoke fluent English, Dimitri Ryleev with a strong, middle-European accent. 'What do you know about the courier?' Ryleev asked.

'His name's Pete Johnston. Salman told me he'd be wearing a red anorak – and he sent me a photo of him so I would be able to recognise him.'

'That was a good idea. You wouldn't want to be giving the case to the wrong guy,' Ryleev said with a toothy grin.

'According to Salman,' Bespalov said, 'Johnston's not very bright, but he uses him as a courier because he's an ex-soldier and he knows how to obey orders.'

A heavy wooden desk stood against the side wall of the cabin. Ryleev bent down and pressed a concealed button underneath the desk, causing a hidden drawer to slide open. He extracted a waterproof rucksack and opened it up to check the contents; a heavy, black attaché case, twenty-five centimetres square and five centimetres thick, with a sturdy metal handle and two combination locks; a set of handcuffs; a torch; a pair of jeans; a woollen sweater and a pair of slip-on shoes.

Bespalov removed his boots and socks, then stripped off his shirt and stepped out of his trousers. He took the wet-suit from the hanger behind the cabin door and pulled it on. Ryleev zipped up the rucksack, then held it up for Bespalov to slip his arms through the straps. Having fastened the retaining belt securely around his waist, Bespalov pulled on a pair of flippers and a face mask with a snorkel attached.

Ryleev walked round in front to make eye contact with Bespalov through his visor. 'Are you ready, Roman?' he mouthed. When Bespalov gave the thumbs up, Ryleev bent down and put his shoulder against the desk, pushing it away from the side of the cabin. Sliding back four retaining bolts, he opened a panel on the seaward side of the boat, just above the waterline.

Bespalov sat down on the edge and balanced there for a moment before lowering himself slowly, silently into the dark waters. Ryleev watched as Bespalov swam powerfully away from the boat and he followed the trail left by the snorkel until it was enveloped in darkness. Closing the side panel, he went back up on deck.

Bespalov crossed Tobermory Bay. By the intermittent light of the moon, he could make out the shape of Calve Island up ahead. He struck out in a slow, powerful crawl, swimming parallel to the coastline. When he was level with the northernmost tip of the island, he turned inland and made his way towards the shore. He crossed the narrow, stony beach, as far as the tree line, before shrugging off his rucksack. He took off his flippers, face mask and wet suit, then unzipped the rucksack and laid the contents out on the ground. Dressing quickly, he slipped the handcuffs into the hip pocket of his jeans and clipped the torch onto his belt. He hid the rucksack and his swimming gear behind a large boulder and covered them with broken branches and twigs. His chest was still heaving from the effort of swimming. He stretched out on his back on the shingle, breathing in and out slowly. When he'd given his lungs sufficient time to recover, he got to his feet, picked up the attaché case and clambered up through the trees. The ground levelled off when he reached the main road and he could see the lights of Tobermory illuminating the night sky to the north. Rain started pattering down as he walked south along the unlit road. He unclipped the flash lamp from his belt and switched the beam on and off at five second intervals. After a few hundred metres his signal was answered by a flash of headlights from a car parked just off the road.

Pete Johnston awoke with a start when the blinding beam from a powerful flash lamp exploded in his eyes. Instinctively, he tried to scramble to his feet, but his heel skidded in the soggy hay and he crashed down on his back on the barn floor.

'It's dangerous to fall asleep, my friend,' the deep voice from behind the torch intoned. 'You never know who might walk in on you.' The dazzling beam was directed straight at Johnston's face. He held his forearm up in front of his eyes to try to shield them from the glare.

'Who the fuck are you?' Johnston panted.

'I believe we have a rendezvous.'

'Why did you sneak up on me like that?'

'I didn't sneak up on you. I walked through the door. You were asleep.'

'Will you stop shining that bloody thing in my eyes.' Bespalov lowered the beam. As his pupils slowly dilated, Johnston could make out the shape of a tall figure. 'Are you the guy who's going to give me something to take to London?'

'That is correct.' Bespalov wedged his torch in the hay with the beam directed towards the barn roof. 'This is what you have to take back,' he said, holding up the attaché case. 'Come over here.'

As Johnston approached him, Bespalov tugged the handcuffs from his hip pocket and looped one cuff through the attaché case handle, snapping it closed.

'Are you right-handed or left-handed?' Bespalov asked.

'Right-handed. Why?'

Bespalov gripped Johnston's left hand and pushed his anorak sleeve up his arm. As he snapped the handcuff closed around Johnston's wrist, his eye caught the array of puncture marks on the inside of his forearm. He twisted Johnston's arm round and glared at him. 'None of that while you're carrying this case.'

Johnston jerked his arm away, gripping the handle of the case and feeling the weight of it tugging at his arm. 'What the hell's in here?' he asked.

'That, as I believe you say, is none of your fucking business.' Bespalov pulled Johnston's anorak sleeve back down over his hand, concealing the handcuffs.

'Is that why I was given an anorak that was too big for me?'

Bespalov ignored the question. 'Your friends in London have the keys for the handcuffs,' he stated. 'And I will send them the combination for the locks on the case. Do not, under any circumstances, tamper with the locks. Any attempt to open the case without the correct combination will result in a very nasty accident.'

'Don't get your knickers in a twist. I won't touch the bloody locks. You just make sure you send the combination to London and leave the rest to me.'

Bespalov bent down to pick up his torch. 'Let's go.'

The rain had eased off. Bespalov took the lead, directing the beam of his flashlight onto the muddy path while Johnston aimed his torch at Bespalov's heels and followed close behind. When they got to the main road, Bespalov turned to face Johnston. 'It'll be dawn in a couple of hours. By the time you've walked to Craignure you won't have long to wait for the ferry.'

The figure in black watched from the cover of the woods as the two men split up. He noticed that Johnston was carrying a briefcase. Flicking the matchstick from one side of his mouth to the other, he checked his watch. He knew there was no urgency to tail Johnston because he couldn't get off the island for another couple of hours, so he decided to follow Bespalov as he headed north, dropping further back when Bespalov started flashing his torch on and off at regular intervals. The twirling matchstick stopped and he froze in his tracks when he saw the answering headlights from a car parked just off the road.

From the deep shadow of the trees, he watched Bespalov climb into the back seat of the car. He made a note of the make of the vehicle and the registration number. He remained in the shadows until the car had disappeared from sight, then he spat out his chewed matchstick and started whistling softly as he backtracked in the direction of Craignure.

By the time Pete Johnston reached Craignure he was mentally drained and physically exhausted. He was wheezing badly and his left arm was aching from the weight of the case. Swollen, grey bags sagged beneath his bloodshot eyes. He sat down on a low, stone wall within sight of the jetty and tugged the packet of cigarettes from his anorak pocket. Tapping one out, he lit up and pulled on it hard as he watched the ferry being loaded. He was the last passenger to go on board. He was surprised at the number of people taking the early morning crossing to the mainland. He went below deck and managed to find a seat, hunching forward on the wooden bench, trying to take the weight of the case on his knees. When he still couldn't get comfortable, he tried leaning back in the seat, balancing the case on his chest and flexing the fingers of his left hand in an attempt to relieve the cramp in his wrist. Closing his eyes, he dozed intermittently throughout the crossing.

The figure in black popped a fresh matchstick into his mouth as he stood on deck, watching the squawking seagulls as they followed the boat.

Johnston made his way up on deck before the ferry docked. As soon as the gangplank was lowered into position, he walked across and made his way to the railway station where he boarded the waiting Glasgow train.

The train pulled out on schedule, but within a mile of the station it slowed down and came to a halt. Johnston rubbed at the grubby window with his anorak sleeve and peered out. He looked anxiously at his watch, knowing he didn't have a lot of time to get from Queen Street to Central Station to catch his connection to London. They had been stationary for about ten minutes when a young, uniformed railway employee came hurrying down the aisle. Johnston grabbed him by the arm.

'What's the hold-up?'

'Safety check on the line. Nothing for six months, now three in a fortnight.'

'How long are we going to be sitting here, for fucksake?'

'For as long as it takes, pal.' Tugging his arm free, he headed towards the rear of the compartment.

It was a further five minutes before the train moved off. Throughout the rest of the journey Johnston fidgeted in his seat, staring continually at his watch.

Sue Paterson was sitting at her kitchen table, pouring skimmed milk onto her bowl of muesli, when her mobile phone rang. She dragged a loose strand of hair away from her face and tucked it behind her ear as she took the call.

'Hi, Sue, it's Tony,' the caller said.

'How did you know I was back?'

'There's not much that escapes the attention of the Glasgow CID.'

'Apart from the odd murderer and rapist?'

'If that's the attitude you're going to take, I'll have you deported to Brussels.'

Sue laughed. 'How are you doing?'

'Pretty good. Hell of a busy, but what's new?'

'I assume Dad mentioned I was back?'

'He said he had to go home early last night because you and Jamie were coming round.'

'That was "early"?'

'Everything's relative.'

'What have you been up to since I left?'

'I've hardly had time to draw breath – working most weekends. However, if I remember correctly, we had a dinner date in February, which you cancelled at short notice because you were heading off to Brussels.'

'You have to admit it was a more original excuse than staying in to wash my hair.'

'I'll grant you that. Are you still on for dinner?'

'When were you thinking of?'

'How about tonight?'

'Tonight!'

'Why not?'

'I'm just back. I've hardly had time to unpack. Would the weekend not be better?'

'The way things are right now, I can't be sure of getting time off at the weekend. And if we make it tonight,' he added, 'that would save you the trouble of cooking a meal this evening.'

'A persuasive argument, indeed. But I don't know if I'd be able to organise a sitter for Jamie. And will we be able to get in somewhere at such short notice?'

'I happen to know where there's a table free.'

'Where?'

'At my place – at eight o'clock.'

'Will you be doing the cooking?'

'Certainly. My specialities are Italian and Indian.'

'I'm impressed.'

'Which do you prefer?'

'I like both – but with a slight preference for Italian.'

'Italian it is.'

'Hold on a minute! It all depends on whether or not I can get a sitter for Jamie. I'll call you back.'

Sue paged through her contacts and clicked onto Sarah's mobile number. 'Remember me?' she asked.

'The prodigal daughter returns! Great to hear from you, Sue. When did you get back?'

'Yesterday.'

'How was Brussels?'

'It was an interesting experience, but I'm glad to be home.'

'We must get together for a coffee soon so you can tell me all about it.'

'Sarah, I realise this is a bit of an imposition, but is there any chance you could babysit Jamie for me tonight?'

'Not a problem. Sean will be over the moon. He's dying to see Jamie. Plus, Sean got bunk beds last month so Jamie can sleep up top.'

'Are you sure Joe won't mind?'

'He's not here this week. He managed to wangle himself a works' jolly in Winchester.'

'Thanks a lot. I'll feed Jamie and drop him off at your place around seven-thirty, if that's okay?'

'Hey! Not so fast. You don't get off as easily as that. Who is he? Do I know him? Is he rich? What kind of car does he drive? Is he single? Is he divorced? How long have you been dating?'

Sue felt herself blush. 'It's nothing like that. It's just a guy I met before I went to Brussels. We seemed to hit it off and he just called me to invite me over to his place for dinner tonight.'

'He doesn't hang about! You've hardly been back in the country five minutes. And the invitation is to his place, is it?'

'It's nothing like that. I think he wants to impress me with his cooking.'

'Maybe that's not all he wants to impress you with.'

'Behave yourself!'

'He's probably going to buy a take-away and try to pass it off at his own cooking. That's the ploy Joe used to use to entice me round to his flat.'

'I don't think he's like that.'

'Don't kid yourself. They're all like that. Anyway, make the most of it. It's not every day you have a built-in babysitter who doesn't mind when – make that "if" – you get home. Mind you, I'll want to hear all about it when you come round to pick up Jamie tomorrow – every single, salacious detail.'

Sue was still smiling as she called Tony's mobile.

Charlie Anderson reversed between two concrete pillars into a tight bay in Pitt Street's underground car park. Checking his watch, he saw it was five to nine. He hurried up the stairs to his office and, as he was taking off his jacket, his eye caught the forensic report on top of the pile of papers in his in-tray. Sitting down, he slipped on his glasses and started to read:

The body recovered from Clyde at seven p.m. on Wednesday 22nd June appears to be that of twenty two year-old Zoe Catherine Taylor, who was reported missing by her mother, Helen Taylor, at ten a.m. that morning. The information provided by the mother included a description of a birth mark on her neck and distinctive butterfly tattoos on her shoulders, both of which match with the corpse. The victim was a trainee with Tracy & Blundell, a firm of accountants in West Regent Street. The cause of death was strangulation and a snapped spinal cord. The bruising around her neck and her splintered fingernails indicate a violent struggle took place prior to her death. The killer used a serrated blade to amputate her left hand at the wrist. The severed hand has not been recovered. One of her shoes, her handbag and her umbrella were found in a boathouse in Glasgow Green. Bloodstains were found on the boathouse floor and the blood group is being cross-checked. The time of death is estimated at between noon and three o'clock on the afternoon of Tuesday 21st June. We will have to wait for the autopsy for formal confirmation but the indications are that she had not been sexually assaulted.

Charlie flicked through the second page of the report, which included Zoe's address and information about her boyfriend, Ryan Ferrie. It stated that her mother had been informed that her daughter's body had been recovered from the Clyde and that her father, Sam Taylor, a long distance lorry driver, was en route from Germany and was expected back in Glasgow on the evening of Thursday 23rd June. Mrs Taylor had been requested to go to the city mortuary, together with her husband, on the morning of the 24th June to formally identify their daughter's body. The report went on to say that the police had not been able to trace Ryan Ferrie. Mrs Taylor had provided the address of the flat that Ferrie shared with Zoe and also the phone numbers for the flat and Ferrie's mobile – neither of which he was answering.

While he was reading, Charlie heard a tentative knock on his office door. 'Come in!' he called out, placing the report back in his in-tray.

Mhairi Orr eased open the door and stuck her head round. 'I'm Dr Orr, Inspector. Am I too early?'

'Not at all,' Charlie said, getting to his feet. 'Can I get you something to drink, doctor? Coffee? Tea?'

'Nothing for me, thanks.'

Mhairi put her briefcase down on the floor and slipped her jacket from her slim shoulders. Her short, brown hair was pulled back from her narrow face and held in position by a silver clasp. She was wearing a midnight-blue blouse that was a perfect match for her straight, knee-length skirt.

Charlie sat back down as Mhairi draped her jacket neatly over the back of the chair opposite his desk. Even in her high heels, he reckoned she couldn't be an inch over five feet tall.

'You wanted to see me, Inspector?' Mhairi said as she settled down on the chair.

'It looks like there could be a serial killer operating,' Charlie stated. 'And if that's the case, as you know, Superintendent Hamilton has issued instructions that you should be consulted. However,

I don't think you'll be able to contribute much at this stage as we have very little to go on.'

Mhairi moved forward onto the edge of her seat. 'What do you have?'

'On Monday morning, an elderly woman was murdered in a gypsy encampment on the outskirts of Port Glasgow. Her body was found in her caravan.'

'I read about that in the papers. Her hand had been cut off, I believe.'

Charlie nodded. 'What you didn't read in the press was that her amputated hand was sent from St Vincent Street post office on Monday morning, in a shoe box, addressed to me.'

Mhairi stretched down for her brief case and took out her iPad. 'I'll take notes as we go along, if that's all right,' she said, flipping back the cover of her tablet and balancing it on her knees.

'Are you aware that a young girl's body was recovered from the Clyde last night?' Charlie asked.

'I heard about that on the news. The report said that her hand had been cut off, too.'

'That's correct.'

'Apart from the fact that both victims had a hand amputated,' Mhairi asked, 'do you have any reason to believe the murders are connected?' She had her eyes cast down, tapping at her keypad as she spoke. 'Might it be possible that a different person carried out a copycat amputation when he, or she, read the press reports about the first victim?'

'Not in this case.' Charlie spoke emphatically. 'The second victim's hand was also sent here. A man gave a parcel to a kid in Sauchiehall Street and told him to bring it here and say it was a present for me. Both hands were delivered in identical shoe boxes, both shoe boxes had a playing card, the nine of diamonds, with a smiling emoticon attached, stapled to the side.' Mhairi glanced up quickly, frowning, before resuming typing. 'We'll need to wait for the post mortem for confirmation,' Charlie continued, 'but it's probable the same instrument was used to cut off both of the victims' hands – some kind of serrated blade. The fact that two murders have been committed – and both victims had their left hand amputated – has been reported in the press, but the information that the hands were sent here, in shoe boxes, addressed to me, with the nine of diamonds and the smiley, isn't in the public domain. There is no doubt that the same person committed both murders.'

Mhairi's fingers skated over her keypad, then she looked up. 'Have you been able to establish any connection between the victims?'

'Not so far. Irene McGowan, a seventy-eight year-old gypsy, was strangled. There appears to have been no physical assault prior to her being murdered. I've just seen the initial report on the second murder,' Charlie said, indicating the document on his desk. 'The victim there was a trainee accountant who worked in the city. It seems she was strangled and her neck was broken. As far as we're aware, there's nothing to link the two victims. Chalk and cheese, you might say.'

'And the only common factor in all this, Inspector – appears to be you?'

'So it would seem.' Charlie let out a sigh. 'Chalk, cheese – and Charlie Anderson.'

'Are there any precedents for this kind of attack?'

'Precedents?'

'Have there been any other murders in Glasgow recently where the killer amputated his victim's hand?'

'As far as I'm aware, there's been nothing like that, here or elsewhere.'

'What do you know about the assailant?'

'Very little. All we have are a couple of sketchy descriptions. The person who murdered Irene McGowan was tall – and he was wearing a cap, on backwards – and the man who gave Zoe Taylor's hand to a kid in Sauchiehall Street was wearing a baseball cap, on backwards.'

'And the same calling card each time, the nine of diamonds and a yellow smiley,' Mhairi said. 'Any idea what that might be about?'

'None at all.'

'He may be wearing the baseball cap because he wants to be noticed, which might mean he's egotistical to the extent of being arrogant. That may be part of his game.'

'What is his game?'

'I've no idea – but we need to find out quickly. I don't think he's finished playing.'

'You think he's liable to strike again?'

'Once serial killers get a taste for it, they rarely stop at two. But already, this is an unusual pattern.'

'In what way?'

'What we normally see with serial killers is a comparatively long interval between the first and second murders, then the attacks become more frequent as his self-confidence grows. But this guy has struck on consecutive days – Monday and Tuesday. He's a man in a hurry.'

'Where do you go from here?'

'My area of expertise is in building up a profile of the killer by analysing the nature of the crime and comparing it to the types of people who have committed similar offences in the past. In order to do that, I'll be looking for patterns in the motivation for the crimes.'

'Such as whether or not he's got a down on womankind because his mother didn't love him or his girlfriend gave him the shove?'

'A more targeted approach than that. Psychological gratification is the driver for most serial killers and usually a specific group is targeted, such as people of the same religion, ethnicity, sex or age group – and there is often sexual contact with the victims.'

'As far as we know, that doesn't appear to be the case.'

'Attention seeking is a prime motivational factor – and the method of killing is usually similar each time.'

'This guy's method of killing was more or less the same – and on both occasions the left hand was amputated, but I'm at a loss to see anything that would link his victims.'

'There must be a link – and that's what I want to establish. To that end, I'd like to see all the documentation you have on the murders: forensic reports, locations, method of attack, as well as the statements from the people who saw the killer, and also the background reports on the victims.'

'I can organise that for you.'

'I'd also like to see the case notes for all serious assaults perpetrated by males on females in the city in, say, the past five years – whether or not the criminal was caught.'

'Do you realise how much data you're talking about?'

'A lot, I would imagine.'

'A hell of a lot. What purpose will it serve?'

'Serial killers don't always start out as murderers. There's often a build-up. They might begin with assaults, perhaps migrate to rapes – and when that no longer does it for them, they up the ante. The cases I'll focus on are those where a female was attacked by a stranger – I think we can rule out domestics – and I'll include all the cases where there was a tendency towards exhibitionism. I'll run the data through my computer module and see if anything resembling a pattern emerges. However, from what we've got so far, Inspector,' Mhairi said, tapping her iPad screen, 'it would appear that the killer only really wants one person to notice. You. So I'd like you to compile a list of all the criminals who might consider they have a score to settle with you.'

'I'll have a go,' Charlie said, scratching at his bald head. 'But I'm warning you, it's going to be a long list.'

'If you could provide me with copies of all the relevant reports and case notes, I'll trawl through them and run a preliminary analysis this afternoon. I'll drop by tomorrow morning to pick up your list and cross-match it with the data to see if that throws up anything. If you need to contact me in the meantime,' Mhairi said, taking a business card from her briefcase and placing it on Charlie's desk, 'those are my home and my mobile numbers and also my office number.'

CHAPTER 6

By the time the train from Oban pulled into Queen Street Station, Pete Johnston had less than fifteen minutes to get to Glasgow Central to catch his connection. He hurried along the platform, across the concourse, and down the flight of stone steps into George Square. The pavement was crowded as he weaved his way down the side of the square and turned into St Vincent Street. He glanced longingly at The Drum and Monkey as he rounded the corner into Renfield Street, then broke into a trot as he crossed Gordon Street and hurried through the main entrance to Central Station.

Johnston stood with his right hand on his knee, bent almost double, breathing heavily as he scanned the large, electronic departures board, searching for the platform number for the twelve o'clock train to London. When he found it, he hurried to the platform. Having memorised his carriage and seat number, he saw he was in the second carriage from the ticket barrier. Clambering on board, he collapsed into his aisle seat in the middle of the compartment, panting for breath. He balanced the attaché case on his knees and leaned back in his seat, breathing in and out deeply as he heard the guard sound his whistle. He felt the shuddering motion as the train started to trundle forward.

Ten minutes out of Glasgow, a tall, bearded figure, carrying a small suitcase, came through the door from the rear compartment. Adjusting his black-framed spectacles, he tugged the peak of his baseball cap low over his eyes as he made his way up the aisle, swaying from side to side with the rocking motion of the train. When he was level with Johnston's seat, he barged into his shoulder.

'Go easy, mate,' Johnston said, holding out a steadying arm.

'Sorry!' Grabbing hold of Johnston's wrist, he thrust a folded slip of paper into his hand before moving on quickly towards the front of the carriage. With a puzzled frown, Johnston unfolded the note. The message was typed in capital letters.

INSTRUCTIONS FROM HASSAM SALMAN.
THERE'S BEEN A CHANGE OF PLAN.
FOLLOW ME TO THE TOILETS.
I HAVE THE KEYS FOR THE HANDCUFFS AND I WILL NOW TAKE CHARGE OF THE BRIEFCASE.

Johnston's eyes flicked up from the page, but the man had already disappeared from sight. His mind started to race. What was going on? Was this some kind of trick? Should he go after him? He licked hard at his lips and read the note again, trying to figure out what to do. How could it be a con? The man knew Hassam Salman's name. He knew about the briefcase and, if he had the keys for the handcuffs, surely it had to be genuine? Deciding he needed to find out what was going on, he stuffed the note into his anorak pocket and pulled himself to his feet, steadying himself with his right hand against the sides of the seats as he swayed his way up the aisle towards the front of the compartment. When he passed through the narrow corridor leading to the adjoining carriage, he saw the toilet door was swinging on its hinges.

'In here!' the insistent voice urged. 'Quickly.'

As soon as Johnston had lurched into the cubicle, the door was slammed shut and the bolt rammed home. There was barely room for both of them to stand upright in the cramped space. The man facing him was now wearing an ankle-length, black, plastic mackintosh and his hands were encased in thin rubber gloves. His baseball cap was twisted round backwards.

'What the hell's going on?' Johnston pulled the note from his pocket and waved it in the taller man's face. 'Who the hell are you and what's all this about a change of plan?'

'You got the message. You've to give me the case.'

Johnston glared at him. 'If I've to give you the case, mate, where are the keys for the fucking handcuffs?'

'I've got them here,' he said, reaching into his pocket. Johnston's bloodshot eyes went out on stalks when he saw the glint of steel and the startled look remained frozen to his features as the stiletto blade was plunged deep into the pit of his stomach. Johnston clawed at his bleeding paunch with his right hand. The blade was wrenched out and driven again and again into his guts, jets of warm, crimson blood splattering against the walls of the cubicle.

When Johnston tried desperately to twist away, the knife was pumped several times into his kidneys. Within seconds, he passed out. There was no room for him to fall to the ground and he slumped forward against the wash hand basin, blood still seeping from his wounds.

Propping the lifeless body in a sitting position on the toilet seat, the assailant took a thin hacksaw blade from his suitcase and used it to saw through Johnston's left wrist, the brittle bone splintering as a fountain of blood cascaded from the lanced arteries and spurted in all directions.

When he'd sawn through the wrist, he tugged off his blood-stained mackintosh and wrapped it around the severed hand. Taking a zip-up, plastic freezer bag from his suitcase, he inserted the still-oozing parcel, then sealed the freezer bag before placing it inside his case. He slid the handcuff over Johnston's dismembered wrist and placed the attaché case, with the handcuffs still attached, inside his case.

He checked his watch. The whole operation had taken less than four minutes – comfortably within his schedule. He picked up the note Johnston had dropped onto the cubicle floor and then went through Johnston's pockets methodically, removing all his possessions and his rail tickets, as well as the ticket stub for the Mull ferry. Tugging off his blood-soaked gloves, he dropped them into his suitcase. He took a long scarf from his case and wrapped it around his neck, using it to cover his nose and his mouth, then he twisted his baseball cap round and tugged the brim low over his eyes. He snapped his case closed and wrenched open the opaque toilet window to check where they were. As the train started slowing down on the approach to Motherwell station, he slid back the bolt on the cubicle door to the accompaniment of the complaining squeal as the engine's brakes started to be applied. Waiting until the train had come to a juddering stop, he picked up his case and stepped out into the corridor, pulling the toilet door closed behind him. He moved quickly through the forward compartment until he got to the far end of the carriage. Opening the door, he stepped down onto the platform and he kept his eyes cast down as he hurried towards the exit, his suitcase tucked firmly underneath his arm. Outside the station, he got into the back seat of a black Ford Focus that was waiting there.

'Did you get it?' the driver asked, as he accelerated away.

'Everything went according to plan.' When they were clear of the station, he carefully peeled off his false beard and removed his spectacles. Taking the attaché case from his suitcase, he slipped it under the passenger seat. 'You know where to drop me off?' he asked.

'Of course.'

The man in black, who had been sitting a few rows behind Johnston, had started to become concerned about the time Johnston was taking in the toilet. As the train rumbled to a halt in the station, he got out of his seat and made his way up the aisle. When he reached the corridor he saw a trickle of blood seeping from under the door of the nearest cubicle. He kicked hard on the toilet door and, as it swung open on its hinges, he was confronted with the gruesome sight. Swearing under his breath, he yanked the door closed and moved quickly up the train, following the trail of bloodstained footprints until they petered out near the open carriage door. He yanked on the communication cord before getting off the train. Hurrying towards the station entrance, he pulled his phone from his pocket and clicked onto a number. He spat out his matchstick as soon as the call was answered.

'This is Farrell,' he snapped. 'I need to speak to Kenicer – right now!'

'Hold on, I'll get him for you.'

'What's the problem?' Mitch Kenicer asked when he came to the phone.

'They got Johnston.'

'Fuck! Where?'

'On the train – at Motherwell Station.'

'The consignment?'

'Gone.'

'How the hell did they manage to get it?'

'They chopped his fucking hand off.'

'Shit! Where are you now?'

'I'm at the station.'

There was a brief pause. 'Are the police involved?'

'Not yet – but they will be soon.'

'Make yourself scarce. Call me later.' The connection was broken.

The guard, who had gone to investigate why the communication cord had been pulled, threw up when he opened the toilet door.

Mitch Kenicer made a call via a radio link to a fishing boat in the North Atlantic.

'What are you playing at?' he demanded.

'What seems to be the problem?' Roman Bespalov asked, a smile on his lips.

'You know very well what the problem is. Someone took out the courier on the train.'

'Did they really?'

'Who the fuck was it?'

'I suppose it must have been our Irish friends.'

'Which "Irish friends"?'

'The Fermanagh Freedom Fighters.'

Kenicer snorted. 'The FFF? How the hell would they be in a position to do that?'

'They bought the same information you did – for the same price. I can only assume they managed to organise something.'

'Our deal was that we would take care of Johnston and Salman when Johnson got back to London,' Kenicer snapped.

'Our deal was that I would provide you with the details of the Iraqis' courier, his itinerary and his schedule. We had no agreement about me not providing the same information to someone else.'

'For fuck's sake! Do the FFF have the combination to open the attaché case?'

'Not yet. But I agreed to sell it to them, if and when they managed to get their hands on the case.'

'You're a bastard, Bespalov!'

Bespalov laughed out loud. 'As a matter of fact, Kenicer, that happens to be correct.'

It was just after one o'clock when Charlie Anderson left Pitt Street by the main entrance and made his way down the hill, stretching and twisting his spine in a figure of eight as he went. The sun was struggling through the high clouds and he could feel the warmth on his face. When he got to the junction with Bath Street he pressed the button on the pedestrian crossing. Waiting until the traffic lights changed in his favour, he crossed the road and headed towards Sauchiehall Street, crowded with shoppers and office workers on their lunchtime break. He joined the queue outside Greggs' the bakers. No matter what time of day, there always seemed to be a queue. It reminded him of something he'd heard on a television programme recently – that in current Glasgow parlance: "Is there a queue at Greggs?" had replaced "Is the Pope a Catholic?" as a statement of the blindingly obvious.

The queue moved quickly – it always moved quickly. When he got to the counter he ordered a cheese and tomato sandwich on wholemeal bread and a bottle of mineral water.

Charlie munched on his sandwich as he walked along the pedestrianised stretch of Sauchiehall Street, mentally compiling a list of everyone who might consider they had a score to settle with him. A few obvious candidates immediately sprang to mind – guys he'd been instrumental in putting away for long jail terms. When he reached an intersection he dropped his sandwich wrapping paper into a waste paper bin and, as he turned the corner, his eye caught an off-licence. On a sudden impulse, he went in and bought a half-bottle of The Famous Grouse and on his way back to Pitt Street, he stopped off at a chemist's and picked up an aerosol of Gold Spot breath freshener.

Charlie collected a black coffee with extra sugar from the vending machine before heading along the corridor to his office. Closing the door behind him, he took a few sips of coffee, then unscrewed the cap from the bottle and tipped a generous measure of whisky into the plastic cup. Spinning the cap back on as he walked across to the metal filing cabinet by the window, he secreted the bottle behind the last hanging file in the bottom drawer.

Charlie turned round with a start when he heard the buzz of his intercom. Crossing to his desk, he pressed the button to make the connection.

'Pauline here, sir. Superintendent Hamilton would like to see you straight away.'

'Isn't this my lucky day?' Charlie muttered to himself. He took a few more sips of coffee before making his way along the corridor, stretching and twisting his neck in an attempt to ease the dull ache at the base of his spine. Glancing over his shoulder as he tramped up the flight of stairs, he took the Gold Spot from his pocket and surreptitiously sprayed it around the inside of his mouth.

When Charlie walked into the office, Hamilton was sitting with his back to him, working at his screen.

Charlie stood just inside the door. 'Pauline said you wanted to see me.'

Hamilton spun round in his swivel chair. 'What's this about another amputated hand being delivered here last night?'

'We don't have anything to go on at this stage.'

Hamilton brought his fist hammering down on the desk. 'Why wasn't I informed?'

'I didn't see any point in disturbing you at home.'

Hamilton's cheeks flushed. 'The Chief Constable phoned me at home last night,' he said, his voice reverting to its customary, measured delivery. 'As you may know, he's on holiday in Austria. He heard about a body being recovered from the Clyde on Sky News. He wanted to be briefed.' Hamilton's tone became the epitome of sanctimonious reasonableness. 'Now how am I supposed to brief the Chief when I haven't been informed that a second amputated hand was sent here yesterday?'

'I was waiting until we had something tangible before I got you involved.'

'How was it delivered?'

'In the same kind of shoe box as before. This time, a guy in Sauchiehall Street paid a kid to bring it here. He told him to say it was a present for me.'

'Which confirms that you're definitely the focal point for this nutter. Don't you have any idea who could be doing this?' Charlie shook his head. 'This is serial killer country, Anderson. You have to get Doctor Orr involved straight away. We need to use her profiling expertise.'

'She's involved already. I had a meeting with her this morning. She's going to analyse the data we have to see if she can come up with anything that looks like a pattern.'

Hamilton stood up and strode towards his office window, gazing out. Charlie recognised the signal that he was being dismissed. 'I need to be kept abreast of all developments,' Hamilton stated without turning round. 'Phone me at home as soon as anything breaks – any hour of the day or night.'

Charlie checked his watch as he trudged back down the stairs. Seeing it was almost two o'clock, he hurried to his office where he found O'Sullivan and Stuart waiting for him.

'Did you find out anything worthwhile in Port Glasgow, sir?' Tony asked.

Charlie took off his jacket and draped it over the back of his chair. 'I spoke to the last person to see Irene McGowan alive – apart from her murderer, that is. A guy called Archie Carter. He told me he saw a man going into Irene McGowan's caravan around eight o'clock on Monday morning.'

'Was he able to give you a description?' Malcolm asked.

'He only saw him from a distance – and his eyesight is dodgy at the best of times. The one thing he did notice was that the guy was wearing a cap, on backwards.' Charlie let out a heavy sigh. 'How did you make out at the post office, Tony?'

'I didn't actually get there.'

Charlie's brow furrowed. 'Why not?'

'It was weird. I'd arranged to meet Renton in St Vincent Street at half-past nine, but just before I set off from home I got a call on my mobile from Crosshouse Hospital in Kilmarnock – from a Doctor Wilson. He told me my Mum was in a coma after a hit and run.'

'Jesus – Tony...'

Tony held up a hand. 'She's fine, sir, she's fine. It's all been a –I don't really know. Doctor Wilson told me that a Mrs Dympna O'Sullivan had been brought into A&E, the victim of a hit and run accident, and she was in a coma. They'd got her name and address from the driving licence in her handbag, and they'd found her address book. My Dad's mobile was the first number in her book, but they hadn't been able to get in touch with him. I was the next "O'Sullivan" in her book, so they tried calling me. When I confirmed Dympna was my mother, the doctor asked me to come to the hospital as soon as I could. I phoned Renton and asked him to handle the post office interviews on his own, then I drove down to Kilmarnock like a bat out of hell. But – and this is the bizarre part – when I got to Crosshouse, there was no Doctor Wilson – and no record of my mother having been admitted to A&E. I got the receptionists to phone all the other hospitals in the area that had A&E departments, but no one knew anything about a hit and run accident. Then I called my Mum – and she told me she'd been at home all morning.'

'Any idea who could've been playing games?' Charlie asked.

'Not a clue,' Tony said.

'There are plenty of morons out there who get their kicks out of wasting police time,' Malcolm suggested.

Charlie shook his head in frustration. 'Did you at least get the lease for your flat sorted out, Malcolm?'

'No problem on that front, sir.'

'Did you find out anything about the significance of nine of diamonds?' Charlie asked.

'There's a lot about it on the Internet,' Malcolm said, 'but nothing that strikes me as being in any way useful. As you know, it's called 'The Curse of Scotland' because of the role it played in the Glencoe Massacre in 1692, and the ongoing feud between the McDonalds and the Campbells at the time.' Malcolm referred to the Wikipedia article he had printed out. 'The McDonalds had looted the Campbells' land and stolen their livestock, so, when the Campbells were billeted in Glencoe, ostensibly to collect taxes, they were out for revenge and they murdered thirty-eight members of the McDonald clan in their beds.

'There are two theories about the nine of diamonds. The popular one is that the order to carry out the massacre was written on the card itself, the other one is that the coat of arms of the Earl of Stair, the Scottish Secretary who ordered the massacre, bears a close resemblance to the nine of diamonds. But what connection either of those theories could have with the murder of an old woman and a young girl is beyond me.'

'I got the initial forensic report on the second victim this morning,' Charlie said indicating the document in his in-tray. 'This time it was a particularly violent attack, though there doesn't appear to have been a sexual motive.'

'Any chance of a DNA identification from the victim's body or her clothes?' Malcolm asked.

'We'll have to wait for the post mortem for confirmation, but as the body was in the Clyde for more than twenty-four hours, I wouldn't pin my hopes on it,' Charlie said. 'She shared a flat in Hill Street with her boyfriend, but the uniformed boys haven't managed to track him down yet. Handle this between you. Start by checking out her apartment. The report says her house keys were in her handbag, so you'll be able to pick them up from the mortuary. While I remember, Tony,' Charlie said, 'did the forensic boys manage to come up with anything on the shoe boxes?'

'Both as clean as a whistle. Identical boxes – Clark's, size nine, men's slippers – no fingerprints. I asked a salesman in the Sauchiehall Street branch if anyone had been in asking for old shoe boxes or buying up slippers in bulk. He took me out back and showed me the bins behind the shop. They were piled high with empty boxes waiting to be collected for recycling. Anyone could have helped themselves.'

'And the playing cards?'

'Bog standard. Literally dozens of outlets in the city.'

'Document everything you've got and send a copy to Doctor Orr,' Charlie said.

'How did your meeting with her go?' Malcolm asked.

'She seems a nice enough wee lassie – and very keen to help. She's gone off with a pile of data to analyse, but I wouldn't bet my pension on her coming up with anything worthwhile. We have to keep her in the loop, but first and foremost we need to – '

Colin Renton's rap on the door interrupted Charlie's flow.

'Any joy at the post office, Colin?' Charlie asked as Renton walked in.

'Not a lot, sir. I spoke to all the counter staff who were on duty on Monday morning, but no one remembers taking the parcel.'

'Hardly surprising,' Tony said. 'They must handle dozens of packages like that every day.'

Charlie's desk phone rang and he picked up.

'News just coming through from Motherwell Station, sir,' the duty officer said. 'A man has been murdered on the Glasgow to London train. His left hand has been cut off.'

CHAPTER 7

Charlie switched the phone to loudspeaker so the others could listen in. 'Could you please repeat what you just told me.'

'I said there's news coming in of a murder on the Glasgow to London train, sir. Someone pulled the communication cord while the train was standing in Motherwell Station and when the guard went to investigate, he found the victim – a middle-aged man – in a toilet cubicle. He'd been stabbed several times – and his left hand had been cut off at the wrist. The severed hand hasn't been found on the train.'

'Has he been identified?' Charlie asked.

'Not so far, sir.'

'What's happening now?'

'The three rear carriages of the train have been cordoned off until the forensic boys arrive and interviews are being organised in the station waiting room to take statements from all the passengers who were travelling in those carriages. We're also checking out the station CCTV footage to find out who got off the train.'

'Thanks for letting me know. Keep me posted on any developments.' Charlie cut the connection.

O'Sullivan, Stuart and Renton all looked at each other. It was Tony who broke the silence. 'Where do we go from here, sir?'

'We maintain focus. This murder may or may not be related to the others. There's been a lot of press coverage of the gory aspects of the first two murders, so we might have a copycat situation on our hands. For now, we'll stick to the plan. You and Malcolm go across to the mortuary and pick up Zoe Taylor's house keys. Check out her apartment and find the boyfriend. And Colin, I want you to get in touch with Central Station and find out if they have CCTV footage of the people getting on board that train. If they do, get it over here.'

When everyone had left his office, Charlie picked up his desk phone and called main reception. 'If anyone turns up at the front desk with a package for me, hold them there. And if a parcel arrives by post, addressed to me, let me know straight away.'

'Yes, sir.'

Charlie took Mhairi Orr's business card from his pocket and dialled her office number. She answered on the second ring. 'It's DCI Anderson, Doctor Orr.'

'I'm afraid I haven't got anything for you yet, Inspector,' Mhairi said. 'My module hasn't established any link between the two murder victims – nor has it come up with a significant probability that the murderer was associated with any of the other recent assaults.'

'You might have to update your system.'

'What's happened?'

'There's been another murder – and another hand amputation. But this time the victim was male.'

'When? And where?'

'This afternoon. On the Glasgow to London train, at Motherwell Station. A middle-aged man. The victim's left hand had been cut off – and the severed hand wasn't found on the train.'

'We can't be certain this is related. It might be a copycat.'

'That was my first reaction, but I dare say we'll know soon enough.'

'How?'

'I'll be waiting in for the postman,' Charlie said grimly.

Malcolm Stuart took the wheel and drove Tony O'Sullivan to Jocelyn Square, waiting in the car while Tony went into the mortuary to pick up Zoe Taylor's house keys. From there, they crossed the city to Hill Street where they found a parking spot not far from Zoe's tenement block. Tony led the way up the staircase. On the third floor landing they saw a name plate bearing the name Zoe Taylor in typed capitals, with Ryan Ferrie scrawled in pencil underneath. Tony pressed the bell push. There was no response. He rang twice more before using the house keys to unlock the door.

Moving slowly down the hall, Tony nudged the lounge door open with his toecap. There was no one there. When he pushed open the kitchen door he saw a man tied to an upright chair in the middle of the room. His head was slouched down on his chest, his swollen face a mass of bruises. His mouth was gagged with a tea towel, held in position by several strips of heavy-duty, adhesive tape lashed around his head. His dressing gown was caked with dried blood. Tony hurried across and felt his wrist. He thought he could detect a faint pulse.

'Call an ambulance, Malcolm,' Tony said. 'As quick as you can. I'll try to find a pair of scissors to cut this poor bugger free.'

Within ten minutes, three paramedics, carrying a stretcher, came running up the staircase. Having quickly examined Ferrie, they fitted an oxygen mask to his face before strapping him onto the stretcher.

'What do you reckon? Tony asked.

'He's not in good shape.'

'Where will you take him?' Tony asked.

'The Southern General. Are you guys coming with us?' one of the paramedics asked.

Tony turned to Malcolm. 'Assuming this is Ryan Ferrie, someone will have to be there to break the news to him about his girlfriend, if and when he comes round. No telling when that might be. There's no need for both of us to spend half the night hanging around the hospital. I can handle it on my own.'

'Are you sure?'

Tony nodded. 'Take the car. I won't need it.'

'How will you get back?'

'There's a rank outside the hospital. I can pick up a cab.'

The paramedics carried the stretcher down the tenement stair-case with Tony following close behind. As the stretcher was being loaded into the ambulance, Tony pulled out his phone and clicked onto Charlie's mobile number. 'We found a bloke in Zoe Taylor's apartment, sir,' Tony said when Charlie answered. 'I assume it's Ryan Ferrie. He was gagged and tied to a chair. He's in a bad way.'

'What happened to him?'

'It looks like he was assaulted in his own kitchen.'

'Is he conscious?'

'No, but there was a faint pulse. We called an ambulance and I'm on my way across to the Southern General with the paramedics right now.'

'Let me know how you get on.'

Malcolm Stuart drove back to Roxburgh Street and found a place to park not far from his flat. There was no knowing, he thought to himself as he got out of the car, when he would next get a night off. No point in wasting the opportunity.

Wandering down to the bottom of Byres Road, he went into the The Three Judges, on the corner of Dumbarton Road. There were only a handful of early-evening customers.

'What are you for?' the barman asked.

'A pint of lager.'

'Don't think I've seen you in here before,' the barman said, eyeing him up and down as he started to pull the pint.

'It's the first time I've been in,' Malcolm said.

'Doesn't sound like you come from around these parts.'

'Is that a problem?'

'Not a problem, pal.' The barman shrugged. 'I was only asking.'

'As it happens, I'm from Sussex.'

'Sussex?' The barman raised an eyebrow. 'That's a long way to come for a pint.' He slid the brimming glass across the bar. 'What brings you here?'

'What brings me to Glasgow? Or what brings me to The Three Judges?' Malcolm asked, placing a ten pound note on the bar.

The barman picked up the note and ostentatiously held it up to the light to study the watermark. 'Take the questions in whatever order you like.'

'A bit of business – and a hell of a thirst,' Malcolm said, lifting the glass to his lips and taking a long pull.

At half-past six Tony O'Sullivan was onto his third cup of watery coffee as he sat on a chair in the corridor outside the ward in the Southern General. He fiddled with his phone, trying to work out if it would be better to cancel his dinner date with Sue now, or leave it a bit longer in case he managed to get away in time. Probably best to give her a call and explain the situation, he decided. As he was scrolling through his contacts, he saw the doctor who had admitted Ryan Ferrie coming along the corridor. Tony got to his feet. 'What's the situation?' he asked.

'He's conscious and he seems all right mentally,' the doctor said, referring to his clipboard. 'But his nose is broken and his mouth's very badly lacerated.'

'Would it be possible for me to speak to him?'

'You can speak to him, but he won't be able to speak to you. His mouth's bandaged up. We've left a slit to assist his breathing, but he can't talk.'

'I'm afraid I have bad news for him.'

The doctor's brow furrowed. 'What kind of bad news?

'You heard about a girl's body being recovered from the Clyde yesterday?'

'Yes.'

'It was his girlfriend.' The doctor shook his head. 'Do you think I should break the news to him now?' Tony asked.

'That's your call, officer. I just patch them up. I'm not a psychologist.' He paused. 'But if you do decide he has to be told now, he's in the second bed on the left.'

Tony found Ryan Ferrie propped up in bed with two pillows jammed behind his back. He pulled the visitor's chair from beneath the bed and sat down. Ferrie half-turned round to make eye contact.

'Ryan Ferrie?' Tony asked, producing his warrant card and showing it to him. Ferrie nodded his head slowly. 'I'd like to ask you a few questions about what happened to you.' Ferrie shook his head as he gingerly fingered his bandaged mouth. 'Are you able to type?' Tony asked. Ferrie looked puzzled as Tony produced his cell phone and clicked onto text messaging. 'I ask the questions – you type the answers – okay?' Ferrie nodded his understanding and took the phone.

'When were you assaulted?' Tony asked.

"tue morning – 8 o'clock," he typed.

'Do you know who attacked you?'

"no – guy rang bell – barged-in – thing over face – bala?"

'A balaclava?'

Ferrie nodded. *"knocked me out – tied me to a chair."*

'Can you describe him?'

"over 6 feet – well built."

'What age?'

"never saw face."

'What about his voice. Did he have an accent?'

"normal Glasgow – like you and me."

Tony forbore to mention that he'd never heard Ferrie's accent. 'Do you know why he attacked you?'

"wanted me to set up mtg for him with zoe – my girl friend."

'Did you?'

"said he'd kill me if not – phoned zoe's office with msg for her –

meet me in boathouse at glasgow green half past twelve – told me to say that then gagged me – laid into me."

Ferrie pointed to the phone. *"my questions, now"* he typed.

Tony nodded. 'Go ahead.'

"did zoe meet him?"

'She did.' Tony made eye contact, shaking his head slowly from side to side.

"what happened?" Ferrie typed feverishly. *"what did he do to zoe?"* He thrust the phone in front of Tony's face and stared at him, wide-eyed. The colour flared in his face. His cheeks bulged.

'I'm very sorry to tell you this. I'm afraid Zoe's dead.'

Ferrie tugged at the bandages around his mouth and tried to speak, small, incoherent, gurgling sounds emanating from his throat. The phone slipped from his fingers onto the bed and his head slumped back onto the pillow.

Tony waited until he was outside the hospital before calling Charlie.

'Ferrie's life's not in danger, but he's been given a real working over.'

'Did you tell him what happened to his girlfriend?'

'Not in any detail, but I did let him know she was dead. I thought he ought to know.' There was silence at the other end of the line. 'Do you need me back in the office tonight, sir?'

'No, that's enough shit for one day. Working twenty-four hour shifts isn't going to get us anywhere. Is Stuart still with you?'

'No, I sent him home earlier.'

'We'll pick up the threads in the morning when we're all fresh – and when we might have some more information about the murder on the train to work on. We'll meet in my office at eight o'clock tomorrow morning. Okay?'

'Sure.'

'I'll give Stuart a call and let him know the arrangements,' Charlie said.

When Malcolm Stuart's mobile rang out unanswered, Charlie left a message, telling him to be in his office at eight o'clock the following morning.

Tony got into the taxi at the head of the rank outside the hospital and gave the driver his address. Checking his watch, he saw it was just after seven o'clock. Just about enough time to get dinner organised, he thought.

'Is this what's you call mood music?' Sue asked, having to raise her voice to make herself heard above the Proclaimers belting out "I would walk five hundred miles." Slipping her jacket from her shoulders, she handed it across.

'Sorry about that!' Tony said, hanging her jacket on the coat stand in the hall. 'The lounge is down there,' he said, pointing. Following Sue into the room, he crossed to the CD player and tweaked down the volume.

Sue produced a bottle of Sancerre and a bottle of Chateauneuf du Pape from her carrier bag. 'I didn't know if you'd prefer white or red.'

'I'm more than happy with either – but I thought you didn't drink?'

'I don't. But that doesn't mean other people shouldn't.'

'Let me stick the white wine in the fridge.'

When Tony came back from the kitchen he found Sue standing by the window, gazing down on the street.

'Tomato juice with Angostura bitters, if my memory serves me correctly?' he said, handing her a glass.

'Ten out of ten – I'm impressed. What are you drinking?'

'G and T,' he said, holding up his glass and chinking it against hers.

'Cheers!' Sue walked across the room and flopped down on the settee. She put her tomato juice down on a coaster on the coffee table. 'Tony, you mentioned on the phone that things are hectic at work these days.'

'There is a lot going on.'

'I hope you don't mind me asking this, but is my father all right?'

'What do you mean?'

'He looked really haggard last night – grey complexion and huge bags under his eyes. He looked as if he hadn't had a decent night's sleep in weeks.'

'He's working hard – and he's under a lot of pressure.'

'What kind of pressure?'

Tony hesitated. 'Did your father talk about his work last night?'

'Apart from the fact that he was very busy – no.'

'Look, Sue – this is something you need to discuss with him.'

'Sorry!' Sue held up both arms in a gesture of surrender. 'I didn't mean to drag you into family problems. Forget I even mentioned it.'

Tony sat down on the settee beside her. 'Tell me about Brussels. How did you get on over there?'

'It was all a bit frenetic, especially for the first couple of weeks. I hadn't fully realised what I had let myself in for. Compared with Dennistoun, the teaching side of it was a doddle. They have no idea what discipline problems are over there. But while Linda was in hospital, I was living in her flat and, in addition to my job, I had to shuttle her three kids – and Jamie – back and forth to school every day, as well as taking them to the hospital to visit their mum every evening – to say nothing of feeding, dressing and entertaining them. I was in a permanent state of exhaustion. It's difficult enough taking care of one kid, but four of them was an absolute nightmare. I don't know how large families cope.'

'It sounds like you could do with getting back to teaching in Dennistoun for a rest.'

'Things calmed down when Linda got out of hospital, even though she was still on crutches for quite some time.'

'How did Jamie settle in?'

'Oh, he was fine. He made a lot of new friends – and his French is coming on really well, considering he's only being doing it for three months. But I could tell he was getting homesick. For the past month his sole topic of conversation has been Partick Thistle's prospects for next season.'

'I didn't know he was a Thistle fan.'

'His grandfather's got him indoctrinated.'

A timer went off in the kitchen and Tony scrambled to his feet. 'I hope you're hungry.'

'I'm famished. My only worry is that my father will call you out before we get to the main course.'

'No way! My mobile's switched off – and I won't be answering the land line tonight.'

Sam Taylor changed down to second gear as he swung his lorry round to edge through the narrow gates of the depot. Somehow, the last few miles always seemed to be the worst, the traffic crossing the Kingston Bridge being particularly heavy this evening, and the incessant drizzle for the past two hours hadn't helped. He pulled up alongside an empty loading bay, then gave two toots on the horn as he reversed slowly until the rear of his vehicle was within touching distance of the ramp. He turned off his windscreen wipers and switched off the radio before cutting the engine and climbing down from the cab, yawning and stretching his stiff back.

A frown formed on his forehead when he looked across the yard. He was expecting Joe to be here to help him unload, but there were two people walking towards him, one of them wearing a police uniform. As they got closer, he saw it was a policewoman, then he suddenly realised the person alongside her was his wife.

Sam broke into a half-run as he stumbled across the yard towards them. 'What is it, Helen?' he called out. 'What's wrong?'

Helen Taylor stopped in her tracks and waited for him. 'It's Zoe,' she said in barely a whisper.

'What about her?'

'She's dead, Sam. She's been murdered.' Tears were flowing down Helen's cheeks. 'I couldn't tell you on the phone.' She was choking on her sobs. 'I just couldn't.'

Sam enveloped his wife in his arms and held her close, silent tears threading down from both his eyes.

The policewoman opened her mouth as if to speak, then turned round and walked slowly back in the direction of the office, leaving them to find whatever comfort they could in their mutual grief.

Sue held her stomach as she flopped down on the settee. 'I couldn't manage another bite. I didn't realise you could actually cook. That meal was fantastic.'

'I'm full of surprises.'

'Your spaghetti carbonara was to die for.'

'Not literally, I hope?'

Sue smiled. 'Where did you learn to do stuff like that?'

'From my mother. Somewhere in the dim and distant past she has Italian blood in her veins. I enjoy cooking, even though I get by most of the time on ready-made meals and take-aways. It's not a lot of fun cooking for one.'

'Did you really make that tiramisu?'

'Of course.'

'You're not joshing me? It wasn't from M&S?'

'How could you?' Tony affected a pained expression as he sat down beside her. 'It's dead easy,' he said, putting his wine glass and the half-full bottle of Chateauneaf du Pape down on the coffee table. 'You break sponge fingers into martini glasses and pour cooled espresso over them, then you mix mascarpone cheese, honey and Marsala in a bowl, add a beaten egg white and dollop the mixture over the sponge fingers. Stick them in the fridge for a few hours and dust them with cocoa powder before serving – et voilà!'

'My God – I'm never, ever going to cook for you!'

'I'm led to believe you do a mean chilli con carne.'

'I'm in the same boat as you where cooking's concerned. I make sure Jamie gets his five a day, but I'm not motivated to prepare anything fancy for myself. I used to enjoy messing about in the kitchen before Paul …' Sue's voice tailed off.

'Are you all right?'

'I'm fine,' she said, taking a tissue from her handbag and using it to wipe away the tear forming at the corner of her eye. 'It's the futility of it… Such a totally unnecessary loss of life,' she said, blowing her nose. 'Why was the other guy driving in that state? Why did Paul have to be on that particular stretch of road, at that particular time?'

Tony reached across and took her hand. 'It can't be easy for you having to bring Jamie up on your own.'

'Hey,' Sue said, pulling back her shoulders and sitting up straight. 'I didn't come here tonight for a counselling session. I came to enjoy myself.'

'How are you doing on that score?'

'So far,' she said, squeezing his fingers, 'so good.'

'Are you sure I couldn't tempt you?' Tony said, holding up the wine bottle.

'No thanks,' Sue said, dragging her hair away from her face and tucking it behind her ear.

Tony put the bottle back down on the coffee table. 'What time do you have to be back for the sitter?'

Sue shrugged. 'No time in particular. Jamie's on a sleepover.'

'A sleepover?' Tony nodded slowly. 'That sounds like a really nice idea,' he said, draining his wine glass.

'Remind me, what was that song you were singing along to when I arrived?' Sue asked.

'When you arrived? I think it must have been The Proclaimers.'

Sue snapped her fingers. 'Oh yes, I've got it.' Looking Tony straight in the eye, she started to sing softly: '"When I wake up, well I know I'm gonna be, I'm gonna be the man who wakes up next to you".'

Malcolm Stuart's pub crawl had taken him half the length of Byres Road, via The Aragon, Tennent's and Jinty McGinty's. It was after ten o'clock by the time he got to The Curlers, where he switched from pints of lager to rum and coke. The bar was crowded and noisy and the heat was making him feel queasy. He finished his drink quickly and went outside, breathing in the cool air deeply. He felt decidedly unsteady on his feet as crossed Byres Road at the pedestrian crossing and headed along Roxburgh Street towards his flat. Whistling an off-key version of "Swing Low, Sweet Chariot", he climbed the tenement staircase. He stood on his doormat, still whistling softly as he fumbled in his jacket pocket for his door keys. When he stretched out a hand to steady himself against the door he found himself stumbling forward as the door swung open on its hinges. He rocked back on his heels to try to regain his balance, the tune dying on his lips. He seemed to sober up instantly as a surge of adrenaline pulsed through his body. He shook his head, trying to clear it. Slipping his keys back into his pocket, he crossed the threshold silently. By the light shafting over his shoulder from the outside landing, he could see his CD player lying on the hall carpet, alongside a cardboard box crammed full of his compact discs. His ears strained to detect any sound.

Slipping off his shoes, he moved on tiptoe towards the lounge. He eased open the door and as soon as he took a step inside he was thumped violently from behind, between the shoulder blades. Staggering across the room, he tumbled head over heels over the back of the settee.

He quickly recovered his wind and scrambled to his feet, the sound of footsteps racing down the staircase ringing in his ears. He vaulted the settee and gave chase but by the time he got down to ground level there was no one in sight. He stood in the tenement entrance, hands on knees, panting for breath, as he gazed up and down the deserted street. Turning round, he plodded back up the stairs in his stocking soles. When he examined his front door he saw the lock had been forced with a jemmy.

CHAPTER 8

Friday 24 June

Charlie Anderson was in his office before half-past six in the morning. He had hardly slept a wink all night, tossing and turning in bed as he'd struggled to recall everyone who could possibly be bearing a grudge against him. He'd gone through all the names he could think of – there were dozens of them. He didn't know if some of them were alive or dead. Some he could eliminate because he knew they were still in prison, others he knew were back on the streets, but there were several instances where he didn't know if they'd been released yet. Something he'd have to check out.

He plucked a sheet of paper from the stack on his printer and placed it in the middle of the blotting pad on his desk. Taking his propelling pencil from his jacket pocket, he wound down the lead and started to compile his list.

Sue was lying on her back, eyes closed, breathing gently as Tony leaned with one elbow on the pillow and watched the rays of morning sunlight, filtering through a crack in the curtains, play on her long, blonde hair which was splayed across the pillow. Slipping from under the duvet, he pulled on his dressing gown and went to the kitchen.

'Breakfast's up!' Tony announced, nudging the bedroom door open with the tray he was carrying.

Sue stirred slowly and sat up in bed. 'What time is it?'

'Nearly seven o'clock.'

'That only counts as half a sleepover.' Sue yawned, stretching her arms high above her head.

'Some of us have work to go to. We don't all have the long, lazy summer holidays of part-time teachers.'

'Mmm… Something smells good.'

'I took a chance on freshly-squeezed orange juice, scrambled eggs with smoked salmon, wholemeal toast and coffee.'

'How did you know that's what I always have for breakfast on Fridays?'

Sue sat up straight in bed as Tony balanced the tray on her knees. He kissed her gently on the forehead. 'Tuck in. No need for you to rush. Take as long as you like over breakfast. There's plenty of hot water and there are clean towels on top of the laundry basket in the bathroom. Just pull the front door behind you when you go out.'

'What do you have planned for tonight?' Sue asked, taking a sip of orange juice.

'Not a lot. However, your father's liable to change that at a moment's notice.'

'If he doesn't, would you be prepared to slum it with chilli con carne?'

'I could be talked into that.'

'Let me give you my address. Do you have a piece of paper?' Tony fetched his notebook and pen from his jacket and handed them across. 'I should warn you,' Sue said as she was writing. 'There are strings attached.'

'You're mixing things up. That's not chilli con carne. It's probably haggis.'

'Very funny! The strings are called Jamie. Before we went off to Brussels, I told him you were an expert on Scottish football. He's got a memory like an elephant and he can't wait to test you out. He's prepared a list of questions already.'

'Any chance of a sneak preview?'

'Good grief! You mean – you'd be prepared to try to con a seven year-old?'

'You don't rise to the dizzy heights of Detective Sergeant in the Glasgow CID if you've got scruples.'

Tony waved across to Malcolm when he saw his car pull up alongside him in Pitt Street's underground car park.

'Did you have a quiet evening?' Tony asked as they were walking up the steps to the main building.

'Not exactly. I decided the opportunity for a Byres Road pub crawl was too good to miss.'

'Good decision. How did it go?'

'Fine – until I got home and found someone trying to burgle my flat.'

'You're joking!'

'If only. I disturbed him in the act and got a thump in the back for my trouble.'

'Did you not manage to nab him?'

Malcolm shook his head ruefully. 'He was far too quick for me. I'd have been hard pushed to lay a finger on him at the best of times, but in the state I was in last night, it was no contest. The bastard was off like greased lightning. The only consolation was that I interrupted him before he managed to nick any of my landlord's precious possessions.'

'Have you reported it to the police?' Tony asked with a grin.

'Of course! I called them straight away. Sergeant McPlod and his lanky sidekick came round first thing this morning to pore over the scene of the crime and take fingerprints, but I won't be holding my breath.'

'I wouldn't make a crack like that about our distinguished constabulary in Charlie's hearing. He came up through the ranks and he thinks very highly of our uniformed colleagues.'

'Thanks for the tip, but I think even the boss would've been unimpressed by this pair.'

'How do you mean?'

'When the Sergeant asked me what I could tell him about the burglar, I said: "Not a lot – apart from the fact that he'd been going through my CD collection, so I reckon we might have a similar taste in music". He must've attended one of Charlie's training sessions because he fastidiously wrote all that down in his notebook – in shorthand.'

'And I wouldn't mention the burglary in front of Niggle either, if I were you,' Tony added. 'He's not going to thank you for bumping up his unsolved crime statistics.'

'I hope both of you had an early night,' Charlie said as Tony and Malcolm walked into his office, 'because it's liable to be a long day.'

'I can't answer for Malcolm,' Tony said, stifling a yawn as he sat down, 'but I was in bed before ten o'clock.'

'I wouldn't have been long after him, if I hadn't been burgled,' Malcolm said, taking the seat beside Tony.

'Burgled?' Charlie said.

'When I got home last night, I interrupted a burglar in the act, but he got away. Fortunately, he didn't manage to steal anything. I called out the uniforms and they came round to my flat first thing this morning. They seemed a very efficient pair – right on top of things.'

Tony hacked at Malcolm's shins below the level of Charlie's desk.

'How did you get on with Ferrie last night?' Malcolm asked, turning to Tony.

'The guy was in a bad way. His nose was broken and his mouth was lacerated – and his condition wasn't improved by me telling him his girlfriend had been murdered.'

'Was he able to give you a description of whoever attacked him?' Charlie asked.

'All he could tell me was that a tall guy, with a Glasgow accent, wearing a balaclava, burst into his apartment and forced him to set up a meeting with Zoe Taylor before punching the living daylights out of him.'

'Okay, let's get a plan of action for the day sorted out,' Charlie said. 'Mr and Mrs Taylor are due at the mortuary at ten o'clock to formally identify their daughter's body.' He turned to Tony. 'Go over there and have a word with them. The usual stuff. Do they know if anyone had been stalking their daughter, anyone phoning her and hanging up, any jealous ex-boyfriends on the scene – you know the score. Malcolm, you do the same at her office. It's Tracy and Blundell in West Regent Street. Talk to her boss and her work colleagues and see if they can cast any light on what might have happened to her.'

Charlie's intercom buzzed. 'Sorry to interrupt you, sir,' Pauline said. 'An email has just arrived with two documents attached – the witness statements from the passengers on the Glasgow to London train and the report on the CCTV footage from Motherwell Station.'

'Print them out for me, please.'

As Charlie disconnected, his desk phone rang. He picked up.

'Renton here, sir. There's been a significant development. We got the CCTV tapes from Central Station. There's footage of all the passengers boarding the London train and we managed to pick out the victim boarding at eleven fifty-eight. The significant fact is that he was carrying an attaché case when he got on board – and the case wasn't found on the train.'

'Thanks for that, Colin.' Charlie recounted to Tony and Malcolm what Renton had told him.

'I've got a session with Doctor Orr this morning,' Charlie said. 'She asked me to compile a list of everyone I could think of who might be bearing a grudge against me.'

'Is Niggle on the list?' Tony asked.

Charlie nodded, sagely. 'I thought about including him, but I decided against it. There's no way he would go around committing murders on his own patch. He's too neurotic about his crime statistics.'

As Keith Tracy approached the front door of his office block, keys in hand, he saw Malcolm Stuart waiting for him in the doorway. Stuart produced his warrant card and introduced himself. 'Are you

Mr Tracy or Mr Blundell?' he asked.

'I'm Keith Tracy. John's on holiday.'

'Could I come in, please? There are a few questions I'd like to ask you.'

Tracy was a mousy, thin-faced creature with a nervous twitch, a pronounced Adam's apple and a permanently worried frown. He nodded his agreement as he fumbled with his key in the lock. 'Of course, officer. Of course.' His voice was shrill. 'But I would appreciate if you could be as brief as possible,' he said as he led the way up the wide staircase. 'I've got a very full schedule this morning.'

Tracy stopped on the first-floor landing and unlocked the heavy, wooden door, ushering Stuart in ahead of him. 'How can I help you?' he asked tugging off his coat as he went into his office.

'It's concerning Zoe Taylor.'

'Zoe?' Tracy stood on tiptoe to drape his coat on the hat stand before scuttling round to the seat behind his desk. 'Do you have news of her?'

Stuart waited until Tracy had settled down on his chair.

'I've very sorry to have to tell you this, Mr Tracy.' Stuart paused. 'I'm afraid Zoe is dead.' Tracy's eyes glazed over and his mouth gaped as if to speak but no sound came forth. 'Did you hear the news last night?' Stuart asked.

'I caught the headlines.'

'Then you know a girl's body was recovered from the Clyde.'

Tracy's eyes widened. 'They said her hand had been cut off,' he mumbled.

'I'm afraid it was Zoe.'

'I just don't… I can't believe it.' Tracy slumped back in his chair, repeating the same phrase over and over again. 'I can't believe it. I just can't believe it.' He picked up a sheaf of papers from his desk and used it to waft his face. 'I knew there was something wrong when Zoe didn't come back to work on Tuesday after lunch. I tried phoning her flat and her mobile several times, but there was no reply. I called her mother on Tuesday evening and she phoned around, but no one knew where Zoe was. Mrs Taylor contacted the police on Wednesday morning to report her daughter missing. I thought Zoe might have had a tiff with her boyfriend, or something like that – perhaps run off. But not – nothing like this.' Tracy fumbled in his desk drawer for a packet of tissues. Tugging one out, he blew his nose noisily. 'I just… I just can't believe it.'

They both heard the sound of the outer office door being pushed open. 'Good morning, Mr Tracy,' a cheery voice called out.

'That's Emma,' Tracy said quietly. 'Zoe's colleague.'

Tracy called Emma into his office. She knew straight away from the expression on his face that something was seriously wrong, When Stuart broke the news to her she started to scream hysterically. It was several minutes before she had calmed down enough to communicate.

'Zoe left the office at lunchtime on Tuesday,' Emma snivelled in response to Stuart's question. 'Ryan had rung earlier that morning. I took the call. I had a feeling something wasn't right. He wasn't his usual self. He normally chats me up when he phones. Just teasing, like. Lots of silly stuff. But on Tuesday he was, like, really brusque – and his voice sounded funny, as if there was something wrong with his breathing. He was barely civil. He wanted to speak to Zoe and when I told him she was in a meeting, he asked me to give her a message.'

'What was the message?'

'She had to meet him at half-past twelve in the boathouse at Glasgow Green. Ryan said it was very important – something about being in a lot of trouble.'

'Did he say what kind of trouble?'

Emma shook her head.

Tony O'Sullivan was sitting in the outer office of the mortuary when Sam and Helen Taylor emerged from the room where they had formally identified their daughter's body. Helen's eyelids were red and swollen, the bags under her eyes grey from lack of sleep.

Her husband was supporting her elbow in the crook of his arm.

O'Sullivan stood up when he saw them approaching and showed them his ID. He offered Helen his chair and she sank down on the seat. O'Sullivan indicated the adjacent chair for Sam.

'I'd just as soon stand, officer,' Sam said quietly.

O'Sullivan propped himself against the edge of the desk and took out his notebook. 'I realise how difficult this must be for you both.' He cast his eyes down. 'But I'm afraid I do need to ask you some questions.'

Sam gripped his wife's hand tightly. 'Go ahead. I need you to find the bastard who did this. And when you do,' he added in a matter-of-fact tone, 'I'm goany strangle him with my bare hands.'

'I know how you must feel, Mr Taylor, but – '

'No you don't, son,' Taylor interjected, shaking his head emphatically. 'You have no idea how I feel.'

'We'll do everything we can to find Zoe's murderer, Mr Taylor.' O'Sullivan paused. 'Do you know if anyone had been bothering your daughter recently?' Taylor looked enquiringly at his wife, who shook her head. 'Do you know if she received any unexplained phone calls? Or if anyone was hanging around in the street outside her flat?'

'You'd have to check with Ryan,' Sam said. 'I'm not around all that much, but I'm sure Zoe would've said something to her mother if there'd been anything like that going on.'

'When did you last see your daughter, Mrs Taylor?'

'On Sunday,' Helen offered. 'Sam was away in Germany. Ryan and Zoe came over to our place for their tea.'

'Would that be Ryan Ferrie, Zoe's boyfriend?'

'That's right,' Helen said.

'What can you tell me about him?'

'Bit of a chancer,' Sam said. 'Never held a job down for more than five minutes in his life, but a decent enough bugger all the same. He moved in with Zoe a couple of months back. He got her a really nice engagement ring. They were planning to get hitched next month.' His voice was on the point of cracking as he grasped his wife's hand tightly. 'Helen was baking their wedding cake last week, while I was away. Zoe was stuck on Ryan and as long as he was treatin' her right, that was fine by me.'

'And was he treating her right?'

Sam Taylor stared at O'Sullivan. 'Unless you're telling me you know somethin' different?' He let go of his wife's hand and both his fists slowly clenched and unclenched. 'Because if you are – ?'

'Not at all, Mr Taylor. Ferrie was attacked in their flat on the morning Zoe was murdered. He's in the Southern General. He was beaten up very badly. We have reason to believe that the person who murdered your daughter was also responsible for assaulting Ferrie.'

'Poor sod,' Sam muttered, relaxing his fists.

O'Sullivan put away his notebook. 'I don't think there's anything else I need from you right now.'

'I've got a question for you, son,' Sam said. 'In the papers this morning, it said the police were waiting for the post mortem results before they could confirm whether or not Zoe's hand was cut off before she was killed.' His voice was a hoarse whisper. 'I need to know.'

'We don't have the results of the post mortem yet.'

'Why did the sick bastard chop her hand off?'

O'Sullivan held eye contact. 'We have no idea.'

A single tear threaded its way down Sam Taylor's right cheek. He helped his wife to her feet and supported her arm as he led her towards the door.

Charlie Anderson's intercom buzzed. 'Doctor Orr is here to see you, sir,' Pauline said.

'Send her in.'

'Do you have your list of names for me, Inspector?' Mhairi asked, taking her iPad from her briefcase before settling down on a chair.

Charlie opened his top desk drawer and produced a photocopy of the list he'd compiled. He handed it across.

Mhairi scanned the twenty or so names. 'You seem to have upset a lot of people in your time.'

'That's not the half of them. I left off the ones who are dead or still doing time.'

'And the five names you've underlined? Is there any particular significance?'

'In my opinion, they're the most likely candidates. But I must stress that's based purely on my gut feeling. I don't have any evidence that would associate them with the murders.'

Mhairi nodded. 'What do you intend to do with the list?' Charlie asked.

'I'll examine the case notes on the crimes for which they were convicted and I'll check for any similarities in methodology and motive vis-à-vis the latest victims. In parallel with that, as you will no doubt recall from my talk at last year's seminar,' Mhairi said, doing her best to suppress a smile, 'I have a sophisticated software package that allows me to cross reference photographs of suspects with CCTV footage. There was no CCTV at the gypsy encampment in Port Glasgow, but there are cameras in the vicinity of the boathouse in Glasgow Green and, for now, I'm working on the assumption that the murder on the London train was the work of the same killer, so I'll include whatever footage I can get from Central Station and Motherwell Station at the relevant times.'

'We already have the CCTV tapes from Central Station,' Charlie said. 'I'll have a copy sent across to you. The victim was identified getting on board and it appears he was carrying an attaché case, which wasn't found on the train.'

'Interesting,' Mhairi said. 'Any idea what was in it?'

'No.'

Mhairi held up the list of names. 'Can you provide me with photographs of these people?'

'There should be mug shots of all of them on file.'

'If you could let me have the photos with the highest resolution, I'll load them into my system and see what that throws up.'

*

'How did it go last night?' Sarah asked, pouring out two cups of coffee.

'Everything went well,' Sue said.

'Well? Is that all I'm getting?'

'He really can cook.'

'Are you sure it wasn't a take-away?'

'A hundred per cent sure. He cooks really well.'

'What else is he good at?'

'What are you talking about?'

'You're blushing,' Sarah said, handing Sue her cup.

'Behave yourself!' Sue took a sip of coffee. 'Was Jamie any bother?' she asked.

'He was as good as gold. He and Sean had to select Partick Thistle's first team for next season. That took a long time, let me tell you. I could hear the whispered arguments still going on long after they were supposed to be asleep.'

'Any sign of life from them?'

'They're both still out cold.'

'I'd better wake Jamie up. My Mum's coming over to my place at eleven.'

'Why don't you let him sleep? You must have a lot of catching up to do with your Mum. I'm sure she'd appreciate having you to herself for a while. I can drop him off at your place when I go shopping this afternoon.'

Sainsbury's in the Braehead Centre was always busy, but today for some reason, the queues seemed longer than usual. Kay Anderson had been waiting in line for five minutes before she got to the check-out. She glanced at her watch in frustration. She'd told Sue she'd be across at eleven o'clock and she was running late.

Kay recognised the checkout assistant as one of her former pupils. 'Why is it so busy this morning, Sally?'

'I've no idea, Mrs Anderson. It's been non-stop from the minute I came on shift. I don't know where they're all coming from.'

As quickly as she could, Kay started piling the contents of her laden trolley onto the conveyor belt. In addition to her regular shopping she'd picked up a carton of chocolate ice cream and a six-pack of Irn Bru for Jamie. She tut-tutted in annoyance when she lifted the ice cream from the trolley and saw the carton was smeared with blood from the sirloin steak, but when she checked the wrapping on the meat it seemed to be intact. Puzzled, she rummaged through the remaining items in her trolley. Her eye caught a plastic bag she didn't recognise. She picked it up, then let out a shriek as a human hand slid from the bag and fell back into the trolley, the fingers lodging in the wire lattice. The last thing she remembered before passing out was seeing a bloodstained nine of diamonds and a yellow, smiling emoticon stapled to the centre of the palm.

CHAPTER 9

Kay jerked her face away from the smelling salts. As she slowly regained consciousness, the security guard's worried expression came into focus.

'Where am I?' she demanded, struggling to sit up straight.

The guard put a restraining hand on her shoulder. 'Better to lie still for a wee bit, Mrs Anderson.'

'Where am I?' she insisted. 'What happened? Who are you?' She tried again to sit up.

'You're in the medical room in Braehead, Mrs Anderson. You had a wee fright, but everything's all right now.'

'How do you know my name?'

'Sally, on the checkout, told us who you were. We called the police and we managed to get in touch with your husband. He's on his way over.'

'There was a hand!' Kay clasped both hands to her mouth. 'It was in my shopping trolley.'

'Just try to lie quiet, Mrs Anderson.'

'Where is my wife?' Charlie demanded.

'Are you Inspector Anderson?' the security guard asked.

'Yes.'

'She's in the medical room. Over there,' he said, pointing. 'The police and a doctor are with her.'

Charlie rapped on the door and walked straight in. Kay was sitting in an armchair, nursing a cup of hot, sweet tea and talking to the two uniformed officers sitting opposite her. The doctor was bent over the adjacent table, writing out a prescription.

Both officers scrambled to their feet.

'How are you?' Charlie asked, hurrying across and taking Kay by the hand.

'I'm all right now – but I got quite a fright. The staff have been very kind. They made me a cup of tea,' Kay said, holding up her cup.

'What happened?' Charlie asked the sergeant.

'From what we've been able to establish, sir, it seems that someone planted a severed human hand in your wife's shopping trolley. The trolley's in the Sainsbury's manager's office. We've sent for a forensic team.'

Charlie turned to the doctor. 'How is she?'

'Your wife's had a traumatic shock, Inspector. She needs complete rest.'

'Can I go home now?' Kay asked.

'As long as someone can stay with you for the rest of the day,' the doctor said.

'I'll make sure of that,' Charlie said.

'These are sedatives.' The doctor ripped a page from his prescription pad and handed it to Charlie. 'Your wife should take two of these as soon as she gets home – and two more before she goes to bed tonight. See how you're feeling in the morning, Mrs Anderson,' he added, turning to Kay. 'There might be a delayed reaction.'

Charlie spoke to the sergeant. 'Do you have any more questions for my wife?'

'Not right now, sir. We might need to talk to her again later.'

'In which case, I'm taking her home.'

Supporting Kay by the arm, Charlie led the way out to his car.

'What about my car?' Kay said as she was about to get into the passenger seat. 'I think I'd be all right to drive.'

'Let's leave it where it is for now, love. We can pick it up later.'

'I need to phone Sue, Charlie. She'll be worried about me.'

'I'll do that,' Charlie said, taking out his mobile and clicking onto Sue's number.

'Sue, it's me.'

'Do you know what's happened to Mum, Dad?' Sue asked straight away. 'She was supposed to be here at eleven o'clock, but she hasn't turned up. I've tried calling her mobile several times, but she's not answering.'

'There was a problem, Sue. Mum got a bit of a fright, but everything's all right now.'

'What happened?'

Charlie hesitated. 'Can you come across to the house?'

'Right now?'

'If you can.'

'Sure.'

On the way home, Charlie stopped outside a chemist's shop and went in to pick up Kay's prescription. When he came back to the car he found Kay sitting with her face buried in her hands, sobbing uncontrollably.

'How's Mum?' Sue asked as she walked through the front door.

'She's sleeping,' Charlie said. 'I gave her a couple of pills and I packed her off to bed.'

'What happened?'

'Someone put a dismembered human hand into her shopping trolley in Sainsbury's this morning.'

'Good God! Deliberately?'

'Hard to see how it could've been an accident.'

'I mean – deliberately into Mum's trolley – as opposed to someone else's?'

'I think so.'

'Why on earth would anyone do that?'

Charlie hesitated. 'Sue, there's something you ought to know. I haven't said a word about this to your mother, but two amputated hands were sent to me in the office this week.' Sue's mouth fell open. 'Someone's out to get me.'

'Who?' Sue asked, shaking her head in disbelief.

'I've no idea.' Sue sank down onto an armchair. 'The doctor said Mum shouldn't be left on her own for the rest of the day – and I have to get back to the office to try to get to the bottom of this. Could you stay with her till I get back?'

'Of course.'

'What about Jamie?'

'He's over at Sarah's place, playing with Sean. I'll phone her and ask her to look after him. She won't mind.'

'I'll give you a call as soon as I know when I'll be able to get back. As I said, your mother doesn't know anything about the hands that were sent to me in the office, so please don't mention anything to her.'

'Don't you think it would be better if she knew what's been going on?'

'Of course it would. And I will tell her – but not right now. She's had a traumatic shock this morning and I don't want to worry her any more than necessary.'

'What is going on, Dad?'

'I wish to God I knew.'

When Charlie got to his office he found a note on his desk, confirming that the hand found in his wife's shopping trolley had been matched up with the victim on the train. Picking up the phone, he called Mhairi Orr. 'As I suspected, Doctor Orr, the latest murder is almost certainly part of the same series.'

'How do you know?'

'The victim's hand has turned up.'

'Sent to you?'

'Not exactly. This time, it was put into my wife's shopping trolley in Sainsbury's – again, with a nine of diamonds and a smiley attached.'

'He's getting more arrogant, Inspector.'

'But, unfortunately, he's not getting careless. No one saw him put the hand into my wife's trolley.'

'Which branch of Sainsbury's was it?'

'Braehead.'

'At what time?'

'Just before eleven o'clock.'

'Can you get in touch with the site management and ask them to provide me with whatever CCTV footage they have? I can include it in my data analysis. I'm also in the process of scanning the photos of the men on your list into my computer module. I'll let you know what that throws up.'

'Thanks. I'll have someone get onto the CCTV for you.'

Replacing the receiver, Charlie summoned Tony and Malcolm to his office.

'We heard about what happened to your wife, sir,' Malcolm said as he walked in. 'How is she?'

'Badly traumatised.' Charlie rubbed at his swollen eyelids. 'Did you get anything useful from Zoe Taylor's office colleagues, Malcolm?'

'Nothing we didn't already know.'

'How about the parents, Tony?' Charlie asked.

'As far as they're aware, there wasn't anyone bothering their daughter.'

'What about the victim on the train?' Charlie asked. 'Has he been identified?'

'Not so far,' Tony said. 'He appears to be in his mid-fifties, but there were no identification papers on him. In fact, no papers or possessions of any kind. Forensics have sent a blood sample off to run a check against the central DNA database, but we haven't got the results back yet.'

'I've had a look through the transcripts of the statements from the passengers on the train,' Charlie said. 'A typical lot. Most of the them were either dozing, reading their newspapers or fiddling with their mobile phones and they weren't aware of anything untoward going on. However, a young girl in the second compartment was bouncing her baby on her knee when she saw a bearded guy, carrying a suitcase, pass through from the rear compartment a few minutes before they got to Motherwell.'

'Was she able to describe him?' Tony asked.

'The only thing she could remember was that he was wearing a baseball cap.'

'Was anything picked on the CCTV footage from the station?' Tony asked.

Charlie referred to the document. 'Only nine people got off the train, one of whom was carrying a suitcase under his arm. He had a scarf covering his face and a baseball cap tugged down low over his eyes. He's almost certainly our man. He got into a black Ford Focus that was parked outside the station. The CCTV picked up the number plate – the car was stolen in Glasgow earlier in the day.'

'If he was carrying a suitcase, could the victim's attaché case have been inside it?' Tony asked.

'That's possible,' Charlie said as his intercom buzzed.

'The Super wants to see you straight away, sir,' Pauline said.

Nigel Hamilton grabbed at the sides of his desk and pulled himself to his full height when Charlie walked into his office. He waved towards the seat opposite. Charlie remained standing.

'Another murder. Another amputated hand. Another nine of diamonds and another fucking smiley face! And this time the hand ends up in your wife's shopping trolley!' Hamilton sank back down onto his seat. 'And to make matters a hundred times worse the media have got wind of the fact that the murderer has been sending his victims' amputated hands to you.'

'How the hell did they get hold of that?'

'I had Fran Gibbons on the blower five minutes ago. An anonymous caller phoned the BBC switchboard at lunchtime and told the operator that two shoe boxes containing amputated hands, adorned with the nine of diamonds and a smiley – had been sent here, addressed to you, and that another hand had materialised in your wife's shopping trolley in Sainsbury's this morning. Gibbons wanted to know if the information was accurate.'

'What did you tell her?'

'I tried ducking the issue, but she wasn't having it. She insisted on getting a straight answer. The story's bound to break sooner rather than later, so I didn't have any option other than confirm that the information she'd been given was correct.

'She told me BBC Scotland are going to transmit a special programme about the serial killer after the ten o'clock news tonight. Exceptionally, they're going to interrupt their Friday evening schedules in order to transmit it because they consider the public need to know what's going on as soon as possible. She asked if we would be willing to cooperate.'

'In what way?'

Hamilton looked away to avoid eye contact with Charlie. 'She wants to interview you on the programme.'

'Interview me?' Charlie felt his mouth go dry. 'Surely that's a job for the press liaison officer?'

'Gibbons knows the amputated hands were sent to you personally, so she wants you on.'

'Did you agree to that?'

Hamilton rolled his eyes. 'We need all the help we can get. The enquiry is going nowhere. Exposure on TV might prompt a member of the public to come forward with some useful information.'

'I'm all for a public information programme. But why do I need to be involved?'

'We have to be seen to be cooperating with the BBC, Anderson. We can't give the impression that we're trying to cover anything up.'

'For Christ's sake! My wife's had a major shock. She needs me to be at home with her this evening.'

'If necessary, we can arrange for someone to be with your wife tonight. You have to appear on the programme.' Hamilton thrust a slip of paper across the desk. 'This is Gibbons' phone number. Give her a call and make the necessary arrangements.'

'I've never done a TV studio interview before.'

'You've been through media training.'

'That was more than twenty years ago!' Charlie tugged at his tie knot. 'And it doesn't prepare you for something like this. I'm on a hiding to nothing. We know sod all about the killer – or his motives – and nothing would give Gibbons greater satisfaction than being able to portray the Glasgow CID as a bunch of headless chickens. When that lady scents blood, she doesn't back off.'

'Of course she'll try to rattle you – that's her job. Just stick to the facts and project a confident image. Try to diffuse the situation and give the impression we're making progress.'

'How?' Crumpling the slip of paper in his fist, Charlie glared at Hamilton, then turned on his heel and stomped out of the office.

As soon as he got back downstairs, Charlie wrenched open the bottom drawer of his filing cabinet and pulled the whisky bottle out with a trembling hand. Grimacing, he glugged down several mouthfuls of the fiery liquid before spinning the cap back onto the bottle and replacing it in the cabinet. He slumped down at his desk and smoothed out the slip of paper containing Gibbons' phone number. He stared at the number for some time before picking up the phone and dialling. 'Could you put me through to Fran Gibbons, please?'

'Speaking.'

'This is DCI Anderson, Glasgow CID. I'm calling about tonight's programme.'

'Thank you for agreeing to participate, Inspector.'

'What time do you need me?'

'The transmission will be going out live at ten thirty-five, straight after the news, but it would be useful if you could come over to Pacific Quay a bit earlier, say around nine o'clock? That would give me an opportunity to go over the format with you and explain what we're trying to achieve with tonight's programme.'

'I'll be there.' Charlie replaced the receiver and pressed his intercom. 'Pauline, find Tony O'Sullivan and tell him I want to see him straight away.'

*

Charlie waved to the seat opposite when Tony walked in

'Just so you know, I've drawn the short straw. The BBC have been tipped off about the amputated hands being sent to me and they want me to appear on television tonight.'

O'Sullivan frowned as he sat down. 'How did they find that out?'

'Some helpful bastard phoned their switchboard and told them that the amputated hands had been sent to me. Fran Gibbons called Niggle and asked for me to be on tonight's programme. Niggle caved in, which means I get the pleasure of being interviewed live on the telly.'

'Ouch!'

'By the way, there's no need to tell the world and his wife that I'll be appearing on the box.'

'Would you not like me to record the programme for posterity?'

'Piss off!' Charlie stretched across his desk and pressed his intercom. 'Pauline, I'm going home now. I need to be with my wife.'

As Charlie leaned forward to speak into the intercom, Tony thought he could detect the smell of whisky.

'Best of luck for tonight, sir,' Tony said, getting to his feet.

As he pulled Charlie's office door closed behind him, Tony noticed one of his shoe laces was undone. When he dropped down on one knee to re-tie it, he heard the metallic squeak of the drawer of Charlie's filing cabinet being wrenched open. He switched knees and re-tied his other shoe lace unnecessarily, to the sound of the drawer being slammed shut. Getting to his feet, he dusted off the knees of his trousers as he walked slowly along the corridor.

Mhairi Orr stared at the message on her screen. *One match identified*. She felt her heart rate quicken as she clicked onto the *Provide match details* icon.

The message came back: *Photograph of James McKendrick cross-referenced with Glasgow Central Station CCTV footage on the morning of Thursday, 23rd June. Match probability of 98.2%.*

'It doesn't get better than ninety-eight per cent,' Mhairi muttered to herself as she picked up Charlie's list, which was lying on her desk. McKendrick wasn't one of the names Charlie had underlined, but it was a match nevertheless. She flicked through the pile of photos and pulled out McKendrick's as she clicked onto *Show CCTV footage*.

The video started playing, highlighting a tall, slim man hurrying across the crowded station concourse. The time-line running along the bottom of the screen showed him being picked up on camera as he came through the main station entrance at eleven twenty-eight a.m. He stopped and looked up at the departures board, then went back to the ticket booths. Having purchased a ticket, he walked past the platform for the London train and continued towards the top of the station where, at eleven forty-three, he was seen boarding the eleven fifty train to Stranraer.

Mhairi froze the image and stared despondently at the screen. She re-wound the footage and zoomed in on the best shot she had of the man's face, comparing it to the photograph she was holding in her hand. She concluded it was definitely him. She wondered if it would've been possible for him to have got off the Stranraer train and switched to the London train without being picked up on camera.

Switching to the CCTV footage of the people passing through the barrier to board the London train after eleven forty-three, she requested a match with McKendrick from then until the time the train departed. The response of *No match* came up on her screen.

Cursing under her breath, Mhairi used Google to find the time-table for the Stranraer train. She made a note of all the stations it stopped at along the way.

Charlie was surprised to see Kay's car standing in the driveway when he pulled up outside his house. When he went inside he found Kay sitting on the settee, sipping a cup of tea. Sue was perched on the armchair opposite her.

'How are you, love?'

'I slept for a couple of hours. I'm feeling a lot better now.'

'How did your car get here?'

'Sue drove me over to Sainsbury's so I could pick it up.'

Charlie's brow furrowed. 'I'm not sure you should've been driving.'

'Don't fuss, Charlie. I had a bit of a fright, but I'm all right now.'

Charlie made eye contact with Sue, who nodded. He sat down on the settee beside his wife. 'Kay, there's more to this than you know.'

'What are you talking about?'

'The psychopath who put that hand into your shopping trolley has also sent two amputated hands to me at Pitt Street.'

'My God!' Kay's teacup rattled in its saucer as she put it down on the coffee table with a trembling hand. 'What's going on, Charlie?'

Charlie took Kay's hand and gripped it tightly. 'We're doing everything we can to find out who's responsible for this, but so far we've drawn a blank. I have to appear on television tonight and I'm supposed to diffuse the situation and reassure the public that there's nothing for them to worry about – though God knows how I'm going to be able to do that.'

'Do you have any idea who could be doing this, Charlie?' Kay asked.

'Not a clue, but until this madman's under lock and key, I don't want you staying here on your own.'

'I'll be all right,' Kay insisted.

'I'm not prepared to take that risk. He managed to find you in Sainsbury's. If he's capable of doing that, he's capable of finding out where we live. I think you should go across to Elderslie and stay with Grace for the time being.'

'Dad's right, Mum,' Sue chipped in.

'What about you, Charlie?' Kay asked.

'I'm staying here. There's no way I'm going to let this bastard drive me out of my own house.'

'That's exactly how I feel.'

'I know you do, love. But do it for me – please. I'd be worried sick at the thought of you being here on your own.'

'That makes sense, Mum,' Sue said. 'And if Dad has to be in the television studio this evening, it would be a good idea for you to go across to Aunt Grace's straight away.'

Kay hesitated, then let out a resigned sigh as she got to her feet. 'I'll do it, Charlie. But just for your peace of mind.' She crossed the room and picked up the phone. 'I'll give Grace a call and let her know I'm coming across.'

'Do you want me to drive you, Mum?' Sue asked.

'No, I'm fine. I'll take my car.'

'Are you sure?'

'Of course.'

'In which case,' Sue said, glancing at her watch. 'I'd better be on my way. I have to pick Jamie up from Sarah's.'

Charlie's mobile started ringing as Sue was leaving. He took the call.

'It's Doctor Orr, Inspector.'

'Do you have anything for me?'

'Nothing of use, I'm afraid. I thought we might've had a break-through because one of the men on your list, James McKendrick, was picked up by the CCTV cameras in Central Station yesterday morning. But I'm afraid it seems to have come to nothing, because he boarded a train to Stranraer. I've requested CCTV footage from the stations that train stops at en route to try to establish where he got off.'

'What now?'

'As soon as I get the CCTV footage from Sainsbury's I'll load the data into my module and re-run it. I'll be in touch.'

'Thanks.'

'I've thought of another question, Mum. It's awesome!'

'Don't start on Mr O'Sullivan the minute he walks through the door, Jamie. Give him time to get his coat off.'

'When is he coming?'

'He said eight o'clock.' Sue glanced up at the kitchen wall clock. 'He should be here any time. Are you sure you've set the table properly?'

'Of course.'

'Have you put out napkins?'

'Yes.'

'Knives and forks on the correct side?'

'Mum!'

'Then pour me a tomato juice and get yourself an Irn Bru.'

The door bell rang as Jamie was taking his Irn Bru out of the fridge. Sue slipped off her pinafore and smoothed her hair behind her ears as she walked down the hall to open the door.

'Did you manage to find the place without any problem?' she asked.

'You can't go wrong with a sat nav,' Tony said, producing a bunch of red roses from behind his back and handing it across.

Sue held the flowers up to her face and inhaled the perfume. 'Thank you! They're lovely.'

Tony smiled at Jamie as he came out of the kitchen and stood shyly at the end of the hall. 'You must be Jamie,' he said, striding towards him and shaking his hand. 'I hear you're a bit of an expert on Scottish football.' Tony handed him a parcel. 'I thought you might like this.'

Jamie took the parcel tentatively and looked at Sue. 'Can I open it, Mum?'

'Of course you can.'

Jamie ripped away the wrapping paper. 'Next season's strip!' He squealed with delight as he held up the Partick Thistle jersey.

'I hope it fits,' Tony said. 'Don't worry if it doesn't. I've kept the receipt and they can change it for a different size.'

'Can I try it on, Mum?' Jamie asked excitedly.

'Go ahead.'

'This is too much,' Sue whispered as Jamie was pulling the shirt over his head. 'You do realise that all that's on the menu tonight is chilli con carne?' she said, winking.

'What? No afters?'

'Not tonight,' she said, nudging Tony in the ribs with her elbow.

'Look Mum!' Jamie said, spinning round and round. 'Can I keep it on?'

'As long as you don't spill anything on it.'

'I won't.'

'Will you take a photo of me in it, Mum, so I can send it to Sean? He'll be dead jealous.'

'We'll do that tomorrow. Have you thanked, Mr O'Sullivan?'

'Thank you very much, Mr O'Sullivan. It's the best present ever.'

'How about you call me Tony?'

'Thanks, Tony.'

'Come through to the lounge and have a drink,' Sue said. 'G and T okay?'

'Sounds perfect.'

'Ice and lemon?'

'Please.'

'I'll put these into water straight away,' Sue said, smelling the roses again. 'Jamie, why don't you ask Tony some of your football questions while I get him a drink?'

Tony sat down on an armchair while Jamie squatted cross-legged on the carpet in front of him, notebook and pen in hand.

'First question. Who was Partick Thistle's best ever goalkeeper?'

'No doubt about it – Alan Rough.'

'Who was their best left winger?'

'Let me think about that,' Tony said, stroking his chin reflectively. 'I reckon it would have to be Davie McParland.'

'What was the score when Thistle played Celtic in the 1971 League Cup Final?'

'How could I ever forget? 4-1 for Thistle. I also happen to know it was 4-0 for Thistle at half-time. Do I get a bonus point for that?'

'No. Who was the Partick Thistle manager who played in Celtic's European Cup winning team?'

'Bertie Auld.'

'Thistle's all-time top goal scorer?'

Tony scratched at his head. 'There, you've got me.'

'It was Willie Sharp. Who was Thistle's – '

'Jamie,' Tony interrupted. 'Are there any questions that aren't about Partick Thistle?'

Jamie looked bemused. 'No. Why?'

'It's time to give Tony a break,' Sue said as she came into the room and handed Tony his drink. 'You can try him with some more questions after dinner.'

'Thanks,' Tony said, taking the glass.

'How did he do, Jamie?' Sue asked.

'Not bad. But he didn't know Willie Sharp was our all-time top goal scorer.'

'Tut, tut,' Sue said. 'Definitely no afters for Tony tonight!'

Just before nine o'clock, Charlie crossed the foyer of the BBC Scotland headquarters in Pacific Quay.

'My name's Charlie Anderson,' he said to the receptionist. 'I'm here to see Fran Gibbons. She's expecting me.'

'I'll let her know you're here, Mr Anderson.' The receptionist picked up the phone and called an extension. 'Fran will be using Studio C on the fourth floor,' she said as she replaced the receiver. 'Someone's on their way down to collect you.'

Charlie's eye was caught by the long, rust-coloured, reception desk. 'That's an unusual piece of furniture,' he said.

'Everyone asks about it.' The receptionist smiled as she took a visitor's badge from the top drawer. 'It's actually a girder from one of the shipyards on the Clyde.'

'Really?' Charlie said, running his fingertips along the cold steel. The receptionist handed Charlie his badge. 'If you wouldn't mind wearing that at all times while you're in the building, Mr Anderson.'

'Haven't we met before, Inspector?' Fran Gibbons rose from behind her desk and took Charlie's hand in a firm grip.

'Not as such. I was in the room when Superintendent Hamilton gave his press conference on Monday.'

'Oh, yes. I knew I recognised you from somewhere.'

Charlie judged her to be in her early forties; strong features, black hair piled haphazardly on top of her head and held in position by a wooden clasp, tight jeans and a grey, polo-neck sweater. She appeared to be wearing no make-up, apart from a touch of mascara.

'It's good of you to step into the breach at such short notice.'

Charlie nodded noncommittally. 'What ground do you want to cover?'

'The public wants answers to the obvious questions.' Fran gestured towards the chair opposite. 'Do the police have any idea who the serial killer might be? How does he select his targets? What's his motivation for chopping off his victims' hands after he kills them? And, on a personal level, what's the connection between the murderer and you and your family?'

Charlie eased himself down onto the chair. 'The questions are a lot more obvious than the answers, Miss Gibbons.'

'Just so we don't get off on the wrong foot, Inspector, I don't respond to *Miss*. My preference is to be called Fran. At a pinch I can live with Ms Gibbons and I can handle any random expletives that come to mind, but, please, not *Miss*.'

Charlie shrugged. 'As you wish.'

'Off the record, do you have any idea who the killer might be?'

'On, or off, the record, the answer's the same – it's "no".'

Fran broke eye contact and thumbed through the sheaf of papers on her desk. 'Let me explain what we're trying to achieve with this programme. What we want to do is cut through the hysterical hype that appeared in the tabloids this morning. We want to inform the public in a responsible way about the murders and advise them what precautions they should be taking while the killer's still at large. I'll give you the opportunity to reassure the viewers that the police are on top of the situation – and I'd then like to touch on the human interest angle – how it's affecting you and your family.'

'Let me get one thing straight. It will not surprise you to know that I'm pissed off that this maniac is targeting me and my family. I'm worried sick about what he might do next and I'm frustrated as hell that I haven't a clue who he is or why he's doing this, but there's no way I'm going to give him the satisfaction of admitting any of that on air.'

'I wouldn't expect you to.' The large, hazel eyes didn't blink. 'Let me explain the format.' Fran checked her notes. 'The programme is scheduled for thirty minutes. We'll kick off with a recording we made this afternoon. Basically, it's a scene-setter where I give a factual resume of the circumstances surrounding the murders, including what we know about the victims' backgrounds. That runs for just under fifteen minutes. By the way, has the man who was killed on the train been identified yet?' Charlie shook his head. Fran referred back to her timetable. 'We'll then show five minutes of clips from a selection of man-in-the-street interviews I did in Argyle Street this afternoon. That will leave ten minutes for me to put questions to you.'

'Do I get to see the questions in advance?'

'There isn't a predetermined list. I don't work that way. Anyway, it's better for you if you don't know what's coming. Trust me on that. If you tried to rehearse your answers you would come across as stilted. When you're in front of the camera, the best approach is to take your time and give a considered, frank response to each question.'

Fran glanced at her watch and got to her feet. 'There are a few things I need to sort out before we go on air. I'll take you over to make-up, then you'll have time for a coffee in the Green Room before the programme.'

Charlie fidgeted in his seat while powder was dusted over his bald cranium, then dabbed at his forehead and the grey pouches beneath his eyes.

'A touch of lipstick, Inspector?' the cheerful make-up assistant enquired. Charlie glowered at her. 'Only joking!'

'I'm not in the mood.'

'Sorry.' Picking up a clothes brush, she flicked the traces of fine powder from the shoulders of his jacket. 'The Green Room is straight along the corridor.'

'Is there a toilet I can use?'

'I'll show you,' she said crossing to the door. 'It's round the corner over there, on the left,' she said, pointing. Going into a cubicle and locking the door, Charlie took his hip flask from his pocket and swallowed a long, slow swig of whisky. Screwing the cap back onto the flask, he sprayed *Gold Spot* around the inside of his mouth.

'It's way past your bedtime, Jamie.'

'Can I not stay up a wee bit longer, Mum?' he pleaded. 'I've only got another ten questions to ask Tony.'

'The questions will keep for another time,' Sue said, ruffling Jamie's hair. 'Say goodnight to Tony and get yourself ready for bed.'

'Goodnight, Tony. And thanks again for the jersey,' Jamie said, stroking the sleeve lovingly.

'I'm looking forward to the day I'll see you running out of the tunnel at Firhill wearing one of those.'

'I won't be wearing this strip. I'm going to be a goalkeeper, like Grandad.'

'Bed!' Sue said, pointing towards the door. 'Go on. I'll be up in a minute.'

Jamie picked up his notebook and pen and trotted up the staircase. 'Don't forget to brush your teeth!' Sue called up the stairs after him.

'Give me a few minutes to get him settled,' Sue said. 'Help yourself to wine.'

'No more for me, thanks. I'm already flirting with the limit for driving.'

Sue picked up the remote control. 'I'll put on the telly so you can catch the ten o'clock news.'

Tony turned down the volume on the television when he heard Sue coming back down the stairs.

'Is Jamie okay?'

'A bit hyper, but he'll be fine. It was really kind of you to get him that jersey. He's over the moon about it. He wanted to sleep in it. The only way I could get him to take it off was by telling him he wouldn't want it to be crumpled when he shows it off to Sean.'

Sue settled down on the settee beside Tony. 'What time is it?'

Tony checked his watch. 'Ten minutes to go.'

'I hope Dad's going to be okay.'

'I'm sure he'll be fine,' Tony said, putting his arm around Sue's shoulders. Tucking her legs underneath her on the settee, Sue snuggled in.

Charlie found himself alone in the Green Room. He watched the ten o'clock news on a monitor, the lead story being about an amputated hand, with a nine of diamonds playing card and a smiley emoticon attached, having been dropped into a shopping trolley in Sainsbury's in Braehead. This was followed by an update on the recent murders where the victims' hands had been cut off at the wrist, the reporter concluding the item by stating that a BBC Scotland programme about the serial killer would be going out on the network immediately after the news.

When Charlie was called into the studio he saw Fran Gibbons leafing through a clipboard of notes while conversing with a technician. She caught Charlie's eye and waved him across. 'Take a seat, Inspector,' she said, indicating the two black leather chairs facing each other. Both chairs looked to be identical, though Fran's appeared to be several inches higher off the ground.

'I am in the right place?' Fran looked at him quizzically. 'I haven't inadvertently stumbled into a recording session for Mastermind?'

'Do I look like John Humphrys?'

'I would have to say I don't see much resemblance.' Charlie studied the transformation. Black, sling-back, high-heeled shoes; slim ankles, nicely-rounded calves, albeit slightly knobbly knees. Fran was wearing a short, pinstriped skirt and her open-necked blouse was unbuttoned just enough to display a hint of cleavage. Her black hair was sculpted down one side of her face and Charlie noticed the subtle use of blusher to pick out her prominent cheek bone. 'I'm sure my wife would appreciate getting your hairdresser's phone number. It takes her hours to get ready when we're going out.'

Fran smoothed her hair unnecessarily as she pulled a vanity mirror from a pocket in the side of her chair to check her appearance. 'You seem relaxed, Inspector. That's a good sign.'

Charlie pulled a face. 'Relaxed is not the word that springs to mind.'

A floor technician came across and clipped a small microphone onto the lapel of Charlie's jacket. 'Just look at Fran while you're being interviewed, Inspector,' he said. 'Don't look at the cameras.' Charlie nodded.

The studio lights dimmed as the closing news headlines segued into the weather forecast. Charlie was only half-listening, trying to anticipate what questions might be coming his way and how he would respond. The programme was introduced live by Fran and then her pre-recorded tape on the serial killer started running. Charlie moved onto the edge of his seat, his eyes glued to the monitor as Fran's soft, lilting voice gave an account of the gypsy's corpse being discovered in her caravan in Port Glasgow. She went on to describe the young girl's body being recovered from the Clyde and the horrific nature of the murder on the London train. 'In each of these cases,' she stated, 'The victim's left hand was amputated at the wrist.'

The scene switched to Argyle Street where Fran was talking to passers-by about the murders, the recurrent theme being that, if a serial killer is targeting twenty year-old blondes, the general public are shocked, but the majority of the population don't feel threatened. However, when his victims are as disparate as a seventy-eight year old woman, a twenty-two year old female accountant and a middle-aged man, everyone is looking over their shoulder.

'Sixty seconds, Fran, and counting.' As Fran was cued in by the floor manager, the studio lights came up full and Charlie felt the heat as well as the glare. The switch to live action was seamless. Charlie pulled himself up straight in his seat.

'Further upsetting details have come to light.' Fran spoke to camera. 'As reported on tonight's news, an amputated hand materialised in a shopping trolley in Sainsbury's in Braehead this morning, with a playing card, the nine of diamonds, and a yellow smiley emoticon stapled to the palm.' She paused as the director cut to a full-screen shot of the front page of the early edition of one of the Saturday morning tabloids. "*The Curse of Scotland Strikes Again!*" in large, scarlet letters, dripping with blood. 'That shopping trolley belonged to Mrs Kay Anderson,' Fran continued, 'the wife of the chief investigating officer, Detective Chief Inspector Charles Anderson of Glasgow CID. The BBC was contacted by an anonymous caller at lunchtime today and told that the dismembered hands of the first two victims had been sent to DCI Anderson – both of them with the murder's calling card, the nine of diamonds and a smiley. This afternoon, Superintendent Hamilton confirmed to me that the information the caller had given the BBC was accurate – and Inspector Anderson has kindly agreed to be with us this evening.'

The camera panned back slowly to include Charlie in the shot.

Fran swung her chair round to face him. 'Inspector, the city is on edge. What assurance can you give the public that the 'nine of diamonds' won't strike again?'

'While this person is on the loose, I cannot give any such assurance.' Charlie could feel the sweat trickling from the tufts of hair on the nape of his neck and running down the inside of his shirt collar.

'Is there any link between the victims?'

'We have not established one so far.'

'How many officers are involved in the hunt for the killer?'

Charlie was taken aback by the question. 'Er... let me see. Three of us are on the case full time and in addition to that there are several officers working on support activities and forensic analysis.'

'Do you consider that level of manpower to be adequate?'

'Yes... Yes, I think so.'

'You think so?' Fran queried. 'Is it adequate, or not?'

Charlie felt his mouth go dry. 'What... what I mean to say,' he said, trying to lick moisture back into his parched lips, 'is that once you go beyond those kind of numbers, you introduce coordination and communication difficulties.' Charlie sat on his hands to prevent himself pulling out his handkerchief to mop his glistening brow. 'I can call on any additional resources I require, but, quite frankly, I wouldn't know how to deploy anyone else right now.'

'Two amputated hands were sent to you and a third one was put into your wife's shopping trolley. Surely that must mean the killer is known to you?'

'That's a logical conclusion and it's the assumption we're working on.'

'Could it be someone bearing a grudge against you?'

'That seems probable. The problem is I've been on the force for over forty years and in that time I've made a lot of enemies – including some I probably don't even know about.'

'Have there been any eye witnesses? Anyone who might be able to identify the 'nine of diamonds'?'

'There have been three possible sightings. The murderer was

seen at Irene McGowan's campsite on the morning she was killed, but only from a distance. We believe he handed a parcel to a young boy in Sauchiehall Street, although the description the lad has been able to give us is sketchy. And we're reasonably sure he was responsible for assaulting Ryan Ferrie, Zoe Taylor's boyfriend, on the morning of her murder, but on that occasion he was wearing a balaclava to cover his face.'

'Do you have enough of a description to publish an e-fit picture?'

'Unfortunately, no.'

'Why the nine of diamonds? What's the significance of that?'

'Apart from it being known as 'The Curse of Scotland', I have no idea.'

'The smiley?' Charlie shook his head. 'Did your wife see anyone acting suspiciously while she was in Sainsbury's?'

'No.'

'And no one saw the amputated hand being put into her shopping trolley?'

'Apparently not. We've launched an appeal for witnesses, but so far no one's come forward.'

'Was nothing picked up by CCTV cameras in the shop?'

'That's being checked out.'

Fran's line of questioning switched to Charlie's personal feelings about his wife being terrorised by the killer and before he realised it she was turning full-on to the camera and saying goodnight. The title music cut in, the credits started rolling and the studio lights dimmed.

'That wasn't too bad now, was it?' Fran said as the technician come across to pluck the microphone from Charlie's lapel.

Charlie tugged out his handkerchief with a shaking hand and smeared the soggy make-up across his brow. 'Did I survive?'

'The public know when someone's trying to pull the wool over their eyes, Inspector, but you came across as sincere. I told you you'd be better off not knowing the questions in advance. What did you think of the programme?'

'It's hard to judge when you're on the receiving end. I thought that plastering the blood-dripping, Hammer House of Horror tabloid headline across the screen was over the top.'

'Too melodramatic?' Fran smiled disarmingly. 'If you think we were a bit B-movie, you should see what STV do with it.'

'You had me going when you asked how many officers were assigned to the enquiry.'

'I considered asking you if Superintendent Hamilton had allocated another three officers to compiling statistics about the murders, but that might have been below the belt.' Fran's fingers gripped her hairline and tugged off her wig.

'Hey! That's cheating.'

'I don't normally resort to the wig, but it's useful for continuity purposes when I want my hair to look the same as in the pre-recorded item.'

'So there's no hope for my wife, then?'

Fran teased out her crumpled hair with both hands. 'It would appear not.'

'Now that my ordeal by fire's over, how about some reciprocal cooperation?'

'Such as?'

'The anonymous caller to the BBC – what, exactly, did he say?'

'I'm told he identified himself as the 'nine of diamonds' and stated that the first two murder victims' hands, along with his calling card, had been sent to you at Pitt Street – and that a third hand had been put into your wife's shopping trolley in Sainsbury's this morning. He hung up before we could get anything else out of him.'

'What about his accent?'

'Run of the mill Glasgow, I was told.'

'Who took the call?'

'A switchboard operator.'

'Would the call have been recorded?'

'I wouldn't think so. It isn't our practice to record calls.'

'I'd like you to record all incoming calls from now on, in case he phones back.'

'You'd have to discuss that with the Director.'

'Can you arrange for me to see him?'

'I can call his secretary and find out when he's available.'

Sue sat up straight on the settee and picked up the remote control to switch off the television. 'I thought Dad did pretty well, under the circumstances.'

'He did okay.' Tony hesitated. 'Do you think he might've had a drink before he went on?'

'Of course not!' Sue bristled. 'What made you think that?'

'It was just that he seemed a bit confused at one point, which isn't like him.'

'He's under a lot of stress. That's all it was.'

'Sure.'

Sue stared hard at Tony, then settled back with her head on his shoulder. 'What do your instincts tell you?' she asked. 'You must have a theory.'

Tony put his arm around her and started to stroke her hair gently. 'I've got too many. That's the problem. Too many possibilities – with nothing to link any of them to the murders. It's needles and haystacks time.'

A shiver ran the length of Sue's spine as she snuggled in closer. 'You realise we're going to have to tell Dad about you coming here for dinner tonight? There's no way Jamie's going to keep quiet about who gave him his new Partick Thistle jersey.'

Tony continued stroking Sue's hair. 'I'd come to that conclusion. The question is – who's going to break the news to him?'

'I wouldn't leave it to Jamie, if I were you. He'll tell Dad you didn't know who Partick Thistle's all-time top goal scorer was – and then you'll really be in the shit.'

'Would you like me to tell him?' Tony asked.

'I think it might be better coming from me.' Sue got to her feet and crossed to the dining table where she re-filled Tony's wine glass.

'No more for me, thanks,' Tony said, raising both hands in front of his face as Sue brought across the glass 'Not when I'm driving.'

'Are you sure?'

'Am I sure of what?'

'That you're driving?'

'I have a choice?'

'Never let it be said I don't give people a second chance. If you can tell me who Thistle's top goal scorer of all time was, there might be some afters after all.'

Tony smiled as he took the proffered glass. 'What about Jamie?'

'Once he's asleep, he's out like a light – and he never wakes up early.'

Tony took a sip of wine, then put the glass down on the coffee table. Standing up, he took Sue in his arms and started nibbling gently at her earlobe.

'I'm waiting for an answer,' she whispered.

'To what?'

'Who was Thistle's top goal scorer of all time?'

'Willie Sharp,' he breathed in her ear.

'Well done. Would you like to try for a second helping?'

'I'll give it a go.'

'How many goals did Sharp score in his career?'

'Let me think. How about five hundred and twenty seven?'

'Close enough.'

CHAPTER 10

Saturday 25 June

Charlie was sitting in his office, flicking through his mail, when his intercom buzzed.

'I've got the Director of BBC Scotland on the line for you, sir.'

'Thanks, Pauline. Put him through.'

'Fran Gibbons left a message that you wanted to talk to me, Inspector.'

'Thank you for calling on a Saturday morning. It's concerning the anonymous phone call to the BBC yesterday, by the individual who identified himself as the nine of diamonds. In case he contacts you again, I'd like you to record all incoming calls to your Glasgow switchboard.'

'Our legal department would have to clear that, Inspector, but as long as certain conditions are met, I wouldn't anticipate a problem.'

'Such as?'

'We wouldn't be prepared to give you carte blanche access to all our calls. However, I think we could agree to taping the incoming calls and letting you have the recording, if and when this nine of diamonds character phones us again.'

'That's fair enough.'

'And we wouldn't be willing to give an open-ended commitment about recording calls. There would have to be some kind of time limit.'

'How about if you agree to record everything for the next week – and then we take a checkpoint?'

'I can go along with that.'

'Wake up, sleepyhead,' Sue whispered. Fully dressed, she stood by the side of the bed and rocked Tony's shoulder gently. 'I let you sleep as long as I could, but Jamie's liable to wake up soon and when he does I don't want him to find you here.'

'What time is it?' Tony said, yawning as he sat up in bed.

'After nine o'clock.'

Interlocking his fingers, Tony yawned as he stretched both arms high his above his head. 'And here was me hoping to break Willy Sharp's scoring record.'

'Not this morning, you won't. Get up!'

'What about my freshly-squeezed orange juice and scrambled eggs with smoked salmon?'

'It'll be scrambled brains you'll be getting if you're not out of that bed in one minute flat.'

Tony reached across and wrapped his arms around Sue's waist, pulling her towards him. He rested his head gently against her stomach. 'Nine out of ten for last night's meal,' he said.

'What do I need to do to get ten out of ten?'

Sue slammed her hand over Tony's mouth before he could answer. 'I think I heard Jamie getting up,' she whispered, straining her ears. 'I'm sure I did. Get dressed – quickly – and tiptoe down the stairs. Don't stand on the second step from the bottom. It squeaks,' she said, untangling herself from his arms. 'I'll go to Jamie's room and distract him.'

'You mean – you'd be prepared to try to con a seven year-old?'

'Will you be quiet!' Sue said in a forced whisper.

'Okay, okay. I'm on my way.' Scrambling out of bed, Tony pulled on his underpants.

'Leave the Yale lock on the front door on the snib so it doesn't make a noise when you pull it closed behind you,' Sue said, snatching up her mobile phone from the bedside table.

'I'll call you,' Tony whispered, pulling on his shirt and his trousers before planting a kiss on the middle of Sue's forehead.

Jamie was out of bed when Sue rapped on his bedroom door. 'How about you put on your Partick Thistle jersey so I can take some photos of you in it?' she said. 'Then you can choose the ones you want to send to Sean.' When she heard the sound of a car engine starting up, Sue stole a glance out of the bedroom window in time to see Tony's car pulling away from the kerb.

Jamie tugged his jersey over his head and Sue took snaps of him in several poses. 'Pick the ones you want to send,' she said, handing across her phone. Jamie studied the photos carefully and, when he'd made his selection, Sue transmitted them.

'Okay, now get washed and dressed while I fix breakfast.'

As she walked down the stairs to the hall, Sue saw four letters had been posted through her letter box. She unsnibbed the Yale lock and closed the front door as quietly as she could before scooping up the letters and flicking through them. She recognised the first three as all-too-familiar bills, but she stopped in her tracks when she saw the fourth letter was a white envelope, addressed to "Jamie Paterson". Both his name and their address had been typed. Puzzled, she ripped open the envelope.

Charlie's phone rang and he picked up.

'He knows where I live, Dad?' Charlie could hear the panic in Sue's strangulated voice.

'What happened?'

'A letter arrived at the house this morning, addressed to Jamie.'

'What was in it?'

'Just a playing card.' Charlie's grip tightened on the receiver. 'It was the eight of diamonds, with a smiley attached, Dad – and it had a hand-written message on it.'

'What did it say?'

'It said: "Be very, very careful – because the next time, it'll be the nine".'

'Christ!'

'What should I do?'

'You can't stay there, Sue. It's not safe. Where's Jamie?'

'He's getting dressed.'

'I want both of you to get out of the house as quickly as possible.'

'Where will we go?'

'How about Sarah's place? Do you think she'd put you up for a while?'

'I'm sure she would. But what reason can I give her for wanting to stay?'

'Tell her the truth. Phone her and let her know what's happened. You'd better not drive in case you're followed. I'll come across right now and drop you off at Sarah's. Lock the front and back doors and don't let anyone in until I get there.'

'What should I tell Jamie?'

'You mustn't scare him. You'll have to make up an excuse for going to Sarah's.'

'I'm frightened, Dad.' Sue's voice was trembling.

'I realise that, love. But do your best to stay calm – for Jamie's sake. Everything's going to be all right. I'll be there as soon as I can.'

Sue snibbed the Yale lock in the front door and checked to make sure the back door was locked before clicking onto Sarah's number. As soon as she'd finished her call, Sue filled a bucket with water from the tap and slopped it all over the kitchen floor, then she turned the water supply off at the stop cock in the utility room before going upstairs to Jamie's bedroom.

'We've got a bit of a problem, Jamie.'

'What is it?'

'It looks like we've got a burst pipe. The kitchen floor's flooded. I had to turn the water off at the main. I called the plumber and he's going to come round this afternoon to have a look at it. We won't be able to stay in the house until it's fixed, so I phoned Sarah and she's going to put us up for a few days. Grandad's on his way across and he'll drop us off there. I'll leave a set of keys with Nancy next door so she can let the plumber in.'

Sue packed clothes for both of them before stacking some of Jamie's favourite toys and games into a cardboard box. Standing by the lounge window, she peered anxiously round the curtain until she saw Charlie's car turn the corner at the end of the street.

'Okay, Jamie. Grandad's here. Let's go.'

Hurriedly putting her suitcase and the box of toys into the boot of Charlie's car, Sue got into the passenger seat while Jamie clambered into the back.

Charlie checked his rear view mirror continually as they were driving away from the house. The traffic was light. A black Audi 4x4, two cars behind, followed him when he made a right-hand turn, and again when he turned left. When he pulled up at a set of traffic lights he saw it was still there, three cars back. Accelerating hard when the lights turned to green, Charlie pulled up sharply at the kerb in front of a row of shops.

'What are you doing, Grandad?' Jamie asked.

The 4x4 drove on past, but Charlie couldn't make out who was driving through the tinted windows. 'I was going to take the main road, son, but I forgot about the road works. We'll be quicker going the back way.' Waiting until the Audi was out of sight Charlie made a tight U-turn and snaked his way through the side streets.

'How long are we going to be staying here?' Jamie asked as they pulled up outside Sarah's house.

'It all depends,' Sue said. 'As far as I could make out, the leak seemed to be coming from somewhere behind the tiles in the kitchen. We won't know how long it will take to fix it until the plumber finds out where the problem is.'

'I hope it takes him ages!' Jamie said.

Sue smiled. 'I brought across some of your things for you to play with.'

'Did you bring my new jigsaw?'

'Yes.'

'Sean's brilliant at jigsaws. He can help me with it,' Jamie said, as he scrambled out of the car and ran off up the path.

Charlie got out of the car and opened up the boot. 'A leak in the kitchen?' he queried.

Sue pulled a face. 'It was the best I could come up with at short notice. Thanks, Dad,' she added as she lifted out her case and the box of toys.

'Can I give you a hand with those?' Charlie asked.

'No, I'm fine.'

'I'm going across to your Aunt Grace's now to see how Mum's getting on. Give her a call and let her know what happened. And try not to worry too much, love,' Charlie added, giving Sue a hug. 'We will get him.'

'I know you will, Dad.' Sue gave Charlie a quick peck on the cheek before hurrying up the path.

'Tea or coffee?' Sarah asked, watching through the kitchen window as the boys thumped a football around in the back garden.

'Coffee sounds good.'

'What's this all about?'

'You heard about the recent spate of murders where the victims' hands were cut off?'

'Yes. It gave me the shivers.'

'The murderer sent the amputated hands to my Mum and Dad.'

'Christ!'

'And now he's threatening me and Jamie.'

Sarah could see the anxiety in Sue's eyes. 'Are you okay?'

'I'm coping all right. It's Jamie I'm worried about – and I'm even more concerned about my father. He's the one who's in the firing line. I can tell the pressure's getting to him.'

'Well you know you're welcome to stay here for as long as you want. No one's planning to use our spare room until Joe's Mum comes to visit us in the middle of July. Come to think of it, you'd be doing me a big favour if you could stay till the end of July.'

Sue managed a wan smile. 'This is really good of you, Sarah. I do appreciate it. Are you sure Joe won't mind us being here?'

'Depending how long you stay, he might not even know about it. I told you he was off on a work's jolly in Winchester?'

'Yes.'

'They call it a management development course. More like an "improve your golf" course, if you ask me. He won't be back before Thursday at the earliest.'

Charlie Anderson drove across town as fast as the traffic would permit, constantly checking in his rear view mirror to make sure no one was trying to follow him. He joined the M8 and drove past the exit for Glasgow airport before taking the slip road for Linwood and heading out towards Elderslie.

Grace came to the front door when Charlie rang the bell. 'Thank goodness you're here, Charlie,' she said, looking furtively up and down the street. 'Kay's in the front room. Go on through.'

'Thanks, Grace.'

'Would you like a cup of tea?'

'That would be great.'

Charlie walked along the narrow corridor to the lounge as Grace bustled to the kitchen to put on the kettle.

Kay sprang to her feet when she saw Charlie. 'Sue phoned me,' she blurted out. 'She told me about the letter. What's going on, Charlie?'

'The bastard is just trying to scare us.'

'Well he's doing a bloody good job!'

'I know this isn't easy for you, Kay.'

'It's Sue and Jamie I'm worried about.'

'They're safe where they are. There's no way he can know where Sarah lives.'

'How can you be sure of that? He managed to find me in Sainsbury's, didn't he? And he managed to find out Sue's address.' Charlie took Kay in his arms. 'I hate this bastard, Charlie.' Kay choked back her tears. 'Who the hell is he? And why is he terrorising our family?'

Charlie held Kay tightly as she started sobbing.

*

Sue was stacking the lunchtime dishes in Sarah's dishwasher when she heard the familiar ring tone of her mobile phone coming from inside her handbag. She pulled out her phone and looked to see who was calling: *Number Withheld*. She swept her hair away from her face and put the phone to her ear.

'Is that Sue?' The voice was unfamiliar.

'Who is this?'

'Does Jamie like card tricks, Sue?'

'Who is this? What are you talking about?'

'Pick a card, any card. But if Jamie knows what's good for him, he must *never* pick the nine of diamonds.' Sue felt her whole body start to tremble. She gripped the back of a kitchen chair for support. 'How is Jamie this morning?' he asked.

'Who the hell are you?'

A chuckle came down the line. 'Someone who's watching you, Sue. Watching your every move.'

'Stop this – right now, you bastard!' she yelled.

'I have to go now, Sue. I've got a busy day ahead of me. But I'll be back in touch with you later on to see how you and Jamie – especially Jamie – are getting on. You must never let Jamie out of your sight. You know how easy it is for little boys to get lost.'

'Who the hell are you and why the fuck are you doing this?'

'Why don't you ask your old man? He's the great detective, isn't he? By the way, there's no point in getting him to trace this call. I've got more mobile phones than you've had hot dinners and this one will be at the bottom of the Clyde before you even have time to let him know I called. You wouldn't want to waste valuable police time chasing shadows, would you?' A raucous chuckle, then the line went dead.

CHAPTER 11

When he saw the black Mercedes pulling up at the kerb outside his hardware store, Harry Brady depressed the record button on the cassette player on the shelf underneath the counter

Alec Hunter followed Terry McKay into the shop and pulled the door shut behind him. Flipping the sign in the door over to "Closed", he tugged down the blind and slipped the bolt.

'Where's my money?' McKay demanded.

'I haven't got it.'

McKay's eyes narrowed. 'How much would it cost to replace your shop windows if they accidentally got broken?' He produced a crowbar from his pocket and swept it along the counter, smashing a glass display cabinet to smithereens. 'Five hundred quid is chicken feed compared with what we're about to do.'

'Screw the nut, McKay. For fuck's sake!'

'How about that one, Alec?' McKay said, pointing to a large vice on the display stand next to the door. 'Bring it over here.' Hunter picked up the heavy vice and carried it across. 'Fix it to the counter,' McKay instructed.

Hunter placed the vice on the edge of the wooden counter and fastened the clamps securely.

Leaning across, McKay grabbed Brady by the wrist and forced the fingers of his left hand into the jaws of the vice. 'Be careful what you wish for, Brady,' McKay laughed. 'We are, indeed, about to 'screw the nut'. On you go, Alec.'

Hunter leered as he spun the handle to close the vice on Brady's fingers. He made eye contact with McKay as it started to grip and, on McKay's curt nod, he continued forcing the handle round until there was a resounding crack.

Brady let out an agonised yelp. 'For Christ's sake! You've broken my fucking fingers!'

'Surely not?' McKay said. 'How could that have happened?' Brady's breathing was coming in short, laboured gasps. 'Now listen to me very carefully, Brady. Jim McHugh thought he could stop paying – and lived to regret it.'

'Don't you mean "died to regret it"?' Hunter interjected with a wide grin.

'Nice one, Alec!' McKay sniggered. 'As Alec so rightly says, McHugh *died* to regret it. My patience is wearing thin, so if you don't want to go the same way as McHugh, you'll pay me tomorrow. I'll be in lounge bar in The Rock between twelve and one o'clock. Bring the money to me there. And by the way, it's now a grand to make up for the inconvenience you've caused me. And just in case you've got any daft notion about going to the police,' McKay added. 'Remember I know where your daughter lives.'

'Leave Sheila out of this!' Brady gasped.

'Oh, I don't think that'll be possible, will it, Alec?' McKay said. 'You see, Alec fancies shagging the arse off her – and I want to see what she'd look like with a fucking big scar down the side of her face. But when you come to think of it, there's no reason we both shouldn't both get what we want.' McKay turned to Hunter. 'Let's have one for the road, Alec,' he said, pointing to the vice.

Hunter gripped the handle and jerked it through another quarter turn. All the remaining colour ebbed from Brady's features as he slumped across the counter. The sobbing in the back of his throat died away and he passed out in a dead faint.

McKay scribbled a note on a slip of paper and tucked it into Brady's shirt pocket. Nodding to Hunter, they walked out of the shop and got into their car.

Charlie Anderson was waiting at a red traffic light, on his way to the office, when his mobile started to ring. He took his phone from his jacket pocket and flipped it open. When he saw the call was from Sue, he snapped the phone to his ear.

'He called me, Dad.'

'Hold on a minute, love. I'm driving,' Charlie said, dropping his phone onto the passenger seat. As soon as the traffic lights turned to green he accelerated across the junction and pulled over at the side of the road. Snatching up his phone, he slammed it to his ear.

'What happened?'

'He called me on my mobile.'

Charlie felt his mouth go dry. 'What did he say?'

'That he was watching me and Jamie all the time.' Charlie could hear Sue choking back her sobs.

'Did you recognise his voice?'

'No. He said he was going to call me back, Dad.' Sue gulped. 'What should I do?' Her tone was imploring.

'He somehow managed to find out your address, Sue – and he's got hold of your mobile number, but there's no reason to suppose he knows where you are right now. I'm on my way to the office. As soon as I get there I'll arrange for CCTV cameras to be installed at Sarah's house, just as a precaution.'

'I'm frightened, Dad.'

'I realise that, but there's no reason to panic, love. That's what he wants you to do. Just keep taking sensible precautions. Don't let Jamie play outside unless you can keep an eye on him. Don't answer any phone calls unless you recognise the number of the person calling. Contact your mobile phone company straight away and arrange to have your number changed.'

'Should I tell Mum about him calling me?' Charlie hesitated. 'If he's got my number,' Sue added, 'he might have Mum's as well. He might try to call her.'

'We have to stick together as a family to get through this. Phone your mother and let her know what happened. Tell her to get her mobile number changed as well, just in case. To be on the safe side, I'll arrange for CCTV cameras to be installed at your Aunt Grace's house.'

Charlie drove to Pitt Street as fast as he could. As soon as he got to his office, he issued instructions for CCTV cameras to be installed at Sarah's house and at his sister-in-law's.

Sitting down at his desk, his head in his hands, Charlie stared unseeing at his blotting pad. The bastard was out there somewhere, taunting him, laughing at him. Was there really nothing he could do, other than kick his heels and hope that Mhairi Orr's profiling software might come up with something? For fuck's sake! He didn't even believe in profiling. The sense of frustration, of total impotence, was eating away at his guts. He didn't even want to go down to the incident room where he would have to face O'Sullivan and Stuart. What did he have to say to them? He couldn't give them any direction.

Charlie's mind was in turmoil. Should he bite the bullet and go and see Hamilton? Ask him to assign the SIO role to someone else because he wasn't getting anywhere? He'd never walked away from a case in his life. But this was more important than his pride – a hell of a lot more important. His family's lives were on the line. But what could anyone else do that he couldn't? What line of enquiry could they pursue? At least he knew the people on his list – and what they were capable of. He'd have to stick with it, he told himself. He didn't have any other option. Despondently, he took the list of names from his desk drawer and went through them again, one by one, trying desperately to figure out who could be doing this to him – and why.

Ten minutes later, when he got to the last name on his list, he felt mentally drained. He was no further forward. He folded the sheet of paper and slipped it into his jacket pocket. He thought about going home to try to get some much-needed sleep, but the prospect of going back to an empty house was thoroughly depressing. Tugging his phone from his pocket, he paged through his contacts and clicked onto Bert Pollock's number.

'Bert, it's Charlie. What are you up to?'

'Just surfing the channels.'

'I could use a dram. Fancy joining me in James Davidson's'?'

'Fine – eight o'clock?'

'See you there.'

Malcolm Stuart's eyes were glued to the computer screen in the incident room while his fingers danced around the keyboard. He didn't hear Tony O'Sullivan approaching from behind.

'Bit of a whiz at the typing, I see.' Malcolm's fingers didn't slow down as he glanced back over his shoulder. 'I've never got beyond two fingers, myself,' Tony said. 'It's Catch 22. I must have started the touch typing course a dozen times, but just when I think I'm beginning to get the hang of it, I have to break off to type something urgent.'

Getting to his feet, Malcolm pushed his thumbs into the waistband of his trousers, stuck out his stomach and started strutting round the room. Lowering the pitch of his voice, he made a passable imitation of Charlie's accent. 'This touch typing nonsense will never catch on, O'Sullivan. Passing fad. Stick to shorthand and you'll be all right.'

'Ahem! Good evening, sir,' Tony said, forcing a cough.

Malcolm spun round, blushing furiously.

'Fifteen-love!' Tony shouted triumphantly, thrusting up his right arm in a self-congratulatory high five.

'You bastard!' Malcolm reached up to slap his open palm.

'Swearing at a senior officer. That'll cost you a pint.' O'Sullivan looked up at the wall clock. 'Time we were knocking off, Malcolm. All work and no play makes Tony a dull boy. Seven o'clock on a Saturday night is late enough for anybody.'

Malcolm sat down again and spun round to face the terminal. 'I just need to finish this off. It'll only take me a couple of minutes.' He raised his hand to his mouth to stifle a yawn. 'What did you think of the boss on the telly last night?' he asked as he was tapping away at the keyboard.

'Under the circumstances, I thought he did all right.'

'Do you think he'd had a few jars before he went on?' Malcolm asked.

'I wouldn't think so.' Tony frowned. 'What gave you that impression?'

'He looked pretty hot and bothered – and he got flustered over a couple of questions.'

'Probably the studio lights and the pressure,' Tony said. 'I wouldn't have fancied bearding the lioness in her den.'

'I don't know about that.' Malcolm grinned slyly. 'I wouldn't say no.'

'You're getting ideas way above your station, my lad. Anyway, the word on the street is that Fran prefers female company to randy toy boys.'

'Oh, don't spoil my fantasy! I was hoping I might be able to talk her into being my Mrs Robinson.'

'Dream on!' Tony snorted. 'Now if I can bring you back to reality with a resounding thud, what do you have planned for this evening?'

'If you're one hundred percent sure Fran's out of the frame – ' Malcolm gave an exaggerated sigh. 'I'll probably grab something to eat and have an early night.'

'Do you like curry?'

'Sure.'

'How about we pick up a take-away and head back to my place? I've got beer in and maybe I can educate you with a malt or two?'

Malcolm's fingers darted around the keyboard as he filed the document he was working on. 'Best offer I've had all day,' he said, leaning forward to switch off the terminal.

'If we're going to have a session, it would make sense for you to drop your car off at your flat and walk over to my place. It's only about ten minutes. Here's the address,' Tony said, plucking a sheet of paper from the stack on the printer and writing it down. 'I'll draw you a map. It's straightforward,' he said, sketching. 'Up to the top of Byres Road, across great Western Road, along Queen Margaret Drive and Wilton

Street is the second on the right. My flat's on the right hand side of the road, two up, left hand side of the landing. My name's on the bell.' Tony handed across the sheet of paper. 'While you're dropping off your car, I'll pick up a take-away from the Shish Mahal. What do you fancy?'

'I'm easy.'

'How about chicken curry and onion bhajis?'

'Sounds good.'

'Vegetable pakora to go with it?'

'Fine.'

'How hot do you take your curry?'

'I usually go for vindaloo.'

'Have you tried Glasgow vindaloo?'

'No. Is there a difference?'

'I'll put you down for mild, then.'

'What?'

'Just kidding.'

Charlie found a parking bay in the High Street in Renfrew and went into the Fish Bar to get a chicken supper. He was picking at it half-heartedly as he walked along Hairst Street when he saw Bert Pollock pull into a parking space on the other side of the street.

'Fancy a chip?' Charlie said, offering the supper to Bert as he crossed the road.

'No thanks. I've already eaten.' Bert eyed Charlie up and down. 'If you don't mind me saying so Charlie, you look like shit.'

'I don't feel *that* good,' Charlie said, scrunching up the chicken supper and dropping it into the nearest bin.

'What's the problem?'

'I'll tell you inside.'

Bert went up to the bar and ordered two Lagavulins and two half pints of heavy which he carried across to the table where Charlie had installed himself.

'I saw you on the telly last night,' Bert said as he took the seat opposite. 'I thought you handled the situation pretty well.'

'I hated every minute of it. But things have taken a turn for the worse.' Charlie threw back his whisky in one, then tipped the dregs into his beer. 'The bastard has somehow got hold of Sue's address and her phone number and he's terrorising her.'

'How did he manage to do that?'

'Christ only knows!' Charlie picked up his beer and glugged it down. 'Same again?' he asked, getting to his feet.

'I've haven't even touched mine yet,' Bert protested, indicating the drinks on the table in front of him. He put a restraining hand on Charlie's sleeve. 'Getting smashed isn't the answer, Charlie.'

'What is?'

'Take it easy.'

'For Christ's sake,' Charlie said, shrugging his arm free. 'I'm only going to get myself a fucking drink.'

'You weren't joking about Glasgow vindaloo,' Malcolm said, wafting his hand in front of his mouth as Tony came back from the toilet and took his seat at the other side of the kitchen table.

'I used to take vindaloo, but I must be getting old,' Tony said. 'These days I never go for anything hotter than Madras.'

'I think I'll join you next time. That was a lot hotter than anything they serve down south,' Malcolm said, scooping up the last of the pilau rice with his fork. He hesitated with the fork half-way to his mouth. 'Do you mind if I ask you something, Tony?'

'Fire away.'

'Does Dino have a drink problem?'

Tony raised a quizzical eyebrow. 'That's the second time you've mentioned that. Why?'

'A couple of times in the office I thought I could smell whisky on his breath.'

Tony took a slow swig of beer. 'Charlie likes his drink as much as the next man, but I've no reason to think he has a problem.'

Malcolm swallowed his forkful of rice. 'I probably just imagined it.'

'Are you ready for a wee malt?' Tony asked, getting to his feet.

'To quote Colin Renton,' Malcolm said, making a dreadful attempt at a Scottish accent: "Haud me back, Jimmy!"'

Darkness had fallen by the time Harry Brady regained consciousness. When he came round slowly, he found himself slumped across his counter, his left arm and hand completely numb. Gingerly, he gripped the handle of the vice with his right hand and tried to unwind it, but it refused to budge. Taking a deep breath, he summoned all the strength he could muster and gave the handle a sharp tug. The stab of pain that pulsed through his left hand was excruciating and he almost passed out again, however, he had managed to move the handle a quarter turn. Heart pounding, he rested for a minute to recover, then he gripped the handle tightly and forced it through another quarter turn, the searing pain in his left hand easing slightly as the pressure slackened on his crushed fingers. Two more quarter turns – and he managed to free his hand. As he cradled his broken fingers to his chest, he noticed a piece of paper protruding from his shirt pocket. He pulled it out and crossed to the window where he could read the note by the light of the street lamp: *Pay me a grand tomorrow – or we pay Sheila a visit.*

Limping back across the room, he lifted the cassette recorder from the shelf underneath the counter. He rewound the tape and pressed the play button. The recording was crystal clear. Removing the tape from the machine one-handed, he slipped it into his jacket pocket.

'There's no way you're driving, Charlie.' Standing outside James Davidson's, Bert Pollock plucked Charlie's car keys from his hand.

'Give me back my keys,' Charlie slurred, grabbing hold of Bert's wrist. 'I'm okay to drive.'

'You are not okay.'

'For God's sake! It's only a couple of miles.'

'You've got enough on your plate without getting done for drink-driving. Why don't you come back to my place and kip down for the night?'

'I can't. I've got a cat to feed.'

'Then I'll drop you off home. Tomorrow's Sunday, so your car will be fine where it is. You can pick it up in the morning.'

Charlie heaved his shoulders. 'I'm all right to drive.'

'How many haufs was it?'

'Not that many.'

'Aye, right! Come on,' Bert said, pocketing Charlie's car keys. 'I'm just across the road,' he said, pointing as he led the way to his car.

Charlie's slumped low in the passenger seat, his eyes never leaving the wing mirror to make sure they weren't being followed as Bert drove the length of Paisley Road. When they got to Wright Street, Bert turned the corner and pulled up outside Charlie's gate. He handed him his keys. 'I've no idea what the solution is, Charlie, but one thing's for sure – it doesn't come in a bottle.'

Charlie unclipped his seat belt. 'Thanks for the lift, Bert. I'll give you a bell.'

Getting out of the car, Charlie stood on the pavement while Bert executed a U-turn and drove off. He looked up and down the street, seeing no one, before swaying his way up his steep drive. He hesitated at the front door with his house keys in his hand, then went round to the back of the building to check for any sign of a forced entry. It was hard to be sure in the dark, but nothing seemed to be amiss.

The house was cold and unwelcoming. He went through to the kitchen and was fixing himself a cheese sandwich when a clatter behind him made him spin round, bread knife poised. Blakey's plaintive miaow drowned the bang of the cat flap closing behind him. Charlie put down the knife and picked up the purring animal, draping him over his shoulder. 'How are you, my big boy?' he said, scratching at the top of the cat's bony head. Blakey started struggling to get down. 'More interested in food than cuddles, as always,' Charlie said, setting the cat back down on the floor. Opening the cupboard above the cooker, he took the nearest tin of cat food from the shelf and bent down to fork the contents into the bowl by the door, Blakey nudging his hand out of the way as he tried to get at the food. 'You've got more of an appetite than I have, big man,' Charlie sighed. Picking up his sandwich, he took a couple of bites, then dropped it into the pedal bin.

Going through to the lounge, Charlie poured himself a large belt of malt whisky and carried it up to his bedroom.

The pain in his hand had been replaced by numbness as Harry Brady trudged up Gibson Street, his broken fist cradled inside his jacket. He made his way up University Avenue and down the hill on the other side, as far as the Western Infirmary. When he went into A&E he saw there were more than twenty people waiting to be attended to. He went over to the reception desk.

'What seems to be problem?' the receptionist enquired.

Brady held up his hand. 'I think I might have broken my fingers.'

'How did that happen?'

'I was working in the garden when a rock fell on me and crushed my hand.'

'Not a great idea, that – working in the garden in the dark.'

'It wasn't dark when it happened. My hand was trapped under the rock. It took me a long time to get it free.'

'I need some particulars,' she said, selecting a form from under the counter. 'Name, address, GP, next of kin and religion.'

'Religion?'

'It's on the form,' she said, tapping the sheet of paper in front of her. 'And please don't say "Jedi Knight"', she said with a weary sigh. 'It's been a long day.'

'How about "none"?'

'None's fine. I just have to fill in the boxes.'

When the receptionist had completed the form, she indicated the row of blue chairs opposite. 'Take a seat over there and wait till your name's called.'

CHAPTER 12

Sunday 26 June

Checking his bedside clock for the umpteenth time, Charlie saw it was quarter past four. He rolled over and closed his eyes, but sleep wouldn't come. His heartbeat was in overdrive and everything was churning inside his head. Could he be absolutely sure that all three victims had been killed by the same person? His brain was hurting. If so, who could the sick bastard be? Assume nothing without proof, he told himself. The man who went to see Irene McGowan at her campsite was wearing a cap. The guy who gave the parcel to the kid in Sauchiehall Street was wearing a baseball cap. The murderer on the train was wearing a baseball cap. Coincidence? Don't believe in coincidences, deal only in facts. Was he wearing the cap as some kind of act of bravado? Did he want to be noticed? Was he showing off? Was he toying with the police? Charlie rolled over in bed again. How did the guy manage to identify Kay? How did he know she'd be in Sainsbury's on that particular morning, at that particular time? How did he know Charlie's grandson's name was Jamie? He'd addressed the letter to Jamie Paterson. How did he know Sue's married name? How did he find out her address? How did he get her mobile number?

The night dragged by slowly. Long periods of tossing and turning trying to make sense of what was happening, interspersed with short bursts of troubled sleep. Charlie found himself walking the length of an identity parade that snaked away into the far distance. The faces were familiar – all men he'd been instrumental in sending to jail, though he couldn't recall many of their names. A few of them were trying to avoid eye contact, some were sneering at him, others laughing in his face. And each and every one of them was holding out an amputated hand and thrusting it at him as he walked past. A voice some way down the line shouted out: "It wasn't me, Anderson. It was him!" while pointing an accusing finger at the man next to him. Others joined in the chant: "It wasn't me, Anderson. It was him!" The line formed a circle around him and started to close in slowly. "It wasn't me, Anderson. It was him!" A hundred Glaswegian keelies leering at him and, incongruously, every one of them was taunting him in a refined Glasgow accent. "It wasn't me, Anderson. It was him!" A hundred raised voices – a hundred amputated hands – a hundred accusing fingers. The chanting rose in a crescendo. It became deafening.

The screech of the alarm clock going off at six o'clock dragged Charlie from his nightmare with a jolt. He climbed slowly out of bed. His throat was parched. His head was pounding. His pyjamas were soaked in sweat.

Charlie turned the temperature up us much as his skin could bear as he stood under the shower and let the water cascade down his body. Stepping out of the cubicle, he towelled himself down vigorously. He took a jar of Paracetamol from the bathroom cabinet and spilled two tablets onto his palm. Filling a beaker with water from the cold tap, he gulped them down. While he was shaving, he decided to go across to Elderslie to see if Kay was all right before going into the office.

Although he didn't feel in the least bit hungry, he made himself a bowl of porridge in the microwave. Sitting down at the kitchen table, he poured on milk and forced most of it down.

Having whistled outside unsuccessfully for Blakey, he re-filled the cat's empty food bowl and left fresh drinking water by the cat flap.

Rather than catch a bus, Charlie decided to walk to Renfrew town centre to collect his car. It was less than two miles and he needed the walk to clear his head. The sun had already been up for a couple of hours and it was shining in a clear blue sky as he made his way down Paisley Road, with only a handful of vehicles passing him en route. When he got to his car he checked his watch. Quarter past seven – too early to turn up at Grace's. He decided to go for a drive. The Sunday morning traffic was light as he joined the M8 in the direction of Greenock. He continued on past the airport turn-off, following the signs for the Erskine Bridge. There was no traffic behind him as he crossed the bridge and he slowed right down so he could appreciate the magnificent vista of the Clyde estuary as it started to open out at Langbank and yawn its way across towards Dumbarton Rock, clearly visible in the distance on the far bank.

From Duntocher, he headed north, through Dumbarton, past the golf course he used to play on every weekend until the arthritis in his fingers made it too painful to grip a club. When he got to Balloch, at the southern tip of Loch Lomond, he drove up the west side of the loch for half a mile before pulling into a large, deserted, lay-by. He got out of the car and sat on a rock by the side of the road, gazing at the view. In the middle of the loch, the imposing island of Inchmurrin with the ruins of Lennox castle was bathed in the early morning sunlight. In the far distance, on the other side of the loch, the hamlet of Balmaha was starting to wake up.

Charlie took his list of names from his jacket pocket and unfolded it. Taking out his pen, he slowly circled, then re-circled, the five names he'd underlined. He hauled himself to his feet and dropped the sheet of paper onto the ground. He scrabbled around until he found five flat pebbles. Yelling out each of the names in turn, he sent the stones skimming across the surface of the loch, each one propelled more furiously than the last. 'What a complete waste of fucking time!' he shouted to the skies as the last pebble plopped from sight below the surface of the loch. He sank back down on the rock. Snatching up his list, he stared at the names. 'What the hell do you think you're playing at, Anderson?' he growled. 'You have to deal in facts. It's no use trying to *guess* who the killer is!' Crumpling the sheet of paper in his fist, he stuffed in into his jacket pocket and strode towards his car. Getting behind the wheel, he fired the ignition.

On the approach to the Erskine Bridge, Charlie wound his window down a few inches to allow the current of cool air to stream into his face. As he was leaving the bridge, he saw two patrol cars up ahead, parked by the side of the road. A uniformed policeman was flagging down the driver of the vehicle in front of him and directing him into the lay-by. The officer indicated to Charlie to tuck in behind. The thought flashed through Charlie's mind was that he was not in great shape for passing an early-morning breathalyser. He recognised the constable who came across.

'Hi, Frank. What's up?' Charlie asked, depressing the button to wind his window down fully.

Frank straightened his tie. 'Good morning, sir. Sorry to pull you over. I'm afraid we've had a jumper.'

Charlie shook his head. 'Dead, I suppose?'

Frank nodded. 'When you hit the water from that height, it might as well be reinforced concrete. We're having a word with everyone crossing the bridge in case they happened to see anything.'

'Weren't they supposed to be installing barriers to prevent people jumping, after what happened to those two wee lassies a couple of years back?'

'It's in the plan, sir. But work won't be starting on the barriers until sometime later this year.'

Charlie shook his head. 'What time did this happen?'

'About an hour ago.'

'I crossed the bridge in the other direction round about then, but I didn't see anything.'

'Okay, sir. Sorry to have delayed you.'

'Have you managed to identify him?'

'It wasn't a bloke. It was a middle-aged woman. We've no idea who she is.'

Instead of taking the motorway, Charlie turned off onto the narrow, twisting back roads he knew well, through Bishopton and Houston, until he got to Elderslie.

When he rang Grace's door bell, Charlie noticed the lace curtains in the lounge window twitch before Grace came hurrying round to open the front door.

'Come on in, Charlie. Would you like a cup of tea?'

'That would be great.' Charlie allowed himself a smile. He couldn't remember Grace ever greeting him with any other welcome – or him giving any other response. 'How is Kay?' he asked.

'Bearing up. Go on through while I put on the kettle.'

Charlie's mobile started to ring as he was walking down the hall. He checked to see who was calling, then dropped the phone back into his pocket.

Kay put down the magazine she was flicking through and got to her feet.

'Are you all right, love?' Charlie asked, wrapping his arms around her and giving her a kiss.

'I'm okay.' She held him close. 'Did you have a session last night?' she asked.

'What do you mean?'

'I can still smell the whisky on your breath.'

'I had a couple,' he said defensively.

'Don't let him get to you, Charlie.'

Charlie stroked her hair.

'Did anything happen last night?' he asked. 'Was there anyone hanging around in the street outside? Any strange phone calls?'

'There was nothing like that. We did get a call from someone who said he'd be coming round this morning to set up CCTV cameras.'

'That's all right. I arranged for them to be installed here – and also at Sarah's place. Just as a precaution.'

'I spoke to Sue half an hour ago,' Kay said. 'She had a quiet night. No more threatening calls.'

Grace came into the lounge carrying a tray with a pot of tea and three cups and saucers. She set the tray down on the coffee table and started to pour.

'Grace and I have decided we're not going to spend another day cooped up in the house,' Kay stated. 'We've made plans. There's a film on in Paisley we both want to see and we've booked a table for dinner tonight in the new Chinese restaurant that opened in Johnstone last month.'

'That's good,' Charlie said, taking the cup that Grace handed him. 'Just be careful, love.'

When he got to his office, Charlie fished Mhairi Orr's business card out of his pocket and called her work number. The phone rang out unanswered. He checked her card again and tried her mobile.

'It's DCI Anderson, Doctor Orr,' he said when she took the call. 'Sorry to disturb you on a Sunday morning, but I need to update you.'

'Not another murder, I hope?'

'No, but the killer sent a threatening letter to my daughter's house yesterday morning, then he phoned her in the afternoon and tried to frighten her.'

'He's upping the ante, Inspector. He's showing off. This is his way of taunting you, through your daughter. Do you know how he managed to get hold of her address or her phone number?'

'Not a clue.'

'By the way, I've eliminated James McKendrick as a suspect. The CCTV footage from Ayr Station shows him getting off the train at twelve forty on Thursday morning.'

'He wasn't high on my list,' Charlie said. 'And now you come to mention it, I remember hearing something about him moving to Ayr a couple of years ago.'

'No joy from the Sainsbury CCTV either, I'm afraid. There was no recording of the hand being put into your wife's shopping trolley. I tried running a match of the photos of the men on your list against the footage of the people entering the store on Friday morning, but that didn't throw up anything.'

'What's next?'

'From the analysis I've been able to do so far, Inspector, I don't believe we're dealing with a serial killer in the accepted sense of the term.'

'What do you mean?'

'The classical definition of a serial killer is someone who murders two or more people over a period of time, with a significant cooling off period between the murders – that isn't the case with this guy. Serial killers are often social outcasts, working in menial jobs. There are exceptions, such as Harold Shipman who killed fifteen people while working as a family doctor – but cases like that are rare. The majority of serial killers have low IQs and low self-esteem – and there's always a pattern to their selection of victims, be it prostitutes, policemen, Jews, or whatever. In this case, there appears to be no common factor that would link the victims. I don't believe this guy is motivated by psychological gratification in the act of killing itself. I think the murders are part of some other, more complex plan.'

'What kind of plan?'

'I don't know. I'll continue trying to build up a picture of him. From what we know so far, I think we're looking for someone who's ruthless, intelligent, arrogant and self-confident, but with a massive chip on his shoulder that's driving him to extremes.'

'"Intelligent" would eliminate most of the people on my list,' Charlie said.

'I've done an analysis of the crimes committed by the people you identified and, in my opinion, only two of them are possible candidates, neither of them in your top five.'

'Who are they?'

'Only Adams and Gray appear to have the psychological mindset which would be required to commit these murders and, even then, I wouldn't rate either of them at more than a ten percent probability.'

'So, the bottom line is that you don't think the killer is on my list?'

'That's what the analysis is telling me.'

'Does that mean you've reached a dead end?'

'I didn't say that. I'll keep working on the data. Essentially, you and I work the same way, Inspector,' Mhairi said. 'We sift through information to try to establish patterns, identify anomalies and assess probabilities. You use brainpower – while I rely on software.'

'Well I sure as hell hope your software comes up with something soon, doctor,' Charlie said with a sigh. 'Because right now, my brainpower isn't contributing much.'

'I'll be tied up all day tomorrow with lectures at the university,' Mhairi said. 'If anything breaks, leave a message for me on my mobile and I'll get back to you as soon as I can. If I don't hear from you before then, I'll drop in to your office on Tuesday morning and discuss where we go from here.'

'Okay.'

'Would ten o'clock be all right?'

'Fine,' Charlie said, making a note in his desk diary.

When Charlie disconnected, he checked his mobile. There was one recorded voice message: *Hamilton here. Come to my office as soon as you get in.*

'Would the word "please" have killed you?' Charlie muttered to himself as he made his way along the corridor towards the stairs at the far end. Hamilton's office door was open and Charlie walked straight in. 'You wanted to see me?'

'I've been trying to call you at home all morning. Why weren't you answering your phone?'

'I went across to Elderslie to see my wife. She's staying with her sister. I didn't want her to be in the house on her own.'

'I tried calling your mobile.'

'I always switch it off while I'm driving,' Charlie said with a dead-pan expression. 'I just picked up your message.'

'Have you seen the email I sent you?'

'I've just got in. I haven't logged on yet.'

'Check it out. There's been a development regarding the murder on the train. The DNA check revealed the victim to be a guy called

Pete Johnston – and the Met are involved. Superintendent Kenicer of Counter Terrorism Command sent me some background information in an email. I've forwarded it to you, but apparently there's a lot more they're not prepared to put in writing. There's going to be a confidential briefing by conference call in my office at twelve o'clock.'

'I'll round up the team.'

'Their presence will not be required.'

Charlie looked puzzled. 'What do you mean "not required"?'

'This is strictly need to know information.'

'For Christ's sake! My guys are working on a murder investigation. That means they need to know everything that could be relevant.'

'It's you and me, Anderson,' Hamilton rasped. 'No one else. Here – at twelve o'clock. That will be all.'

Tony O'Sullivan woke with a thumping headache. Squinting through slits of eyes at his bedside clock, he saw it was after ten o'clock. When he tried to sit up in bed, the whole room started to spin. He eased his head back down onto the pillow and tried to recall the events of the previous evening. He got as far as pouring two large measures of Highland Park while holding court on the virtues of independence for Scotland. He had a vague recollection of reminding Malcolm how to get from Wilton Street to Roxburgh Street, but he had no memory of showing him out or going to bed.

He rolled over onto his side and shut his eyes tightly, which seemed to slow the room down a little.

Harry Brady fumbled with the belt of his dressing gown as he came down the stairs.

'You must've got home very late last night,' Maisie said as he walked into the kitchen. 'I waited up till after midnight and – '

Maisie broke off when she saw her husband's bandaged hand. 'What happened?'

'I had an accident in the shop yesterday afternoon. I was repairing an electric lawnmower when it fired up unexpectedly and my hand got caught. I broke a couple of fingers. And the queues in A&E at the Western were ridiculous. I didn't get home until after one o'clock, and I didn't want to wake you.'

'Why didn't you call?'

'I tried from the hospital, but my phone was flat.'

'Is it very painful?' Maisie asked.

'It was pretty sore at the time, but it's a lot better now.'

'What would you like for breakfast?'

'Porridge would be good, but I'll have a shower first.'

'Will you be able to manage?'

'I'll be fine.'

Harry plodded back up the stairs to the bedroom. He took the cassette from his jacket and fished the note out of his shirt pocket. Going into the bathroom, he locked the door. He stared long and hard at the note. *Pay me a grand tomorrow – or we pay Sheila a visit.* Weighing the cassette in his hand, he dropped it onto the tiled floor and ground it under the heel of his slipper. Ripping the note to shreds, he dropped the scraps of paper into the bowl and flushed the toilet.

Charlie had asked Pauline to print out Kenicer's email while he went to the vending machine to get a coffee. Stirring in the sugar, he read the text:

> *The Metropolitan Counter Terrorism Command have known the identity of the man who was killed on the train from the outset, but we could not be seen to be involved. However,*

now that your DNA check has identified the victim to be Pete Johnston, I am able to release some background information. Johnston was a private in the British Army until he was invalided out in 1992, officially a victim of Gulf War syndrome, in reality a junkie who was more of a danger to his fellow soldiers than the enemy. I will contact you by phone at twelve o'clock today to brief you further. The SIO in charge of the investigation may be present, but no one else. The information I will be divulging is classified.

Mitch Kenicer
Detective Superintendent
Counter Terrorism Command.

Charlie walked into Hamilton's office just before twelve o'clock, the phone on Hamilton's desk ringing out as he was about to sit down.

'Superintendent Hamilton here,' Hamilton stated as he picked up the receiver. Charlie couldn't hear what the caller said. 'I have DCI Anderson with me. He's the SIO in charge of the murder investigations. I'll put you on the box.' Hamilton switched to loudspeaker mode and replaced the hand set.

'Good afternoon, gentlemen.' A deep, resonant voice filled the room. 'My name is Mitch Kenicer, Detective Superintendent in Counter Terrorism Command.' Hamilton fiddled with the volume control on the loudspeaker. 'I have with me Detective Inspector John Farrell, also of SO15. Are you in a secure environment?'

'The phone line is encrypted,' Hamilton said, 'and the office is soundproofed.'

'Have you both seen the email I sent this morning?'

'Yes,' said Hamilton.

'Then let me fill you in on the details. After he left the army, Pete Johnston financed his heroin addiction by working as a mercenary for anyone who was prepared to stump up for his services. He was involved in conflicts as far afield as Angola, Burma, Sierra Leone and Ethiopia, as well as a stint on the Golan Heights. When he was murdered on the London train, he was acting as a courier for an Iraqi terrorist organisation known as Brothers of the Sword, transporting an attaché case from Mull to London.'

'How did you manage to establish that?' Charlie asked.

'We have Johnston's apartment in London under constant surveillance. We monitor his visitors and we have a tap on his phone. He received a visit last Tuesday from a man called Hassam Salman, one of the leading lights in Brothers of the Sword. The day after Salman's visit, DI Farrell followed Johnston from London to Mull where he observed him meeting a contact in a remote barn and collecting an attaché case.'

'What was in the case?' Charlie asked.

'Anthrax.'

CHAPTER 13

'Anthrax!' Charlie's exclamation reverberated around the office.

'Anthrax spores, to be precise. All the way from Russia. Back in the nineteen eighties, the Soviets created over a hundred tons of spores on Vozrozhdeniya Island,' Kenicer stated. 'Despite signing an agreement to end bioweapon production in 1972, they continued to have an active programme long after that, including the production of weapons grade anthrax. Our intelligence sources tell us that the residents of Sverdlovsk were exposed to an accidental release of anthrax from a biological weapons complex in 1979. Over a hundred people were infected, most of whom died. The accident was covered up by the KGB until Yeltsin went public about it in 1992.'

'Were the Soviets planning to use anthrax as a chemical weapon?' Hamilton asked.

'Not a lot of room for us to take the moral high ground on that score, Superintendent. In the 1940s we contaminated a Scottish island for fifty years by testing the Vollum-14578 strain with a view to using it against the Germans.'

'Of course, it would have to be a *Scottish* island,' Charlie muttered under his breath.

'What was that?'

'Nothing.' Hamilton said, glaring at Charlie. 'Go on.'

'Unfortunately, the spores from Vozrozhdeniya were never destroyed and they have now fallen into the hands of some unsavoury characters.'

'Such as Johnston's contact?' Charlie suggested.

'Precisely. A guy who goes by the name of Roman Timofeivitch Bespalov. DI Farrell followed Johnston to Mull where he observed him meeting someone in a remote barn to effect the handover – either Bespalov himself, or one of his cronies. Farrell got the number of the car that picked this guy up after he and Johnston split up. The vehicle's registered as a taxi belonging to someone called Lachlan Gunn, a resident of Mull. Can you have him checked out?'

'I'll take care of that,' Charlie said, scribbling in shorthand in his notebook.

'Farrell was still shadowing Johnston when he boarded the London train in Glasgow,' Kenicer continued. 'Our intention was to let him carry the consignment back to London where we planned to recover the anthrax and nail his Iraqi friends at the same time. However, someone put a spanner in the works by taking Johnston out on the train and relieving him of the case he was carrying.'

'Do you have any idea who that was?' Hamilton asked.

'We don't have a name, but we know he was a member of an Irish Republican paramilitary organisation called the Fermanagh Freedom Fighters.'

Charlie and Hamilton's eyes met. 'Irish Republicans?' Charlie's tone was incredulous. 'How did you manage to establish that?'

'We also have dealings with the aforementioned Roman Timofeivitch Bespalov. Fisherman by trade, venture capitalist by inclination. Long before the Iron Curtain came down, Bespalov was a role model for western capitalism. Everything is available from him – for the right price. He's heavily involved in brokering arms deals. There's a glut of guns and explosives on the international market these days – the former Yugoslavian republics are awash with them – and the most popular route is from Bosnia-Herzegovina, via Croatia and Slovenia, to Russia. From there, the weaponry is shipped to wherever the buyer wants it delivered.

'Bespalov acts as middle man. He negotiates the price and organises the handover. Anthrax doesn't come onto the market very often and for this particular consignment the Irish and the Iraqis were bidding against each other. The Republican paramilitaries have been strapped for cash for some time – ever since their American funding dried up. There's no way they could match the petro-dollars. However, Bespalov has never been known to turn down anyone's money if he can help it – and he appreciates the value of information. After agreeing a sale with Brothers of the Sword, our Russian friend sold the details of the delivery plan to the FFF. He gave them everything they needed to know; from the scenario of a purportedly crippled fishing boat limping into Tobermory harbour, to the modus operandi for the handover, including a photograph of the courier and the fact that he was a mercenary. He even let them know the attaché case containing the anthrax would be handcuffed to the courier's wrist. Bespalov supplied the Irish with the details of the pick-up point, the route and the schedule – in effect, all the information they would need to intercept the consignment – and he sold them that information for ten percent of the purchase price. He also agreed to provide them with the combination to open the briefcase, if and when they managed to appropriate the anthrax.'

'Isn't this all a bit John Buchan?' Charlie interjected. 'A crippled fishing boat, a secret rendezvous in a remote barn, a briefcase handcuffed to a courier's wrist? For God's sake! If the Iraqis wanted to get a shipment of anthrax to London, why not just tell Bespalov to sail into some quiet cove on the south coast of England and drop it off?'

'It's not that simple, Anderson. For a start, Bespalov would have trouble coming up with a credible justification for sailing in those waters – and even in the middle of the night you couldn't get a boat within ten miles of the British coastline these days without it being monitored by satellite surveillance.'

'I realise I'm in danger of repeating myself,' Charlie persisted, 'but how did you find all this out?'

'We also got the details of the delivery plan from Bespalov – for another ten percent. It made quite a dent in my annual budget, I don't mind telling you. But unfortunately, Bespalov chose not to disclose to us that he'd tipped off the Fermanagh Freedom Fighters until after the event, so we weren't anticipating the hit on the train. Our Russian friend has a nasty habit of playing both ends off against the middle.'

'So,' Hamilton stated grimly, 'what you're telling us is that, at this very moment, somewhere in the Glasgow area, there's an Irish paramilitary faction sitting on a consignment of anthrax?'

'That would appear to be the case.'

'Bloody hell!'

'We're working on damage limitation,' Kenicer said. 'Bespalov is still at sea and we're in radio contact with him. If he's to be believed, he hasn't transmitted the combination for the briefcase to the FFF yet. Straight after this call I've got a meeting with the Home Secretary to determine how far we're prepared to go in bribing Bespalov not to release that information, but that's little more than a holding exercise. Bespalov's a law unto himself and as soon as he thinks he's milked us for all we're worth, he'll sell the combination to the Irish. Nothing is surer.

'I've spoken to Downing Street,' Kenicer continued. 'Their instructions are that any information regarding a stolen consignment of anthrax is to be disseminated on a strictly need to know basis. If the press got wind of the fact that Irish dissidents have got their hands on anthrax on the British mainland it could engender widespread panic.'

'In case you've forgotten,' Charlie interjected, 'we happen to have our own Parliament up here. Have you involved the First Minister?'

'This is a national security affair, Anderson,' Kenicer snapped. 'Downing Street calls the shots. No one who does not need to know will be informed about what has happened – and that includes your First Minister. I'll arrange for Downing Street to confirm those instructions to you in writing, Hamilton.'

'What about my Chief Constable?' Hamilton asked.

'There's no reason to involve him. Besides, he's on vacation.'

'You're very well briefed.'

'I know your boss is in Vienna – and I know when he's due back. I know what hotel he's staying in and, at the touch of a button, I could find out what he did yesterday afternoon, what he had for his dinner, how much he had to drink and who he took to bed.'

'You've made your point.'

'My team have got to know what they're up against,' Charlie protested. 'They need to know what's at stake.'

'That's your call, Hamilton,' Kenicer stated. 'If you consider it necessary for your officers to be told about the anthrax, you're at liberty to brief them. But do understand that you'll be held personally accountable if there's any leak of information at your end.' Hamilton sucked his cheeks in hard. 'This situation will require full cooperation between our organisations,' Kenicer continued, 'if we're to have any chance of discovering the identity of the person who carried out the hit on the train – and tracking down the anthrax – before Bespalov releases the combination to the FFF.'

'Where do we go from here?' Hamilton asked. 'We're already pulling out all the stops.'

'We're dealing with a consummate professional. Whoever took out Johnston on the train knows his business. The kill was clinical and the dismemberment of the hand was essential to relieve him of the case he was carrying.'

'Wouldn't it have been simpler to saw through the links on the handcuffs, rather than chop the guy's hand off?' Charlie suggested.

'Two reasons for not doing that. Number one, a sawn off handcuff, attached to the victim's wrist, might have put you on the right track. Number two, the hit man was working to a tight schedule. As he had no way of knowing what material the handcuffs would be made of, that would have introduced an unknown factor. Sawing your way through good old flesh, bone and gristle is much more predictable.'

Charlie got to his feet and strode towards the office window. 'Is everyone at SO15 as callous as you?' he called out over his shoulder.

'Don't lose your cool, Inspector. If you want to talk about callousness, I suggest you concentrate on the killer.'

'What about the murders of the gypsy and the young girl?' Charlie asked. 'Surely they weren't also carrying something he wanted?'

'Not as far as we know,' Kenicer said.

'And why the nine of diamonds and the smileys?' Hamilton asked.

'I don't see the point of them,' Kenicer said. 'They're probably just red herrings,' he said, cutting the connection.

Charlie and Hamilton looked at each other.

'What now?' Hamilton asked.

'I need to brief my guys about the anthrax,' Charlie said.

'Who do you need to tell?'

'O'Sullivan and Stuart at least. They have to know what we're up against.'

'All right. But only those two. And make sure they understand the need for complete secrecy.'

'What about Doctor Orr? Should I tell her?'

'Definitely not! Under no circumstances must any civilian be told about the anthrax.'

Tony O'Sullivan was dozing on his settee, nursing his hangover, when Charlie's phone call roused him. Charlie then called Malcolm Stuart, instructing both of them to be in the incident room at three o'clock.

Colin Renton popped his head round Charlie's door. 'Have you got a minute, sir?'

'Sure.' Charlie put down his pen.

'Frank told me he stopped you on the Erskine Bridge this morning.'

'That's right. Apparently a woman had committed suicide.'

'I thought you'd want to know that she's been identified, sir. It was Helen Taylor, Zoe Taylor's mother.'

'What?'

'Her car was found in a lay-by in Erskine,' Renton said. 'She left a note on the passenger seat to the effect that she couldn't go on any more. She said she hardly ever saw her husband because he spent most of his time on the road – and that her daughter was the only reason she had for living.'

Charlie felt a lump forming in his throat.

Tony O'Sullivan arrived at Pitt Street just before three o'clock. He was sitting alone in the incident room, cradling a black coffee in both hands, when Malcolm Stuart walked in.

'Is Dino not around?' Malcolm asked.

'Gone for a coffee,' Tony said blowing gently on his drink to cool it down.

When Charlie returned, he closed the door and sat on a chair in the middle of the room. 'The first thing I want to tell you,' he said, 'is that Helen Taylor, Zoe's mother, committed suicide this morning by jumping off the Erskine Bridge.'

'Jesus,' Tony muttered under his breath.

'In my book,' Charlie said, 'that's another murder down to this bastard. But that's not the reason I called you in this morning. Counter Terrorism Command from the Met got in touch with Niggle to let him know that the guy who was killed on the train was a courier for an Iraqi terrorist organisation known as Brothers of the Sword. His hand was chopped off to relieve him of an attaché case that was handcuffed to his wrist.'

Malcolm raised an eyebrow. 'Do we know what was in the case?'

'Anthrax.'

Tony's hand froze with his coffee half-way to his lips. 'Do they know who killed him?' he asked.

'They don't have a name, but they believe the killer belonged to, or worked for, an Irish republican paramilitary organisation called the Fermanagh Freedom Fighters.'

'Bloody hell!' Tony stretched forward to put his coffee down on the table with a shaking hand.

'I can't emphasise too strongly the need for confidentiality,' Charlie stated. 'Niggle has authorised me to brief the two of you, but no one else. If we need to enlist any additional resources to assist us with the murder enquiries, they must not be told about the anthrax. If the press were to get a sniff of the fact that Irish paramilitaries have got their hands on a consignment of anthrax on the Scottish mainland it could start a major panic. So apart from you two, no one else gets told about it – not even little Miss Profiler. That includes colleagues, girlfriends and mothers. Is that clear?'

With only a fifteen minute break to grab a sandwich, the brainstorming session lasted until after midnight, by which time flipchart pages containing lists of events, times, potential motives and possible suspects covered the incident room walls.

'Three murders, three amputated hands, three nines of diamonds and three smileys. And nothing to link any of them,' Malcolm mused. 'That's just not possible – there has to be a connection.'

'Maybe all three victims came from Auchtermuchty?' Tony suggested.

'If that's the level we've descended to,' Charlie said, looking at his watch and rolling down his shirt sleeves, 'it's time to call it a night.' He got to his feet and stretched his aching back. 'I could do with some kip. I reckon we all could.'

'The murderer wanted to get his hands on the attaché case,' Malcolm said, 'so there's a logical reason for him killing the soldier – and I can think of reasons why someone might want to kill a young girl – but it's completely beyond my comprehension why anyone would want to murder some old tinker. Unless it's a...' Malcolm paused, a look of comprehension slowly spreading across his features. He leapt to his feet. 'Eureka!'

'What is it?' Tony said.

'I've figured out the reason for the smileys,' Malcolm said excitedly.

'Go on!' Charlie demanded.

'First, he kills a *Tinker*, then a *Taylor*, Zoe of that ilk, then a *Soldier*. I think he's playing games with us, sir. The smiley is a smiley with a capital 'S'. George Smiley? The John le Carré novels?'

'Jesus Christ!' Charlie said, sinking back down onto his chair.

'So where does he go from here?' Tony asked. 'Has he finished killing – or will his next target be a sailor?'

'That's the nursery rhyme,' Malcolm said. 'In the le Carré version, the next one in the sequence is a spy.'

'That's all I need,' Charlie said with a quick shake of the head. 'I'm really looking forward to telling Special Branch that I want the names of all the spies they have operating in Scotland so I can arrange protection for them.'

'The reason the soldier was killed was to relieve him of his attaché case,' Malcolm said. 'But maybe the killer doesn't realise we know about that.'

'What are you driving at?' Charlie asked.

'If he thinks we don't know about the case, then those first two killings might've been a diversionary tactic to throw us off the scent. If Smiley assumed we'd cotton onto his Tinker, Tailor, Soldier theme eventually, then maybe he was trying to deflect us from the real reason for him murdering the soldier. Maybe he was hoping we'd deploy our resources towards protecting spies and sailors, or whatever, instead of focussing on the attaché case and what was in it?'

'Killing two innocent women as a diversionary tactic would require a seriously twisted mind,' Tony said.

'That goes without saying,' Malcolm said.

'Why the nine of diamonds?' Charlie asked.

'I don't know,' Malcolm said, sitting back down.

'That was good work, Malcolm. I'd better update Niggle straight away,' Charlie said, picking up the phone. 'Anytime of the day or night, he said.'

Having woken Hamilton, Charlie told him about Malcolm's le Carré theory.

'I suggest we all head off home now and get some sleep,' Charlie said, replacing the receiver. 'We'll pick up the threads in the morning.'

'Well done, Malcolm,' Tony said, yawning and stretching as he got to his feet. 'Goodnight all. Sweet dreams.' Flinging his jacket over his shoulder, he headed along the corridor in the direction of the staircase. Malcolm remained seated.

'No home to go to, son?'

'Could I have a word, sir?'

'Fire away.'

'I don't know how to put this.'

Charlie furrowed his brow.

'It's this Irish Republican business, sir.' Malcolm shifted uncomfortably on his seat.

'What are you trying to tell me?'

Malcolm's face flushed. 'I went back with Tony to his place last night. We had a couple of beers and then we got stuck into the whisky. After he'd had a few, Tony started going on about this Catholic and Protestant thing. How Pitt Street's riddled with Freemasons. How his prospects depend more on the school he went to than his ability as a copper. How he got knocked back for promotion first time round because he was a Catholic. Lots of stuff like that. Then, after we'd sunk a few more, he started playing CDs of Irish rebel songs.'

'Is that it?'

Malcolm hesitated. 'I was thinking back to Thursday morning, when Johnston was killed on the train.'

'Go on.'

'Tony was supposed to be interviewing the post office staff in St Vincent Street with Renton that morning, but he told us he got a call on his mobile from someone who claimed to be a doctor in Kilmarnock – and who told him his mother had been involved in a hit and run accident. But when he got to the hospital, it turned out to be a hoax.'

'So?'

'If it was a prank call, by someone wanting to waste police time, how did the caller get hold of Tony's mobile number?' Malcolm paused. 'I thought – what if Tony wanted an excuse not to go to the post office, sir, in case… in case someone recognised him?' Malcolm stared at the floor to avoid eye contact with Charlie. 'Or what if Tony got on the London train…?' His voice tailed off. 'I just thought it should be checked out,' he mumbled, his gaze fixed on the floor. 'If I'm out of order, sir, I'm sorry.'

'Is that it?' Malcolm glanced up and nodded quickly. 'I don't for one minute believe Tony's involved in any of this,' Charlie said, 'but you're not out of order. Nothing is sacrosanct. Good detective work requires every line of enquiry to be followed up. It's only by eliminating the impossible that we get to the truth.'

'I wouldn't want Tony to think that I – '

'No need to concern yourself on that score,' Charlie interjected. 'Tony will be told what he needs to be told. You were right to get it off your chest. Now go home and get some kip. You look as if you could do with it.'

All the way home in the car Charlie's mind was racing, trying to come to terms with what Malcolm had said. He knew Tony had a chip on his shoulder about religious discrimination in the force. He knew Tony's family had Irish Republican leanings. He also knew Tony considered himself hard done by when his promotion to sergeant had been deferred for a year. And something had been nagging at the back of his mind ever since he'd seen Tony handing over a cheque to Kylie. Her husband was a known Republican activist. What had that cheque been for? There could be an innocent explanation. Tony might've been settling his bar tab. But was it likely he'd do that with a cheque? Whatever the reason, it didn't mean Tony had become an IRA sympathiser, far less a contract killer. Charlie told himself that there couldn't be any substance to Malcolm's suspicions, however, he also told himself he wouldn't be doing his job if he didn't have it checked out.

When he pulled up in his driveway he glanced up at his bedroom window. There was no welcoming light to greet him. He tugged the Sunday Herald from the letterbox in the front door as he turned his key in the lock. The house felt cold. He opened the back door and whistled for Blakey, but there was no sign of the cat. The food bowl by the cat flap was empty. He took a tin of cat food from the cupboard above the cooker and, tugging the ring pull from the can, he forked the contents into the bowl.

Although he didn't feel hungry, he knew he ought to eat something. He found a wedge of Cheddar cheese in the fridge and munched on it as he went through to the lounge where he tipped a generous measure of whisky into a tumbler before going back to the kitchen to add a splash of water from the tap. Tucking the newspaper under his arm, he carried his drink up the steep staircase. He gave his teeth a cursory brush and changed into his pyjamas. Propping himself up in bed, he sipped at the whisky. He struggled to concentrate on the sports pages, but try as he might, his mind kept returning to the conversation he'd had with Malcolm Stuart.

CHAPTER 14

Monday 27 June

When he drifted back to consciousness, Charlie had a foul taste at the back of his mouth. He was still propped up in bed, the newspaper wedged between his fingers. The bedside lamp was still on, the half-drunk whisky sitting on the bedside table. He peered at his alarm clock and saw it was almost four o'clock. He set the alarm for seven, then swallowed the rest of the whisky in one gulp before switching off the lamp and pulling the duvet up to his chin.

Charlie cut two thick slices of brown bread and popped them under the grill before putting on the kettle to make himself a pot of strong tea. Sitting at the kitchen table, buttering his toast, he made up his mind. He was convinced Tony couldn't be involved in any of this, but it still had to be checked out. It was how he'd worked all his life – the only way he knew – sifting through a sea of conflicting data, eliminating the impossible and challenging the improbable in order to get at the truth.

The sun was shining and the sky was clear apart from a few wisps of high, fluffy cloud drifting aimlessly under the influence of a light, swirling breeze. He decided not to go via Glasgow and pick up the M77. Although the motorway would be quicker, he preferred the scenic route. The Monday morning traffic was heavy as he drove, stop start, across the centre of Paisley, past the Abbey, then through the Glenburn housing estate before starting the steep climb towards the Gleniffer Braes. This had always been one of his favourite spots

– at least, until a few months ago when a body had been discovered in a clump of trees halfway up the hillside. As he drove past the copse, his gaze was drawn towards the spot where the victim had been found. He recalled vividly arriving at the scene to identify her mutilated body. The sick feeling in the pit of his stomach returned.

Charlie wound down the car window to clear his head, taking deep breaths of the fresh, clean air as he drove along the crest of the Braes. When he reached the hamlet of Lugton, he took the left fork in the direction of Stewarton and continued on the road towards Kilmarnock.

When he arrived at Crosshouse Hospital, he managed to find a parking space at the far end of the car park, then walked back to the main entrance. There were two girls sitting behind the reception desk, one of them dealing with a middle-aged man who was trying to find out what ward his father was in. Charlie showed his ID discreetly to the other receptionist.

'How can I help you?' she asked with a smile.

'Would it be possible to talk to someone who was on reception last Thursday morning?' Charlie asked.

'Just a minute,' she said, stretching for the clipboard under her desk. 'Thursday morning, you said.' She ran her finger down a column of names. 'That would've been Lorna.' She indicated her colleague. 'And Maurice Struthers. Maurice is on his day off today.'

'Thanks.'

Charlie waited until the person Lorna had been dealing with had walked away before showing her his ID. 'Last Thursday morning, Lorna,' Charlie said, 'did a guy in his late twenties – tall, slim, red hair – come here looking for information about his mother who had supposedly been brought into A&E, the victim of a hit and run – but it turned out to be a hoax?'

Lorna took off her tortoiseshell spectacles and twiddled with them in her fingers. 'I don't recall anything like that happening.'

'Think hard. It's important. I need a definite answer.'

'Then, no.' She shrugged. 'The answer's definitely no.'

'Are you absolutely sure? He would have asked to see Doctor Wilson.'

'We don't have a Doctor Wilson.'

'What about your colleague who was on duty with you?' Charlie looked at the other receptionist. 'Maurice Struthers, you said?' She nodded. He turned back to Lorna. 'Could Maurice have dealt with this guy without you knowing about it?'

'I suppose that's possible.' Lorna sounded highly sceptical. 'But I very much doubt it. As you can see, we sit alongside each other.'

'Perhaps you might have been away from the desk at the time? In the toilets – or on a coffee break?'

'I suppose that could have happened,' she said, 'though I'd be very surprised that Maurice didn't mention anything about it when I got back. I've got Maurice's mobile number. Would you like me to give him a call and ask him?'

'Please.'

Lorna took her phone from her jacket pocket and paged down her contacts' list. 'Maurice? It's Lorna. Sorry to disturb you on your day off, but the police are here making enquiries about last Thursday morning when we were on together. Did you talk to a guy in his late twenties who thought his mother had been brought into A&E as a hit and run victim, but it turned out to be a hoax?' Lorna made eye contact with Charlie and shook her head. 'You're quite sure? Did anything like that happen on Thursday – or any other day last week?' Again she looked at Charlie and shook her head. 'Was there anyone here asking to see a Doctor Wilson?' There was a pause while Lorna listened. 'I know we don't have a Doctor Wilson, but was anyone asking for him?' Lorna shrugged her shoulders. She ended the call, slipping her phone back into her pocket. 'Nothing like that happened, Inspector. Not on Thursday, or any other day last week.'

Charlie put his foot down on the motorway on the way back to Glasgow, trying to make sense of what was going on. Could he have misheard which hospital Tony had been called to? He very much doubted it, but he'd have to check. He wasn't at all happy at the idea of Tony telling him a pack of lies about going to Crosshouse, but that didn't make him an IRA sympathiser. There were a hundred and one reasons he might have wanted to sneak time off, Kylie, the red-headed barmaid in *Òran Mór*, being but one of them. Perhaps he had nipped over to her place for a bit of early morning hanky-panky after her husband had gone to work?

He allowed himself a wry smile as he recalled the antics of Kirton and Malone. It must have been the best part of thirty years ago. Two coppers on the beat. For more than ten years, every Friday afternoon, between three and four o'clock, Kirton got Malone to cover for him while he supposedly went to visit his mother in a retirement home. In fact, he was nipping over to Bearsden to have it off with Mrs Malone, safe in the knowledge that her hubby would be fully occupied.

Would it be better to confront O'Sullivan with the facts and have it out with him? Or should he give him enough rope to hang himself? Charlie decided to play it by ear.

Charlie's mobile phone rang as he was getting out of his car in Pitt Street's underground car park. He saw the call was from Harry Brady. Connecting, he put the phone to his ear.

'Jack Williams isn't prepared to play ball, Charlie. He's too scared of what might happen to his missus.'

'Are you still willing to take the stand?'

'There's no point to it, Charlie. As you said yourself, if it comes down to my word against theirs, they'll walk.'

'I'm not going to let this drop, Harry. There are other things that can be done – such as setting up hidden CCTV cameras in your shop. But this isn't something we should be discussing over the phone. I'll come across to your place and we can talk it through.'

Brady hesitated. 'Not right now. I'm on my way out. I'm meeting my brother for a pint.'

'Will you be in the shop this afternoon?'

Brady hesitated. 'Yes.'

'Okay if I drop by?'

Brady gave a resigned sigh. 'I suppose so.'

Tony tried calling Sue's mobile, puzzled when he got a response to the effect that the number he was calling was no longer in service. He checked her number in his notebook and punched it in again, only to receive the same recorded message.

Harry Brady was walking along Woodlands Road towards The Halt Bar when a car pulled up at the kerb alongside him. The rear door was flung open, blocking his path. When he stepped to one side to avoid walking into the door, the man who had been following him appeared at his shoulder. Grabbing Brady by the wrists, he rammed his arms halfway up his back and bundled him into the back seat of the Mercedes before climbing in after him.

'What the hell are you playing at?' Brady demanded.

The driver didn't turn round. 'We're not playing, Brady,' he said.

Harry recognised Terry McKay's wheezy voice the instant before the cosh crashed into the base of his skull.

Charlie looked up the phone number of the Tobermory police station and made the call.

'DCI Anderson, Glasgow CID here. Would you put me through to whoever's in charge today.'

'That's me, sir. Sergeant Jerry Condron. What can I do for you?'

'Do you know a taxi driver on Mull called Gunn?'

'Sure. That'll be Lachlan.'

'Late last Wednesday night, he picked a man up on a remote stretch of road a couple of miles north of Craignure. I need to know who his passenger was.'

'I'm on duty until seven o'clock, sir. If you like, I could drop in and have a word with Lachlan on my way home. He lives round the corner from me.'

'I'd appreciate that, Sergeant. Give me a call and let me know what you find out. Do you have a pen?'

'Yes.'

Charlie recited his mobile number.

Harry Brady heard the twitter of birdsong as he came round. He felt a dull, throbbing pain at the base of his skull. He massaged the back of his neck with his right hand as he slowly opened his eyes, struggling to focus. 'Where the hell am I?'

'Hell's not a bad guess.' He recognised Terry McKay's voice.

Blinking his eyes, Brady found he was sitting on a wooden garden bench, wedged between McKay and Hunter. When he looked around he saw they were in a high-walled garden at the back of a large, detached, stone-built house.

'I waited for you in The Rock until after one o'clock yesterday,' McKay wheezed. 'Why didn't you put in an appearance?'

'You know why. I don't have the money.'

'That's not good enough, Brady. What kind of signal would it send to the others if word got out that I'd let you off the hook?' Brady didn't respond as he continued to massage the back of his throbbing neck. 'And you thought you could get away with telling your daughter to make herself scarce?' McKay laughed. 'How naïve can you get?'

Brady's hand froze on his neck. 'What are you talking about?'

'I thought you might try to stop us having a chat with Sheila, so I sent Alec over to keep an eye on her house. When he saw her coming out the front door last night, he offered her a lift. Well, "offered" might not be the right word – perhaps, "persuaded her to accept a lift" would be more like it.'

'Fuck you, McKay! What have you done with her?'

'Nothing – yet. She's upstairs,' McKay said, pointing towards a second-floor window with the curtains tightly drawn. 'Once we've dealt with you, Alec and I are going to toss up to see who gets first shot at her – and when we've both had our way with her, we're going to dump her body in the Clyde.'

'If you as much as lay a finger on her,' Brady shouted, trying to scramble to his feet. 'I'll strangle you with my bare hands!'

'You mean, with this one?' Hunter said, grabbing hold of Brady's bandaged left hand and crushing it in his fist. 'I don't think so.' Brady screamed in agony.

'You just don't learn, do you?' McKay said, taking his inhaler from his inside jacket pocket. Cupping both hands in front of his mouth, he depressed the plunger. 'You're as pig-headed as McHugh.'

McKay slipped his inhaler back into his pocket and produced a flick knife. Snapping the blade open, he tested the point with his thumb before holding the tip against Brady's throat. 'This is your last chance, Brady. Either you pay me today, or you and your daughter will face the consequences.'

'I don't have the fucking money!'

'That is not the right answer,' McKay said, twitching the blade. 'Think about Sheila.'

'If either of you lay a hand on my daughter, I'll fucking well kill you.' Brady's voice was shaking. 'I mean it, so help me God!'

A cruel smile played on McKay's lips as he pricked the tip of the blade into Brady's neck. 'Have it your own way,' he said, plunging the knife deep into Brady's jugular, causing a jet of warm blood to spurt out. He looked up towards the sky. 'It might be time to help him, God.'

As the death rattle echoed in Brady's throat, Hunter produced a hacksaw blade.

'It's the left hand, Alec,' McKay said.

CHAPTER 15

Charlie Anderson pulled up outside Harry Brady's hardware store in Woodlands Road. He could see the door blind was down. He got out of the car and tried the door handle. It was locked. He checked the time on his watch. Just after four o'clock. The card in the window said the opening hours were from 09h00 to 12h00 and 13h00 to 18h00, Monday to Saturday. When he peered through the window, there appeared to be no one inside. He hammered on the door and rattled the handle. Taking out his phone, he called Brady's number. There was no reply.

Sergeant Condron walked along the narrow street of terraced houses, stopping in front of a red-painted door. When he rang the bell, a tousle-haired, teenage girl came trotting down the stairs to open the door.

'Is your father in, Alice?' he asked.

'Dad! It's Sergeant Condron!' she called out. Turning her back, she traipsed back up the steep staircase, leaving Condron standing on the doormat.

An unshaven, tubby figure appeared from the lounge. 'What can I do for you, Jerry?'

'I've got a couple of questions for you, Lachlan. All the way from the Glasgow CID.'

'It must be important, then. Come on in.'

Lachlan Gunn moved aside to allow Condron to step into the cramped hall. Closing the front door, he led the way to the lounge. 'What's it about?' he asked, waving towards an armchair.

Condron sat down and took out his notebook and pen. 'The Glasgow boys want to know if you were driving your taxi late last Wednesday night.'

'Wednesday night?' Gunn scratched at the back of his head. 'Aye, as a matter of fact, I was.'

'They want to know who your passenger was.'

'I haven't a clue. A bloke came round to my garage on Wednesday afternoon and booked me to pick someone up on the main road, a mile south of Tobermory, at three o'clock on Thursday morning. My instructions were to drive him down to Scallastle Bay, to the track leading to Drumairgh Cottage. I was told to wait there for him, then drop him back off where I'd picked him up.'

'Do you know the guy who made the booking?'

'Never seen him before in my life.'

'Did you not find that a bit strange?'

'Bloody weird, if you ask me. But he was paying in advance, in cash, and with the amount of money he was putting on the table, he could be as weird as he liked as far as I was concerned. He told me where to park my cab at three o'clock in the morning and said I was to wait there until I saw someone coming along the road, flashing a torch on and off.'

'Did you recognise the guy you picked up?'

'Never seen him before. Big bloke – heavily built – carrying a briefcase. When he got into the cab he didn't say a word. I drove down to Scallastle Bay, as I'd been told. He got out of the car and walked up the dirt track towards Drumairgh Cottage and about half an hour later he came back down the path with someone else. He'd given his briefcase to the other guy, who headed off in the direction of Craignure. My passenger got back into my cab and I dropped him off at the pick-up spot.'

'Anything else you can tell me?'

Gunn shrugged. 'That's it.'

Condron closed his notebook and got to his feet. 'Thanks, Lachlan.'

Charlie was sitting at home, watching the television news and nursing a glass of Glenmorangie, when his mobile rang.

'Sergeant Condron here, sir.'

'Thanks for calling back, Sergeant. What do you have for me?'

Condron recounted what he'd found out from Lachlan Gunn. 'Sorry if it's not much help, sir.'

'Thanks, anyway.' Disconnecting, Charlie took a long, slow sip of whisky.

Tuesday 28 June

Charlie again slept badly. He was up, showered, shaved and dressed before seven o'clock. Having decided to skip breakfast, he glanced up at the low clouds as he was locking his front door. At least the rain was holding off. When he turned towards his car, which was parked in the driveway, his eye caught something jammed under the windscreen wipers.

He walked towards the car, then his jaw sagged when he made out the shape of a human hand with a soggy playing card jutting out from between the index finger and the thumb.

CHAPTER 16

Charlie was in his kitchen making a pot of tea when there was a sharp rap on his front door.

'I'm finished now, sir,' Sergeant McLaughlin said, stripping off his polythene gloves.

'What do you make of it, Eddie?'

'Male, middle-aged. The hand is swollen and badly bruised and at least one of the fingers looks like it's broken. We'll remove the wedding ring back at the lab and see if that gives us anything.'

'When do you reckon the hand was amputated?'

'More than twelve hours ago, less than twenty-four. Hard to be more precise at this stage.'

'I'm going into the office this morning,' Charlie said. 'Let me know as soon as you can if you find out anything from the ring.'

'Will do.'

When he got to his office, Charlie found a single sheet of paper lying on his desk. He slipped on his reading glasses and scanned it quickly. Picking up his phone, he called Mhairi Orr's mobile. Her phone rang out several times before switching to the answering service. He left a message, asking her to come to his office as soon as she could. Replacing the hand set, he summoned O'Sullivan and Stuart.

'Another amputated hand turned up this morning,' he stated when they walked in. 'With another nine of diamonds and another smiley attached – this time, delivered to my front door.'

'Bloody hell!' Tony muttered. 'I thought that would be the end of it – once he got his hands on the anthrax.'

'I've got the initial report from forensics,' Charlie said, indicating the sheet of paper on his desk. 'Male, probably in his forties. Third and fourth fingers of his left hand were broken. The hand was amputated using some kind of hacksaw, but the shredding marks on the skin and the wrist bone indicate that the blade had a wider serration than the one used on the three previous victims.'

'He might have changed his blade because the old one was blunt – or broken,' Malcolm suggested.

'Or it could be a copycat killer this time,' Tony offered.

'Both possibilities are feasible,' Charlie said. 'There was a wedding ring on the fourth finger of the hand,' he added. 'It was inscribed inside with – ' He read from the report: *From M.B. to H.B. With all my love – 23 10 92.*

'Were his fingers broken before or after the amputation?' Malcolm asked.

'We don't know at this stage. But "H.B",' Charlie mused. He checked a phone number in his diary, then picked up his hand-set to dial, drumming his fingertips rhythmically on his blotting pad as the call rang out. A female voice answered. 'Could I speak to Harry Brady, please?'

'Who's calling?'

'This is Charlie Anderson. I'm a golfing friend of Harry's dad.'

'This is Maisie, Mr Anderson. I'm Harry's wife. I'm afraid he's not here right now.'

'When will he be back?'

'I don't know – in fact, I'm worried about him.'

'Why is that?'

'He was supposed to be meeting his brother in the pub at lunchtime yesterday, but he didn't show up. He didn't come home last night and he's not answering his mobile. I'm sorry to dump all this on you, Mr Anderson, but I'm at my wits' end. '

'That's all right.'

'If you do manage to get in touch with him, would you please ask him to phone home straight away?'

'Of course.'

Charlie replaced the receiver slowly. 'Harry Brady didn't show up for a lunch-time pint with his brother yesterday – and I know for a fact that he didn't open up his shop yesterday afternoon – and he didn't go home last night. His wife's name is Maisie,' he added grimly.

'Harry Brady? Isn't he the guy who came to see you last week?' Tony said.

Charlie nodded. 'He told me Terry McKay was putting the squeeze on him for protection money. He said he was prepared to take the stand and testify, but when I spoke to him yesterday morning, he told me he was backing off.'

'Do you reckon Brady could've run foul of McKay?' Tony asked.

'That has to be favourite.'

'Do you think McKay could be the serial killer?' Malcolm asked.

'That could make sense. He's a vicious enough bastard.' Charlie shrivelled his brow. 'I sent him down for ten years for GBH, so it's perfectly possible that he wants to get his own back on me. But as far as I know he's never had any connection with paramilitaries. And I couldn't imagine what would link him to Irene McGowan or Zoe Taylor. Neither of them is even a remote candidate for his protection rackets.'

'What about the Tinker, Tailor, Soldier pattern?' Tony asked.

'Coming up with something like that would be out of McKay's league,' Charlie said. 'I doubt he could recite two lines of a nursery rhyme, never mind being *au fait* with the works of John le Carré.' Charlie rubbed hard at his chin. 'And the nine of diamonds is still bugging me. There must be a reason for it.'

'Should we tell Maisie Brady we think we've found her husband's hand?' Malcolm asked.

'God only knows!' Charlie said 'I've seen people faint when they've been asked to identify a dead body. I can't begin to imagine how Maisie Brady would react if we were to ask her to identity her husband's severed hand. I'll need to take advice on how to handle this. I'm hoping to see Doctor Orr this morning. I'll bounce it off her.'

As Tony was leaving the office he checked his mobile and saw he had received a text from a number he didn't recognise. As soon as he read the message, he called the number.

'I tried phoning you a couple of times yesterday,' he said, 'but all I got was a message saying your number was no longer in service.'

'I'm getting more scatter-brained by the minute,' Sue said. 'I was wondering why you hadn't called. It completely slipped my mind that I'd changed my mobile number. I was starting to think that maybe you didn't want to...' Sue's voice tailed off.

'Are you kidding? How could think for one minute that I wouldn't call while I'm still in the running to beat Willie Sharp's all-time scoring record?'

Sue smiled. 'It's good to hear your voice.'

'And yours.'

'By the way, I checked it out on Wikipedia,' Sue said. 'Willie Sharp's scoring record was only two hundred and twenty nine.'

'You can't trust everything you read on Wikipedia,' Tony said. 'To be on the safe side, I think we should stick with five hundred and twenty seven.'

'Behave yourself!'

'How are you bearing up?'

'I'm okay. Sarah's been a great help. And Jamie's as happy as a sandboy as he's got Sean to play with all day. It's my Dad I'm worried about. How is he?' Sue asked.

'The frustration of battering his head off a brick wall is getting to him. Especially as everything's so close to home. By the way, have you said anything to him yet about... you know... us?'

'There hasn't been a suitable opportunity,' Sue said.

'I think it might be better to leave it like that for the time being.'

'Why?'

'He's got more than enough on his plate right now. Another hand turned up this morning. Your father found it jammed under the windscreen wipers of his car, outside his house. And this time we think it might belong to someone your Dad knows.'

'Jesus!'

Mhairi Orr declined Charlie's offer of a coffee as she shrugged off her jacket and draped it over the back of a chair in his office. Sitting down, she opened her brief case and took out her iPad.

'Thanks for coming across,' Charlie said. 'The reason I wanted to see you is that another amputated hand turned up this morning – again with the nine of diamonds and a smiley attached. It was delivered to my house. By the way, one of my guys came up with an explanation for the smileys.'

'Which is?'

Charlie recounted Malcolm's theory.

'Sounds plausible,' Mhairi mused. 'It's compatible with his egotistical profile.'

Mhairi closed the cover of her iPad and sat up straight in her chair.

'So we're asking ourselves if the latest murder is a continuation of the same series or something else entirely?'

'The pattern has changed. This time the victim was probably someone I know – a guy called Harry Brady.'

'Does he have any connection with sailors or spies?'

'Not as far as I know.'

'How confident are you that's it's him?'

'To all intents and purposes, I'm certain. Brady has been missing since yesterday. There was a wedding ring on the amputated hand and there are initials and a date inscribed inside the ring. The initials tie up with Brady and his wife, Maisie, and the date is more or less right for their wedding day.'

'But you haven't found his body?'

'Not yet – and I'd appreciate your advice as to whether or not we should break the news to his wife at this stage?'

'I'm not a behavioural psychologist, Inspector. My expertise is in analysing data and establishing patterns, not anticipating how people will react to any given set of circumstances.'

'I'd still value your opinion.'

'My gut reaction is that you shouldn't contemplate going down that road. Not until you're one hundred percent sure. Ninety-nine point nine percent isn't good enough. You're talking about unimaginable trauma for his wife. People react in different ways when they find out a loved one is dead but, by and large, they find a way to cope with it. For some, it's immediate hysteria, for some it's floods of tears, for others it's introversion and denial. It can take time, but as long as there's a body that can be identified, there's an element of closure. However, in this case, all you've got is an amputated hand. If you were to show Maisie Brady her husband's wedding ring, of course, she'd be able to identify it. But where do you go from there? She'd want to know where you got the ring. Can you be *absolutely* sure it was Harry Brady's hand? Is it possible that someone could have taken Brady's wedding ring from him and put it on another victim's finger? That's what his wife will want to believe. And to prove to her that's not the case, you would have to show her his hand.'

'She'll have to find out the truth sooner or later.'

'Are you absolutely certain she could identify her husband's hand?'

'Surely?'

'Are you sure you could identify your wife's hand, Inspector? Are you even positive you could recognise your own?' Charlie stared at the back of his liver-spotted hand. 'It's not like recognising a face,' Mhairi said. 'Many hands look similar. Of course, you could be *reasonably* sure – but one hundred percent? Remember, Maisie Brady will be in denial. She won't want it to be her husband's hand, so she'll try to convince herself it isn't. Is there some way you could get a DNA sample of Harry Brady and match it with the hand?'

'That would be difficult without collecting something from their house.'

'And even if you did manage to establish that it is his hand, the problems don't end there,' Mhairi continued. 'The next stage of Mrs Brady's denial would be to refuse to accept that he's dead. You may be convinced that he's dead, but it's perfectly possible for a person to have a hand amputated and still be alive. That's the straw she would cling to.'

'What's the bottom line?'

'My advice would be to say nothing to her until you find her husband's body.'

'And leave her hoping he might walk through the door at any minute?'

'It's either that or run the risk of her having a breakdown. Once you've got a body she can identify, she can start to come to terms with her husband's death – but only once you have a body.'

'Thanks for the advice.' Charlie drummed his fingertips on his desk. 'Do you think this is the same killer, doctor?'

'I don't have an opinion on that. If you could let me have all the data you have, I'll update my computer module and see what that throws up.'

Mhairi got to her feet and slipped her jacket over her shoulders. As she was leaving the office, Pauline buzzed through. 'Fran Gibbons from the BBC called while you were in your meeting, Inspector. She said it was urgent. She asked if you would phone her back as soon as possible.'

Charlie dialled Fran's number. It was answered on the first ring. 'Ms Gibbons?'

'Thank you for calling back so quickly, Inspector. I need to talk to you urgently.'

'Go ahead.'

'Not on the phone. Can I come to your office?'

'Er, yes… I suppose so.'

'I'll jump in a taxi. I'll be there in fifteen minutes.'

Charlie was nursing a black coffee when Fran Gibbons rapped on his office door and walked in. 'What's the panic?' he asked.

Fran closed the door behind her and pulled a playing card from her handbag. 'This was delivered to the BBC half an hour ago. A young boy walked up to the reception desk in Pacific Quay and handed it over. He told the receptionist it was for Fran Gibbons, then ran off. By chance, I happened to be in the building, preparing an item for a programme next week. See what's written on it,' Fran said, placing the card on Charlie's desk.

Charlie's bushy eyebrows merged in a frown as he fished in his shirt pocket for his reading glasses. Slipping them on, he studied the hand-written words scrawled across the face of the nine of diamonds: *Ask Charlie Anderson if he knows what I'm going to do with the anthrax.*

Charlie whipped off his glasses. He stared at the card, then at Fran.

'What's this all about, Inspector? Do you understand the reference to anthrax?' Charlie licked hard at his lips, but didn't respond. 'Are you going to tell me what this is all about?'

'I am not going to tell you anything.'

'It's only a matter of time until the story breaks.'

'You cannot use this!' Charlie flung his glasses down onto the desk.

Fran raised both arms in a conciliatory gesture. 'Browbeating me is not the way to keep the lid on this, Inspector. Two BBC receptionists have already seen the card and read the message, as well as the kid who handed it in. It would make a lot more sense if you were to cooperate. That way you could be sure of getting a sympathetic hearing.'

Charlie crunched his closed fist down on the desk. 'You do not seem to appreciate the seriousness of this, Ms Gibbons.'

Fran met Charlie's glare full on. 'I will, once you explain it to me,' she said, sitting down on the chair opposite Charlie's desk. Crossing her legs, she smoothed down her short, denim skirt.

Charlie stared into the probing hazel eyes. 'This is a matter of national security. I'm not at liberty to discuss it with you.'

'Let's start with an off the record briefing and we can take it from there.'

'Off the record or on the record, the answer's the same.'

'You haven't thought this through, Inspector. I didn't have to bring that card here. Whoever sent it to me clearly wants to get the story into the public domain. For all we know he might have sent the same message to STV, and perhaps to the newspapers. If we don't run the story, it's perfectly possible someone else will.'

'I need to discuss this with my boss.'

'Superintendent Hamilton?' Charlie nodded. 'So he can assign two officers to work out the statistical probability of STV running the story before we do?' Fran shook her head dismissively and picked up the pen lying on Charlie's desk. She scribbled on his notepad. 'This is my mobile number. I'll expect to hear from you as soon as you've spoken to Hamilton.' Fran got to her feet and stretched across the desk for the playing card.

'I'll hold onto that, if you don't mind,' Charlie said, placing a restraining hand on top of hers.

'Be my guest.' Charlie lifted his hand away. 'Just so you know,' Fran said, tapping her handbag. 'I have a photocopy.'

Charlie took the stairs two at a time. He strode into Hamilton's office without knocking and pulled the door closed behind him.

Hamilton spun round from his screen. 'What is it?' he demanded.

'We've got a serious situation on our hands. Fran Gibbons has been tipped off about the anthrax.'

'Fucking hell! How much does she know?'

'Someone handed this nine of diamonds into the BBC within the last hour, Charlie said, placing the card on Hamilton's desk. 'Gibbons came to see me to find out what's going on.'

'What did you tell her?'

'That I'd discuss the situation with you and get back to her.'

'She mustn't be allowed to break this story under any circumstances.'

'I realise that, but she did make the relevant point that if the BBC's been tipped off, then who's to say the other TV channels and the newspapers haven't as well?'

'We have to nip this in the bud. Organise communiqués to all radio, television and press contacts and instruct them that this story's off limits.'

'It goes wider than that. We can't be sure the English nationals haven't been told. We need to let SO15 know what's happened and get them to issue a nationwide D-notice.'

'Right.' Hamilton grabbed his phone. 'Margaret, get Mitch Kenicer of the Met's Counter Terrorism Command on the line for me – right away.'

'The story is D-noticed, Ms Gibbons,' Charlie said.

'You don't hang about, Inspector,' Fran said, transferring her mobile to her left hand so she could pick up her pen.

'All broadcasters and newspapers have been advised accordingly.'

'How long do you think you can keep the lid on it?'

'Probably not for long, but at least it'll buy us some time.'

'I'd be prepared to bet you lunch that the story will be on the Internet before the day is out.'

'That's outwith my control.'

'As I had the decency to warn you before the story broke, surely that entitles me to an off the record briefing?'

Charlie hesitated. 'Not on the phone.'

'How about that lunch?'

'Òran Mór?' Charlie suggested.

'Twelve thirty?'

'I'll see you there.'

Nigel Hamilton was sitting in front of his terminal, replying to an email, when he heard a tentative knock on his open office door.

'Come in!' he called out, swinging round in his seat.

'I hope I'm not interrupting you, sir?'

'What do you want, Stuart?'

'Could you spare a minute?'

Having driven up and down the side streets looking for somewhere to park, Charlie had to settle for a spot in Dumbarton Road. From there, he had to walk the length of Byres Road to get to Òran Mór.

When he went into the bar he spotted Fran Gibbons sitting beneath a stained glass window, two alcoves along from where he'd had lunch with Tony. She was reading a paperback and nursing a tonic water.

'It's quiet in here today,' Charlie commented, looking around as he took the seat beside her.

'It wasn't ten minutes ago,' Fran said, putting a bookmark in her place and closing her book. 'The place emptied a few minutes ago when everyone trooped downstairs for "A Play, A Pie and A Pint".'

'Would you like to eat in the restaurant?' Charlie asked.

'I'd be just as happy having something here.'

'What do you fancy?' Charlie asked picking up the menu card from the table and handing it across. 'I can recommend the cullen skink.'

Fran scanned the choices. 'I'll settle for a cheese sandwich.'

'What would you like to drink?'

'I'm fine,' she said, holding up her tonic water.

Charlie crossed to the bar and ordered two cheese sandwiches and a pint of Guinness. Kylie took his order, but showed no sign of recognising him from his previous visit. Having paid for the food and his drink, he waited until the Guinness had settled before picking up the glass and carrying it across to the alcove.

'So, Inspector,' Fran said quietly, 'what's all this about anthrax?'

Charlie looked around to make sure no one was within hearing distance. 'You understand that this is strictly off the record?'

'Of course.'

'A consignment of anthrax spores was smuggled into the country last week. It was being transferred to London by a courier when it was intercepted.'

'Can I assume the courier was the guy who was murdered on the London train?' Charlie nodded. 'Who's in possession of the anthrax now?'

'We believe it to be in the hands of a dissident Irish Republican group.'

'Really?' Fran exhaled softly. 'How much anthrax are we talking about?'

'We have no idea. All we know is that a consignment was intercepted.' Charlie broke off as the barman arrived with their sandwiches on a tray, which he put down on the table in front of them.

Fran waited until the barman had moved out of earshot. 'The victim on the train had his hand amputated. Do you know why?'

'We believe the anthrax was in an attaché case handcuffed to his wrist.'

'In which case, I can understand that there was a reason, albeit grisly, for cutting off his hand. But what's the connection between that murder and the first two?'

'We don't know for sure, but we suspect they may have been a diversionary tactic.'

'Do you know why the amputated hands were sent to you?' Charlie shook his head. 'Surely you must have some idea who's trying to terrorise you and your family?'

'Not a fucking clue.' Snatching up his Guinness, Charlie took a long, slow swig.

CHAPTER 17

'We can't arrest Terry McKay without substantive evidence,' Hamilton stated. 'His legal team would make mincemeat of us.'

'I'm sure he murdered Harry Brady,' Charlie said.

'What about the other victims?'

'We don't have anything to connect him with them. But one murder charge is enough to be going on with.'

'Do you have any reason to believe McKay has links with the FFF or any other Irish paramilitary organisation?'

'No. But he's never been fussy about whose money he takes. Kenicer's theory is that the Irish hired a contract killer to do their dirty work for them. McKay's muscle, Alec Hunter, would fit the bill perfectly.'

'That's all hypothetical. And even if your suspicions are correct, we wouldn't be able to offer any proof.'

'Maybe not at this stage, but I still think it's worthwhile bringing McKay and his sidekick in for questioning.'

'That is not a sensible approach. It wouldn't get us anywhere.'

'It's worth a try.'

'You're not listening to me, Anderson. I told you – that would get us nowhere!'

Charlie summoned O'Sullivan and Stuart to his office.

'We're going to pull McKay and Hunter in for questioning. Hunter's not the sharpest tack in the box and if we split them up, it's possible we might get something out of him. Harry Brady told me they do their collection round in Woodlands Road on Tuesday afternoons.' Charlie checked his watch. 'We'll meet downstairs in the car park at two o'clock.'

Charlie took the wheel with O'Sullivan and Stuart in the back seat. He drove down Pitt Street, along Bath Street, then swung right at the Charing Cross traffic lights before filtering left into Woodlands Road. Driving slowly, he found a place to park between Ashley Street and Arlington Street, twenty metres from Harry Brady's hardware store.

'From what Brady told me, this is more or less the middle of their patch,' Charlie said, switching off the ignition. 'It's just a matter of hanging about and waiting for them to put in an appearance.'

They had been sitting in the car for more than half an hour, Charlie's fingertips drumming incessantly against the steering wheel as he continually checked his watch. Glancing into his rear view mirror for the umpteenth time, his fingers froze in mid-tap when he saw two tall figures striding along the pavement towards them. 'This is it, boys,' he said. 'Get ready.'

Charlie kept his eyes fixed on his rear view mirror as the distance between the approaching figures and the car diminished. When the two men were almost level with the vehicle, he flung open the driver's door and stepped out onto the pavement in front of them while O'Sullivan and Stuart scrambled out from the rear seats and moved round behind them.

'Nice day for a walk,' Charlie said.

McKay and Hunter stopped in their tracks. 'What the fuck do you want, Anderson?' McKay wheezed, glancing back over his shoulder at O'Sullivan and Stuart.

'When did you last see Harry Brady?'

'Who the fuck's Harry Brady?' McKay said.

'You're trying to tell me you've been collecting protection money from someone for the past five years and you don't even know his name?'

'You're talking through the hole in your arse, Anderson. As usual.'

'I noticed that you walked straight past Brady's shop just now. Didn't even give it a sideways glance. How did you know he wouldn't be there?'

McKay's left eye twitched as his hand snaked towards his inside jacket pocket. Stuart was the first to react, bending low and launching himself horizontally, taking McKay around the hips and driving him like a human battering ram into the red sandstone wall. There was a dull thud as McKay's skull crunched into the wall, his neck twisting at a grotesque angle. He lay motionless on his back, his eyes open wide, staring unseeingly, as a trickle of blood leaked from the corner of his gaping mouth. There was a stunned silence, broken only by the sound of Stuart's rapid breathing as he lay prone, his arms still wrapped around McKay's thighs.

O'Sullivan stepped forward to help Stuart to his feet. Stuart's features were chalk white. He turned to Charlie. 'You saw him, sir?' His look was imploring. 'You saw him reaching for his gun?'

'He was going for his fucking inhaler!' Hunter shouted. 'Terry never carried a gun in his life. That was murder, Anderson – and you fucking know it!'

Charlie made eye contact with O'Sullivan.

'I saw his hand move, sir.'

'This is a stitch up!' Hunter roared. 'That was cold-blooded fucking murder!'

Charlie exchanged a nod of recognition with the uniformed officer who was sitting beside the door of the interview room in Pitt Street.

'They're queuing up to give evidence,' Charlie said as he walked across to the table in the middle of the room where Alec Hunter was sitting, his eyes glued to the floor. 'At the latest count, half a dozen shopkeepers in Woodlands Road are prepared to testify that McKay and you have been running a protection racket for the past five years.'

Charlie eased himself down onto the chair on the opposite side of the table. 'The forensic boys have given the hacksaw blade we found in the boot of your car the once-over and they found your prints on the handle and traces of Harry Brady's DNA on the blade. You can either sit there like a cat who's lost his tongue or you can try to save your miserable skin.' Hunter continued to stare fixedly at the floor. 'I know you and McKay killed Brady. Why did you kill the others?'

Hunter looked up quickly, meeting Charlie's gaze full on. His eyes were flashing. 'I don't know anything about any others.'

'Come off it! Four victims – all of them with their left hands amputated – and all four hands sent to me and my family. And you're trying to tell me you don't know anything about them? Pull the other one.'

'They were nothing to do with me.'

'Have it your own way.' Charlie shrugged. 'One murder rap – or four. It doesn't make a great deal of difference.'

'I didn't kill Brady.'

'Give me a fucking break, Hunter! Your prints are on the handle of the hacksaw and Brady's blood is on the blade. That's better than a signed confession.'

'Okay, okay. I was there when Brady was killed – and I did cut off his hand. But he was already dead when I did that. I didn't kill him.'

'Are you telling me McKay killed him?'

Hunter hesitated, then nodded quickly. 'He stuck his flick knife into Brady's throat.'

'I want that in writing.' Hunter's eyes clouded over. 'Why did McKay kill him?'

'Brady refused to pay his protection money. We told him we'd got hold of his daughter and we threatened to do her in, but he still wouldn't pay up.'

'Did you have her?'

'No. I went round to her place to try to get her, but she'd done a runner. Brady must have tipped her off.'

'Why did you chop Brady's hand off?'

'McKay told me to do it.'

'What did you do with his hand?'

'We drove over to your house and stuck it under your windscreen wipers.'

'Why?'

'McKay wanted to scare the shit out of you.'

'Did McKay tell you to chop the hands off the other victims as well?'

'I've already told you. I don't know anything about any others.'

'Who are you trying to kid? It was the same routine every time. Someone was murdered, their left hand was chopped off and it was sent to me or my wife. Are you trying to tell me there's another nutter like you running around the city?'

'How often do I have to say it? I know fuck all about any other murders.'

'Could McKay have killed those people when you weren't there?'

'I don't know. All I know is they were nothing to do with me.'

'What did you do with Brady's body?'

'We buried it.'

'Where?'

'In the Campsies.'

'Are you ready to take us to it?'

Hunter nodded slowly, then his gaze sank back down to the floor.

Charlie got to his feet and went across to the door. 'Arrange for this one to be transferred to Barlinnie,' he said to the uniformed officer.

'What the hell were you playing at, Anderson?' Hamilton seethed. 'I expressly forbade you to arrest McKay and Hunter.'

'At least six shopkeepers in Woodlands Road are prepared to testify that they've been paying protection money for the past five years. Hunter is going to turn Queen's evidence. He's admitted chopping off Harry Brady's hand and he's prepared to point the finger at McKay for Brady's murder. By my reckoning, that's a result.'

'That does not justify you countermanding my instructions!'

'I knew from Brady that Tuesday afternoon was McKay and Hunter's pick-up time in Woodlands Road. I didn't want to miss the opportunity. I tried to call you to clear it with you,' Charlie lied, 'but your phone was engaged.'

'What about the other murders? Has Hunter admitted his involvement?'

'He claims to know nothing about them, but we're still working on him.'

'Do you believe all four murders are down to McKay and Hunter?'

'I don't know. If the Tinker, Tailor, Soldier theory is correct, Brady's murder doesn't fit into the pattern. And it appears that a different hacksaw blade was used on the fourth victim, though that, in itself, isn't conclusive.'

'I think it likely that McKay and Hunter were responsible for all four,' Hamilton stated. 'Copycat murders and mutilations are rare – and McKay had every reason to want to get his own back on you because you sent him down for ten years. If the FFF had come to McKay looking to hire a contract killer, he would've been prepared to offer them Hunter's services if the price was right.'

Charlie frowned. 'If Hunter was the hit man, what does he stand to gain by admitting his involvement in Brady's murder while denying all knowledge of the other three?'

'You said Hunter has admitted to chopping Brady's hand off, but he's claiming it was McKay who killed him?'

'That's correct,' Charlie said.

'He knows we've got incontrovertible proof from the hacksaw that he was responsible for cutting off Brady's hand, so pointing the finger at McKay might be a ploy on his part to try to avoid facing a murder rap. Keep the pressure on him and see if you can get him to crack.'

'What's the situation with Malcolm Stuart?' Charlie asked.

'There will have to be a disciplinary hearing,' Hamilton said. 'In your assessment, was his action justified?'

'When we confronted McKay and Hunter in the street, McKay's hand definitely moved towards his inside jacket pocket. I realised he was reaching for his inhaler, but Stuart thought he was going for a gun and he reacted accordingly. It all happened in a split second.'

'How are the press treating it?'

'The breaking news on television is calling it an understandable mistake. McKay had few friends in the media, it seems.'

'I'm holding a press conference at nine o'clock tomorrow morning. Make sure your team are all present in case there are specific questions for them.'

'How did it go upstairs?' Tony asked when Charlie got back to his office.

'As well as could be expected, under the circumstances. I got a bollocking for ignoring Niggle's instructions and going after McKay and Hunter, but the fact that Hunter's prepared to turn Queen's evidence ameliorated the situation somewhat. Niggle thinks McKay and Hunter were responsible for all four murders and pinning them all on them will allow him to close out four murder investigations in one fell swoop. As far as he's concerned, that's a higher priority than establishing the facts. He's holding a press conference at nine o'clock tomorrow morning and we all have to be there to witness him lording it over the media. One thing you can be sure of, he'll be milking it for all its worth.'

'Would it be worth our while having another go at Hunter?'

'It can't do any harm.'

'Perhaps it's just as well it ended the way it did,' Tony said. 'The prospect of having McKay back on the streets, even in twenty years' time, is something we could all do without.'

'Fair comment,' Charlie nodded.

'I reckon Malcolm's going to have trouble coming to terms with what happened, considering McKay wasn't carrying a weapon,' Tony said.

'Did you think McKay was going to draw on us?' Charlie asked.

O'Sullivan shrugged. 'His hand moved toward his inside jacket pocket. I'm sure of that. A split-second decision. If Malcolm hadn't gone for him, I might well have. Will Malcolm be okay?'

'As a matter of procedure, there will be a disciplinary hearing. The question that has to be addressed is whether or not the force he used was proportionate. Hard to say how that will go.'

'Do you need me for anything else today?'

'Why? Have you got another hot date lined up?'

'If only! My father called me half an hour ago to let me know my Mum's not feeling great.'

'Not another hit and run?' Charlie fixed Tony with a stare.

'Nothing like that. Dad thinks she might have a touch of summer flu. I'd like to go down to Saltcoats and try to cheer her up.'

'Niggle's press conference is at nine o'clock tomorrow morning and it's a three line whip. We all have to be there. Why don't you wait until after the conference and go down to see your mother then? You can have a couple of days off in lieu of overtime – you've earned it.'

'Okay, thanks. I'll do that.'

'In which case, let's go across to Barlinnie now and have another go at Hunter.'

'Dates and time, Hunter,' Charlie stated. 'Dates and times.'

Alec Hunter, sitting on the opposite side of the table in the interview room, eyed Charlie and Tony suspiciously. 'What are you talking about?'

'If you're going to stick to your story that you had nothing to do with the first three murders,' Charlie said, 'you're going to have to come up with a credible alibi for what you were doing at the time those murders took place.'

Tony referred to the sheet of paper in his hand. 'Monday, twentieth June at nine a.m. – Irene McGowan. Tuesday, twenty first of June at twelve thirty – Zoe Taylor. Thursday, twenty third of June at twelve o'clock – Pete Johnston. Where were you and what were you doing on those days, at those times?'

'You must be joking!' Hunter shook his head. 'I don't keep a fucking diary.'

'It was only last week,' Charlie said. 'It's in your own interest to think hard about where you were, because if you can't account for what you were doing, we're going to throw the book at you for all four murders.'

'Jesus Christ!' Hunter rubbed hard at his chin. 'I was with Terry McKay most of the time.'

'You're not helping your cause,' Tony said.

'Wait a minute!' Hunter snapped his fingers. 'You said one of them was last Tuesday?'

'Yes.'

'At half-past twelve?'

'That's right,' Charlie said.

'I was with McKay in Woodlands Road.'

'Is there anyone who can vouch for that?'

'Tommy Matheson, in the chippie. We normally do our rounds on Tuesday afternoons, but we went across early last Tuesday, just after half past twelve, to lean on Matheson because he was behind with his payments.'

'For your sake, you better hope he remembers your visit,' Tony said.

'He'll remember it all right,' Hunter said sheepishly, his cheeks reddening. 'I dipped his fingers into his deep-fat fryer.'

There was an early-evening chill in the air when Charlie and Tony walked out of the gates of Barlinnie and headed towards their cars, which were parked side by side.

'By the way,' Charlie called across as he was unlocking his door. 'Remind me. What hospital was it that you were sent to on a wild goose?'

'Crosshouse,' Tony said. 'Why?'
'I just wondered.'

CHAPTER 18

Wednesday 29 June

Charlie got to his office before eight o'clock. He was tugging off his jacket when he noticed a sealed envelope with his name printed on it, lying in the middle of his blotting pad. He slit the envelope open with his paper knife and slipped on his reading glasses. Sitting down, he read the hand-written page.

Grabbing his phone, he dialled a number. 'We'll go with Plan B,' he stated tersely.

Charlie slouched on the long wooden bench at the back of the interview room, Malcolm Stuart by his side. At the front of the room, Superintendent Hamilton was basking in the television camera arc lights as he sat in front of a battery of microphones.

'Where the hell's Tony?' Charlie whispered in Malcolm's ear.

'I haven't seen him all morning, sir.'

As the wall clock flicked across to nine o'clock, Hamilton got to his feet to deliver his prepared statement. When he'd finished speaking, he sat down and announced that he was prepared to take questions. They came thick and fast.

'Do you have proof that Terry McKay was involved in all four murders?'

'Alec Hunter has confessed to being present when McKay slit Harry Brady's throat. He took us to where they'd buried Brady's body.'

'Has Hunter admitted his involvement in the other killings?'

'Not at this stage, but we're still questioning him. However, the similarity of the modus operandi means it's likely that McKay and Hunter were the perpetrators of all four murders.'

'What was their motive?'

'That has still to be established, although it's clear that the animosity McKay bore towards DCI Anderson was a significant factor.'

'Was Terry McKay resisting arrest when he was killed?'

'That matter is subject to an inquiry. I am not prepared to speculate on the outcome.'

'Was McKay carrying a gun?'

'Again, pending the inquiry, I'm not in a position to make any comment.'

'What's the situation regarding DC Stuart?' Malcolm felt his throat go dry.

'As a matter of procedure, there will be a formal investigation by the Complaints and Disciplinary Branch, following which the Procurator Fiscal will make the decision as to whether or not to initiate criminal proceedings.' Malcolm's fists clenched involuntarily. 'However,' Hamilton continued, 'what I can tell you is that two experienced officers were present at the scene of the incident and they both saw McKay reach for what was presumably a weapon.' Malcolm's fists slowly relaxed. 'The arresting officer, DCI Anderson, is with us this morning.' Hamilton waved his hand in the general direction of the back of the room. A sea of faces turned round and Charlie was momentarily blinded by cameras flashing in his direction. 'I would like to take this opportunity to offer my congratulations to DCI Anderson and his team for the excellent job they did in identifying Terry McKay as Harry Brady's killer. Of course McKay's death was regrettable,' Hamilton droned on, 'however, those who live by the sword…'

Hamilton's squeaky voice seemed to rise a notch with every crowing response, his tone becoming ever more triumphalist. 'Year to date, my division has an excellent record of solving serious crimes on our patch. I doubt you'll find a better performance anywhere in the country. Wouldn't you agree, Miss Gibbons?' he said, grinning inanely at Fran who was sitting in the front row.

'*Miss* Gibbons,' Charlie muttered to Malcolm. '*Big* mistake.'

'Once again, you seem to be manipulating the statistics, Superintendent,' Fran retorted.

Hamilton studiously ignored her comment and waved his hand to take a question from a reporter in the middle of the room.

When the questions had died to a trickle, Charlie whispered to Malcolm. 'I'm going to make myself scarce. I don't want to have to face the vulture pack at the end of the session. If anyone asks, I was called away urgently. I'll see you back in my office when it's over.' Getting to his feet, he slipped quietly from the room.

Charlie had his head buried in paperwork when Malcolm walked into his office fifteen minutes later. 'Did I miss anything interesting?' Charlie asked, screwing the top back onto his fountain pen.

'Just the cat polishing off the cream, sir. Any news of Tony?'

'He got a puncture on the way to work and the stupid idiot's spare was flat. He had to call out the AA. He didn't get here until five minutes ago. He's gone for coffees.'

Tony nudged the office door open with his toe cap. 'Hi, Malcolm. Sorry, I didn't get you one,' he said, placing the two plastic cups he was carrying on cardboard coasters on Charlie's desk.

'We've all worked too many hours recently,' Charlie said, standing up and arching his back. 'I think we've earned ourselves an afternoon off – and I fancy something a bit stronger than coffee. How about a wee libation, boys?'

'I wouldn't take a lot of persuading, sir,' Malcolm said, grinning as he glanced at Tony.

'How about you, Tony?' Charlie said.

'Count me in. What about Renton? Shouldn't we invite him?'

'Colin had to go to the dentist's this morning,' Charlie said. 'His wisdom tooth was giving him gyp.'

'I've got an idea,' Tony said, snapping his fingers. 'How about we go across to my place? Despite Malcolm's last visit, the malt supplies are still in a reasonably healthy state.'

'Look who's talking,' Malcolm said. 'I wasn't the one pissed out of my brains at two o'clock in the morning!'

'Love-fifteen,' Charlie said.

Tony drove his car up the ramp out of the Pitt Street car park with Malcolm in the passenger seat and Charlie in the back.

'Do you think you'll be appearing on the telly again this week, sir?' Malcolm said, twisting round in his seat to face Charlie.

'Not if I can help it.'

'If you do,' Tony said, 'I suggest you ask for a bit more make-up. Your cheeks were turning a delicate shade of pink towards the end of the programme.'

'You're getting far too big for your boots, my lad,' Charlie growled. 'Just for that, I'm going to put a fucking big hole in your malt supplies.'

As they were hopping from one red traffic light to the next along Great Western Road, Charlie tapped Tony on the shoulder. 'Drop me off at the tobacconist on the corner. I fancy a big Havana.'

'I didn't know you smoked.'

'I haven't touched the weed in years, but I'm going to make today an exception. Anyone care to join me?' They both declined as Tony pulled up by the kerb to let Charlie out.

Tony found a place to park at the end of Wilton Street, then he and Malcolm climbed the tenement staircase together. 'You know where the whisky supplies are kept,' Tony said as he was unlocking his apartment door. 'Go ahead and choose your poison while I go for a leak.'

Tony eased his apartment door open quietly to let Charlie in. Placing his index finger across his lips, he pointed in the direction of his half-open bedroom door. They both moved silently across the hall.

'Is this what you're looking for?' Charlie asked.

Malcolm was on all fours on the bedroom floor, tugging a suitcase out from under Tony's bed. When he heard the gruff voice behind him, he spun round. Charlie was framed in the doorway, a pair of wrap-round sunglasses in one hand, a baseball cap in the other. Tony was standing by his side, a hacksaw blade in his left hand, his right arm fully extended with a pistol trained on Malcolm's head.

Malcolm scrambled to his feet. 'What the hell's going on?'

'How about you answer that question?' Charlie said.

'I… I was just…'

'You were just, what?' Tony said.

Malcolm's eyes narrowed. 'Why don't you go and fuck yourself!'

'Now we're getting somewhere,' Charlie said. 'Why did you pick on Tony to frame? After all, he comes from your side of the divide.'

'Calls himself Irish!' Malcolm spat out the words. 'He's worse than useless! He lets the Orange bastards tramp all over him and all he does is whinge about missing out on his promotion.'

Tony strode across the room and grabbed Malcolm by the shoulders. Spinning him round, he dragged his hands behind his back and snapped on the handcuffs.

Charlie led the way down the staircase to Tony's car. He guided Malcolm's head down as he pushed him into the back seat and climbed in after him. Tony got into the driver's seat and fired the ignition.

'Where to, sir?'

'Maryhill nick. I'll call ahead and let them know we're coming,' Charlie said, pulling out his mobile.

Charlie recognised the sergeant behind the desk 'Take very good care of this one, Dave. He's big trouble.' Charlie turned to Malcolm.

'Malcolm Stuart,' he intoned. 'I am arresting you for the murders of Irene McGowan, Zoe Taylor and Pete Johnston. You do not have to say anything. However, it may harm your defence if you do not mention, when questioned, something you later rely on in court. Anything you do say may be given in evidence.'

As soon as he got back to Pitt Street, Charlie hurried up the stairs to his office. Checking a phone number, he picked up his handset and called Fran Gibbons.

CHAPTER 19

Charlie and Tony sat side by side in Nigel Hamilton's office, waiting for the four o'clock conference call with the Met's Counter Terrorism Command to come through.

'How the hell did Fran Gibbons manage to get hold of the story?' Hamilton fumed. 'I've just had the Chief on the blower and he's spitting blood. He got home from holiday this afternoon and he switched on the television just in time to catch Gibbons delivering a breaking news exclusive about Malcolm Stuart being a three-time serial killer.'

Charlie and Tony exchanged a puzzled glance. 'I've no idea.' Charlie shrugged.

Hamilton shook his head in exasperation. 'Why wasn't I informed about Stuart's involvement before I went in front of the press?'

'I didn't find out until it was too late,' Charlie lied. 'I was called out of the press conference to take an urgent call from Tony.'

'I was planning to go down to Saltcoats for a couple of days to see my mother as soon as the press conference was over,' Tony interjected. 'So before coming in to work this morning, I went to pack a few things. When I took my overnight bag out from under my bed, I found a pair of blue, wraparound sunglasses and a baseball cap inside, as well as a hacksaw blade. There was no sign of any forced entry to my apartment. I racked my brains as to who could have put them there and I came to the conclusion that the only person who'd been in my flat since I'd last used my overnight bag was Malcolm Stuart. He came round to my place last Saturday for a few drinks and he must've smuggled the stuff in and planted it in my case, probably when I went to the loo.'

'When Tony told me what he'd found, he suggested we could either confront Stuart with the evidence, or bait a trap for him. I opted for Plan B.'

'It looks as if he was trying to frame me,' O'Sullivan said.

Hamilton nodded. 'That certainly seems to have been his intention. He came to see me yesterday and told me he suspected you of having Irish Republican leanings. He laid it on pretty thick. He told me he'd been to your place on Saturday and he said that, after you'd had a few, you started playing Irish rebel songs.'

'The lying bastard!'

'Stuart told me he'd come to me over your head, Anderson, because he thought you were too close to O'Sullivan to be objective. He tried to convince me there was enough evidence to justify searching O'Sullivan's flat and he asked me to issue a warrant.'

'And did you?' Charlie asked.

'Of course not!' Hamilton blustered. 'I told him I'd have to review the situation with you.'

'Planting the evidence to frame Tony was clearly part of Stuart's plan,' Charlie said, 'but that wasn't without its risks. Stuart was the one pointing the finger and if Tony could manage to prove his innocence, suspicion was liable to fall on him. However, when Terry McKay committed a copycat murder, Stuart saw the possibility of letting him take the rap for all four. For that to work, he had to make sure McKay wouldn't be able to confess to one murder while denying all knowledge of the others. When he got the opportunity to take McKay out in the line of duty, with two police officers as witnesses, he must have thought all his Christmases had come at once. In retrospect, I can see now that the way he drove McKay's head into the shop doorway was way over the top, but in the heat of the moment it looked like an accident.

'The only fly in Stuart's ointment,' Charlie continued, 'and it was one hell of a big fly – was that he'd already planted the sunglasses, baseball cap and hacksaw blade in Tony's overnight case. He was probably planning to break into Tony's flat to recover them when we presented him with the opportunity to retrieve them on a plate, at the same time giving him enough rope to hang himself.'

'I should have been consulted before firearms were issued.'

'I didn't want to interrupt you in the middle of your press conference,' Charlie said. 'But when I reflected on how clinically Stuart had taken out McKay, I thought we'd better go in prepared, so I asked the Assistant Chief Constable to authorise issuing a handgun.'

'What does Stuart have to say for himself?' Hamilton asked.

'He had an initial outburst when we arrested him, but since then he's clammed up completely. I'm planning to – '

Charlie's flow was interrupted by the buzz of Hamilton's intercom.

'I have Superintendent Kenicer of Counter Terrorism Command on the line for you, sir.'

'Put him through, Margaret.' Hamilton transferred the call to the loudspeaker. 'Hamilton here,' he announced. 'I have DCI Anderson and DS O'Sullivan with me.'

'Good morning, gentlemen,' Kenicer's voice boomed. 'I believe you've arrested Malcolm Stuart and charged him with murder. Well done! A nasty piece of work, if I may say so.'

'You know him?' Hamilton queried.

'We've known Stuart was bad news from the day he applied to join the Met. We knew from the outset he was an Irish Republican sympathiser – it runs in his family – and while he was at LSE he fell in with a bunch of hardliners from the Fermanagh Freedom Fighters.'

'How do you know all this?' Charlie asked.

'We have a mole within the FFF who keeps us informed.'

Charlie stared incredulously at the loudspeaker. 'In which case,' he demanded, 'why didn't you block Stuart's application?'

'Dissident Irish factions, along with many other terrorist organisations, are continually on the lookout for opportunities to infiltrate the Establishment, Inspector. If we were to reject the likes of Stuart, they'd only plant someone else. Much better the devil we know to keep an eye on. For example, within the Met itself, we've recently identified a mole with links to Hizb ut-Tahrir. Once such people have been pinpointed, we're in a position to feed them whatever information, or disinformation, suits our purposes. Much more worrying is the situation with Hezbollah who are clearly being leaked information and we've no idea where it's coming from.'

'Why did you withhold that information from us?' Charlie demanded.

'A lot of things will fall into place, Inspector, when I explain the background.' Kenicer's tone was patronising. 'When the Fermanagh Freedom Fighters got the details of the handover plan for the anthrax from Bespalov, Stuart volunteered for the mission to intercept the courier. However, for that to happen, his handlers had to arrange for him to be posted to Glasgow. His hands-on training had originally been scheduled as six months in Liverpool, followed by six months in Manchester, until someone rather high up in the Met came up with the idea of fostering good relationships with their Scottish counterparts by offering to send Stuart up north for a spell. We've had our suspicions about that gentleman for some time.'

'Do you have enough to make it stick?' Charlie demanded.

Kenicer laughed out loud. 'Not at all in our interests, Inspector. Another devil we now know.' Charlie shook his head in exasperation. 'Stuart had a specific reason for volunteering to take on the assignment,' Kenicer stated. 'It was personal. He wanted to get his revenge on you.'

Charlie's eyes narrowed. 'What are you talking about?' he said.

'He held you responsible for his father's death.'

Charlie stared at the loudspeaker. 'His father?'

'Does the name George Campbell mean anything to you?' Kenicer asked.

'Ye…es,' Charlie stammered. 'I think so. Sent him down for terrorism. Twenty-odd years ago. IRA. Not the front line stuff, he was a more of a fixer, arranging false passports, safe houses, fund raising – stuff like that.'

'That's the guy. It was twenty three years ago, to be precise. Some of the tabloids christened him George…'

Charlie interrupted. 'George Smiley Campbell.' He glanced at O'Sullivan. 'He was this little, insignificant, grey man. Like the character. He died in prison.'

'He fell in the shower and cracked his head wide open – at least, that was the official explanation,' Kenicer said. 'No one at the time believed it was an accident. It was far more likely to have been retribution for slipping up and revealing the network. After Campbell was convicted, his pregnant wife, Agnes, was subjected to hate mail and several threats were made on her life. Eventually she packed her bags and went to live with her sister in Sussex. She reverted to her maiden name in order to make a fresh start and Agnes Stuart's son, Malcolm, was born in Brighton.'

'George Campbell's boy?' Charlie's eyes widened.

'Stuart's mother told him what had happened to his father – and he held you personally responsible.'

'I only gathered the evidence,' Charlie protested. 'It was the court and the jury that convicted him.'

'That's not how Stuart saw it. As far as he was concerned, as well as being instrumental in his father's death, you carried the can for his mother getting some pretty scary stuff sent to her in the post. He decided to give you and your family a taste of the same medicine.'

'The nine of diamonds!' Charlie exclaimed, making eye contact with Tony. 'The Curse of Scotland, Tony. The revenge of the Campbells!'

'You cotton on fast, Inspector,' Kenicer said. 'That type can never resist the egotistical touch.'

It was Hamilton who broke the stunned silence that ensued. 'What I fail to understand, Kenicer, is that your people knew from the outset that Stuart was a Republican fanatic, yet you did nothing to prevent him coming up here and causing mayhem?'

'You have to keep these things in perspective, Hamilton. We knew Stuart was a Republican sympathiser – and we knew strings had been pulled to have him assigned to Glasgow. However, we didn't know why. Bespalov didn't tell us he'd sold the anthrax delivery information to the FFF until after Johnston had been murdered on the train. It was only then we made the connection.'

'But from that point on,' Charlie insisted, 'you knew the score.'

'As soon as we realised it was Stuart who had taken out Johnston, I sent DI Farrell to Glasgow to search his apartment to try to recover the anthrax.'

'That wouldn't happen to be the guy Stuart disturbed trying to nick his CD player?' O'Sullivan chipped in.

'As a matter of routine, my people always remove an item of value when they break into premises. It makes it look like petty theft. Farrell had time to give Stuart's place a thorough going over before he was disturbed. He didn't find the anthrax, however, he did find incontrovertible proof that Stuart was responsible for the murder on the train.'

'What was that?' Charlie asked.

'He found Johnston's amputated hand in the freezer compartment of his fridge.'

'Jesus!' Charlie felt a shiver travel the length of his spine. 'Let me make sure I've got this straight. You knew all along that Stuart was a Republican sympathiser. You also knew from the outset that Stuart's real name was Campbell, so you must have figured out the Curse of Scotland connection of the nine of diamonds, but you kept us in the dark about that – even to the extent of telling us you thought it was a red herring. What was all that crap you were spouting about this investigation requiring maximum cooperation between both our organisations? You've been playing bloody games with us!'

'I have one, and only one, priority, Anderson,' Kenicer snapped. 'And that's to recover the anthrax before it can be used to cause carnage. From the moment I knew Stuart had appropriated it, my men had him under surveillance and his phone was tapped. If I'd let you know we were on to him you might have spooked him and any chance we had of recovering the anthrax would have flown out of the window.'

'In which case,' Charlie demanded, 'what would have happened to Stuart if we hadn't uncovered the fact that he was the serial killer?'

'I dare say he'd have returned to London to continue his training, probably with a commendation from the Glasgow CID.'

'This is fucking ridiculous!' Charlie sprang to his feet. 'You mean to say you would've condoned a murderer working in the Met?' Charlie ignored Hamilton's pained expression as he waved at him to sit down. 'Stuart attempted to frame Sergeant O'Sullivan by planting incriminating evidence in his flat,' Charlie persisted. 'He tried to talk us into issuing a search warrant. What would have happened to O'Sullivan if we'd carried out a search and discovered the evidence?'

'You tell me, Inspector. If you'd concluded there was a case for O'Sullivan to answer, the judicial process would've run its course.'

'You wouldn't have intervened?'

'Be realistic. We can hardly go around knobbling judges. The most we could have done under those circumstances would have been to ensure the Home Secretary was properly briefed, if and when the case was referred to her office.'

'That is fucking preposterous!'

'You're entitled to your opinion, Anderson, but my priority is national security. I need your cooperation now, Hamilton,' Kenicer stated. 'DI Farrell and I will be flying up to Glasgow this evening. I want to interrogate Stuart first thing in the morning to try to find out what he did with the anthrax.'

'The guy's committed four murders on our patch,' Charlie said. 'We're perfectly capable of carrying out any interrogation that's required – both about the murders and the anthrax.'

'The murders are your problem, Hamilton,' Kenicer said, 'but as far as the anthrax is concerned, he's more likely to talk to us.'

'How do you figure that out?' Hamilton asked.

'He's close to his sister and his mother. We can explain to him the repercussions of not cooperating more succinctly than you can.'

Charlie's cheeks turned scarlet and his breathing quickened. He planted his hands wide apart in the middle of Hamilton's desk. 'No fucking way!' he mouthed in Hamilton's face.

'I can't overstate the importance of this, Hamilton,' Kenicer said. 'There's a consignment of anthrax in the hands of Republican terrorists and we need to do everything in our power to recover it before they can use it. Farrell and I need to interrogate Stuart. After we've finished with him, you can question him all you want about the murders. Where is he being held?'

'Right now, he's in a cell in Maryhill police station,' Hamilton said, 'but we'll be transferring him to the Terrorism Detention Centre in Govan this evening.'

Charlie stretched further across the desk and stared at the microphone, his florid cheeks becoming redder by the minute. 'Do you want to borrow our water board, Kenicer?' he growled, 'or will you be bringing one of your own?'

'I don't like your attitude, Inspector.'

'And I don't appreciate your high-handed approach, Kenicer,' Hamilton interjected sharply. 'My guys have been busting a gut trying to identify a serial killer, while all the time you were withholding vital information. It's a bit rich expecting us to cooperate now.'

'I'm not asking for your cooperation, Hamilton,' Kenicer snapped. 'I'm telling you the way it's going to be. Farrell and I will be at the detention centre in Govan at eight o'clock tomorrow morning to interview Stuart. If you're not prepared to accede to that request, I'll go over your head.'

'Then that's what you're going to have to do. I won't tolerate my people being messed about like that.'

Muttering a curse, Kenicer broke the connection.

'Thanks for that,' Charlie said gruffly.

'I don't expect it will make one whit of difference,' Hamilton said with a resigned shake of the head. 'A pound to a penny the Chief will be on the line to me within five minutes, bending my ear and instructing me to toe the line.'

Half an hour later, Charlie got a phone call requesting him to go back up to Hamilton's office.

'As expected,' Hamilton said as Charlie walked in. 'Kenicer and Farrell will get their own way.'

'I want to be present while they interrogate Stuart,' Charlie said.

'That isn't on. You heard what they said. They're insisting on talking to Stuart on their own.'

'In which case, I want a go at Stuart as soon as they're through with him.'

'No.'

'What did you just say?' Charlie's tone was incredulous.

'I said – no, Anderson. You're too personally involved in this to be objective.'

'But I'm the SIO!'

'I will handle the interview myself,' Hamilton stated.

'For Christ's sake! There are a load of questions to which I need answers!'

'Write them down – and I'll ask them.'

As soon as Charlie got back to his office he called Grace's number and asked to speak to Kay.

'It's over, love. We've got him.'

'Thank God for that! Was it Terry McKay?' Kay asked.

'He was involved, but it's complicated. I'll tell you all about it tonight.'

'Does that mean I can go home now?'

'Yes. Call Sue and let her know she can go home too. There are a few loose ends I need to tie up here. I'll get home as soon as I can.'

Charlie looked up Mhairi Orr's office number, and dialled.

'There's no need to spend any more time on the case, Doctor,' Charlie said. 'We've got him.'

'That's a relief!' Mhairi said. 'Did the same person commit all four murders?'

'One person was responsible for the first three, but Brady's murder was a copycat.'

'Was it one of the guys on your list?'

'No. It was someone who wasn't even on our radar. He has no track record. There's no way your computer module could have picked him up.'

'From a professional point of view, I'm pleased about that.'

'But ten out of ten for your analysis. Ruthless, intelligent, arrogant and self-confident, with a massive chip on his shoulder, sums him up perfectly.

'I must say,' Charlie added, 'that, even though it didn't give us a result this time round, I was impressed by the way your software was able to pick up James McKendrick in Central Station.'

'It is a powerful tool, Inspector.'

'I may well be requesting your assistance again in the not too distant future.'

'Any time.' Mhairi smiled at her phone as Charlie disconnected.

Charlie buzzed through to Pauline. 'Find Tony O'Sullivan and ask him to come to my office.'

A few minutes later, Tony stuck his head round the door. 'You wanted to see me?'

'I've got a bone to pick with you,' Charlie said, crumpling his plastic coffee cup in his fist and dropping it into the waste paper basket. 'And I'm warning you. I've had just about all the crap I can take for one day, so I don't want any more from you.'

'What are you talking about?'

'I want the truth. Where did you slope off to last Thursday when you claimed to have gone to Crosshouse Hospital on a wild goose chase?'

Tony gave Charlie a puzzled look. 'I didn't slope off anywhere. I went to Crosshouse, like I said.'

'Don't give me that nonsense! I want to know where you went. Who were you shagging? Was it Kylie?'

'I don't know what you're talking about.'

'For Christ's sake!' Charlie slammed his fist down on his intercom button. 'Pauline, get Crosshouse Hospital on the line for me. Straight away.' Tony gazed at the floor until the phone buzzed a few moments later. Charlie snatched up the receiver. 'Is that Crosshouse reception?'

'Yes.'

'This is DCI Anderson of Glasgow CID. Could you please tell me who's on duty this afternoon?'

'Me, Tracey Strang, and Maurice Struthers.'

'How long are you on for?'

'Another couple of hours.'

'Thanks.' Charlie cut the connection. 'Come on, you,' he said, pulling himself to his feet. 'You and I are going for a drive.'

There was an uncomfortable silence all the way down the motorway to Kilmarnock. When they pulled up in the car park outside Crosshouse Hospital, Tony unclipped his seat belt and turned in his seat to face Charlie. 'Are you going to tell me what this is all about?'

'Come with me!' Charlie instructed, flinging open his door and getting out of the car.

Charlie marched up to the reception desk with Tony following close behind. He flashed his ID. 'DCI Anderson, Glasgow CID,' he said. 'I called earlier. Are you Maurice Struthers?'

'Yes.'

'Do you recognise this man?' Charlie asked, stepping aside.

'I'm sorry, sir,' Maurice said, looking dubious. 'Should I know you?'

'My name's O'Sullivan. I came here last week looking for my mother.'

'Of course!'

'You do know him?' Charlie spluttered, pointing at Tony.

'I wouldn't say I know him,' Maurice said. 'I met him last week when he came here looking for a Doctor – was it a Doctor Nelson?'

'Wilson,' Tony said.

'Wilson. That's right. Something about your mother having been involved in a hit and run accident, wasn't it?'

'Yes.'

'How is your mother?'

'She's fine. It turned out to be a false alarm.'

'Why did you claim to know nothing about this when Lorna phoned you on Monday?' Charlie demanded.

'I don't know what you're talking about.'

'I came here on Monday when Lorna was on duty. She told me she didn't know anything about a man coming here and making enquiries about a Doctor Wilson last Thursday.'

'There must be some mistake. Lorna and I spent fifteen minutes ringing round to see if Mr O'Sullivan's mother had been admitted to an A&E department in one of the other hospitals in the district.'

'So why did Lorna deny all knowledge of it? Why did you deny all knowledge of it when she phoned you on Monday?'

'I really don't know what you're talking about. Lorna didn't phone me on Monday.' Maurice frowned 'We are talking about the same person?' he said. 'Lorna Campbell?'

'Did you say Lorna Campbell?' Charlie sucked his breath in hard and straightened his tie knot. 'Could you give me her address, please.'

'I don't have it. You'd have to talk to the admin. manager. Her office is down the corridor,' he said, pointing. 'It's the second door on the left.'

When Charlie rang the door bell of the semi-detached house on the outskirts of Ayr, Lorna Campbell came to the door. She shrank back when she saw who was standing on her doorstep.

'I think you have some explaining to do, Miss Campbell,' Charlie stated.

'I didn't mean to cause any trouble. Honestly!' she pleaded. 'It was supposed to be just for a joke.'

'I don't see anyone laughing,' Charlie said.

'Malcolm asked me do it for him – as a favour.'

'Malcolm Stuart?' Lorna nodded. 'Are you two related?'

'He's my cousin. He told me he was going to send someone down to the hospital last Thursday – and that the guy would be looking for a Doctor Wilson. He said he just wanted to get him out of the way for a couple of hours so he could do up his flat for a surprise birthday party.'

'So you didn't phone Maurice Struthers while I was at Cross-house on Monday morning?'

Lorna bit her bottom lip. 'I panicked when you showed me your ID.' Her voice was trembling. 'I had no idea the police would be involved. I just pretended to call Maurice,' she said in a hushed voice. 'I didn't actually click onto any number.'

'Did you not get in touch with your cousin to find out what was going on when you realised the police were involved?' Charlie asked.

'I tried calling Malcolm as soon as you left. I wanted to know what the hell he was playing at. But all I got was a message telling me his mobile number was no longer in service.'

'A complete mystery,' Tony mused. 'Where was Tony O'Sullivan last Thursday morning? That appeared to be your *Key Question*. However, rather than take the word of a trusted colleague, you decided to condemn him out of hand on a mere shred of circum-stantial evidence.' Tony was enjoying himself on the drive back to Glasgow.

'If you spend half your time shagging barmaids,' Charlie growled, 'what else can you expect?'

'Another totally unjustified assertion, based on no evidence. How was it Doctor Orr described the killer?' Tony said. 'Intelligent and self-confident, if I remember correctly. Easy to see how you made the mistake.'

'Sod off!'

'So it was Stuart who phoned me last Thursday and sent me off on the wild goose chase to Kilmarnock.'

'That figures,' Charlie said. 'He wanted to make it look like you had made up an excuse to avoid going to St Vincent Street post office in case someone might recognise you – and he also tried to sow a seed in my mind that you could have been responsible for the murder on the train. For that to be even remotely credible, he had to make sure you didn't have an alibi for the critical period of between twelve and one o'clock on Thursday. What time did you say you got the call?'

'Just after nine o'clock.'

Charlie nodded. 'His timing was spot on. If you allow a couple of hours for you to drive to Kilmarnock and back, including enough time to sort things out at the hospital, that would mean you could've been back in Glasgow in time to get on board the twelve o'clock train and take out Johnston – and still be able to turn up for our two o'clock meeting.'

'I must say, he does a good Glasgow accent,' Tony said. 'I thought he was Scottish when he phoned me, and so did Ryan Ferrie when he broke into his flat and duffed him up.'

'Not surprising he can do the accent,' Charlie said, 'considering his family come from Ayrshire.'

'As a matter of fact, he does a good impersonation of you, sir.' Tony added, grinning.

'Does he really?' Charlie grunted. 'I must ask him to do it for me sometime.'

Charlie pulled up at the bottom of his driveway and switched off the ignition, smiling when he saw Kay's car parked by the side of the house. He hurried up the drive and turned his key in the lock.

'Anybody home?' he called out.

'I'm in here.'

When Charlie went into the lounge he found Kay sitting on the settee with Blakey curled up in her lap. 'He's been complaining

241

vociferously that he hasn't been getting his share of t.l.c. lately,' Kay said, stroking gently at the purring cat's head.

'Him and me both,' Charlie said, stripping off his jacket.

Kay lifted Blakey from her lap and put him down gently on the cushion beside her. She got to her feet and stood on tiptoe to give Charlie a kiss and a cuddle. 'Tell me all about it,' she said.

'Can we start with a cup of tea?'

'I'll put the kettle on,' Kay said, 'while you make your peace with Blakey.'

CHAPTER 20

Thursday 30 June

Scotland's Major Crime and Terrorism Investigation Unit was established in the wake of the unsuccessful attempt to bomb Glasgow Airport in 2007 and, round about the same time, the Scottish Terrorism Detention Centre was set up in a fortified police station in Govan, opposite Bellahouston Park.

In a ground floor interrogation room in the centre of the building, where no natural light could penetrate, Malcolm Stuart sat propped on the edge of an upright chair in front of a rectangular steel desk that was bolted to the floor. Stuart's right wrist was handcuffed to a rail running along the side of the desk.

The police officer, sitting against the wall of the claustrophobic room, got to his feet when he heard the door being unlocked.

Mitch Kenicer, a squat figure with a bull-like neck and a completely shaven head, acknowledged the officer as he walked in. John Farrell, tall and loose limbed, with a thin face and sharp features, did likewise. Both men were wearing dark suits and open-necked, white shirts.

'We'll handle this now,' Kenicer said. 'Wait outside.' The police officer left the room and pulled the door closed behind him.

The spent matchstick between Farrell's thin lips stopped twirling as he whispered something in Kenicer's ear, then both men strode across the room and sat down on the opposite side of the desk from Stuart.

Kenicer fixed Stuart with a stare. 'Where is the anthrax?' he demanded.

'I don't know what you're talking about.'

'The fuck you don't. Where is the anthrax you took from Pete Johnston?'

'I took a guy's attaché case. I've no idea what was in it.'

Kenicer exhaled noisily. 'Okay, let's start again. What did you do with the case you took from Pete Johnston?'

Stuart hesitated. 'I don't have to say anything without my lawyer present.'

'He's on his way.'

'Then I'll wait till he gets here.'

'This is off the record. That thing isn't on,' Kenicer said, jabbing his thumb in the direction of the wall-mounted camera positioned high in the corner of the room, 'and the recording equipment isn't switched on, so cut the crap and answer the question.'

'I know my rights. I don't have to say anything until my lawyer gets here.'

'Don't come the smart arse with me.' Kenicer slammed his fist down on the desk. 'I don't give a fuck about your rights. As a matter of fact, you don't have any. I want to know what your mates are planning to do with the anthrax.'

'With a bit of luck, they'll send it to you in a Christmas card.'

Kenicer leaned across the desk. 'Listen to me very carefully, you miserable little piece of shit. I don't give a fuck about what happens to you. You're going down for life, whether you answer my questions or not. But I need to know what your pals are going to do with the anthrax – and I need to know now.'

'Why don't you go and fuck yourself?'

'That's not very polite,' Farrell interjected, the matchstick flicking rapidly from one side of his mouth to the other. 'Do you know where your sister is right now?' Stuart frowned. 'She's on holiday in Mexico,' Farrell continued. 'And she's due to fly home at the weekend. Oh, dear! She's going to be stopped at customs on the way out of the country – and they're going to find several thousand pounds' worth of heroin hidden in the lining of her suitcase. That is not good news.'

Kenicer leaned back in his chair and clasped both hands behind his neck. 'Which one of them do you reckon will get out of jail first, John?' he asked.

'It'll probably be his sister, sir, but it'll be a close call.'

'At least you have the relative comfort of a British jail to look forward to,' Kenicer said, swinging his legs up onto the desk, 'whereas your sister will be facing the prospect of spending half her life rotting away in some unspeakably grotty Mexican hell hole.'

'I hear that good-looking British birds are very popular over there,' Farrell offered, 'both with their fellow prisoners and the jailers. It won't matter much whether she's lezzie or straight, she'll never be short of a shag.'

Stuart gripped the side of the desk with his free hand, so hard that his knuckles turned white. 'You can't get away with that.' His eyes were blazing. 'I'm going to tell my lawyer what you threatened to do and if anything like that happens to my sister, he'll be able to prove she was framed.'

Kenicer dropped his feet to the floor with a thud. 'If you tell your lawyer that, of course it won't happen.' Kenicer smirked and spread both his arms wide. 'But in that case, something else will. What do you reckon, John? Will some deranged bastard throw acid in his sister's face when she gets back to Brighton? Maybe a nutter will break into her apartment and beat her up and rape her? Or do you think she might be so distraught about her brother being arrested for murder that she'll top herself by jumping off the end of Brighton Pier?' Stuart's hand went limp and all the colour drained from his face. 'We're not playing games, Stuart,' Kenicer snapped. 'Either you cooperate with us or your sister will suffer the consequences. And once we've dealt with her, your mother will be the next one on our list.'

Stuart licked hard at his dry lips. 'I've no idea what they're planning to do with it,' he said in a hushed tone.

'Who are "they"?'

'I don't know.'

'I don't have time for this crap!' Kenicer yelled.

'I don't know any names,' Stuart protested. 'There's a cell system. I only have one contact – and all I know is his codename.'

'Which is?'

'Galway Bay.'

'What do you know about him?'

'Nothing. I've never met him.'

'How does he give you your instructions?'

'He phoned me a couple of couple of weeks ago and told me there was a mission pending which would require someone to be assigned to the Glasgow CID. I volunteered for it.'

'What was the mission?'

'I was sent a letter that included a photograph of a middle-aged man. I was told to wait by the ticket barrier of the twelve o'clock train from Glasgow Central to London on the twenty third of June and look out for him. I was told he'd be wearing a red anorak and carrying an attaché case. When I saw him, I was to follow him onto the train. The letter I got included a typed note, purportedly from someone called Hassam Salman, which I was to give to the guy when we were ten minutes out of Glasgow. The note said that I had the keys for the handcuffs attached to his wrist – and it told him to follow me to the toilets and transfer the case to me. When he came to the toilets, I was to kill him, saw off his hand and take the case that was handcuffed to his wrist.'

'What were you told to do with his hand?'

'There was nothing about that in the instructions. Taking it was my idea.'

'Why?'

'I wanted to scare the shit out of Anderson.'

'What did you do with the attaché case?'

'My instructions were to get off the train at Motherwell and get into a black Ford Focus that would be waiting for me outside the station. I was to put the case under the passenger's seat and the driver would drop me off at my flat. I've no idea what happened to the case after that.'

'What's the procedure if you need to get in touch with Galway Bay?'

'He contacts me. I don't have any way of getting in touch with him.'

'Bullshit! You must have some way of contacting your handler in an emergency.' Kenicer stared long and hard at Stuart as Farrell started whistling a slow, off-key rendition of *Down Mexico Way*.

Stuart swallowed hard. 'If I tell you how I contact him,' he stammered, 'will you guarantee to leave my sister out of this?'

'You're not in any position to negotiate,' Kenicer said. 'But what I will guarantee is that, if you don't tell me how to contact him, your sister will be well and truly fucked. Both metaphorically – and physically.'

Stuart again licked hard at his lips. 'I've got a mobile number I can use in an emergency.'

'What is it?'

'You've got to promise to lay off my sister.'

'Stop wasting my time, Stuart. Give me the fucking number,' Kenicer demanded, pulling a notebook and pen from his jacket pocket. Stuart recited the number and Kenicer jotted it down. 'This had better be kosher, for your sister's sake.'

'It is.'

'We'll be able to trace this cell phone,' Kenicer stated, tapping the page in his notebook with his pen, 'but if you fuck things up by trying to contact Galway Bay and warning him off, don't expect to see your sister again.'

'One more thing,' Farrell said as they were getting to their feet, 'If you want your sister kept out of this, you'd better cooperate fully with Hamilton on the murder enquiries. You're going down for life whatever happens, so plead guilty to everything he throws at you. The last thing we need is the case going to a trial, and awkward questions about Counter Terrorism Command involvement being asked. That could open up a very unwelcome can of worms.'

Kenicer and Farrell walked across to the door and rapped on it. 'We might need to talk to him again later,' Kenicer said to the police officer when he opened up, 'but for now, you can tell Hamilton he's all his.'

The fishing vessel was ploughing its way through the heavy waters of the North Atlantic, under the influence of a strong westerly wind. Roman Bespalov was at the wheel when Dimitri Ryleev came up from below to tell him there was a call for him from Mitch Kenicer. Bespalov handed control over to Ryleev and went down the spiral staircase to his cabin to take the call.

'What can I do for you?' Bespalov asked. The radio signal was strong.

'Have you sent the Fermanagh Freedom Fighters the combination for the briefcase?'

'Not yet.'

'You must not send it to them.'

'"Must not?" Did you just say "must not"? Surely what you mean is – you would prefer me not to send it to them? And if I agree to that – you would like to give me something in return.'

Kenicer hesitated. 'How much?'

'I like to deal in round numbers. Let's say – another ten percent.'

Kenicer cursed under his breath. 'If I go along with that,' he said, 'will you guarantee not to send the Irish the combination for the case?'

'If the money is in my Swiss account within the next twenty four hours, I'll give you an unequivocal guarantee that the FFF will never be able to use the anthrax. You have my word on that. The word of an officer – and a bastard.' Bespalov laughed as he broke the connection.

There were four chairs lined up behind the one-way mirror that looked down on the detention centre interview room where Malcolm Stuart was handcuffed to the table. He was deep in whispered conversation with Tom McPherson when Nigel Hamilton walked through the door. Charlie settled on the chair at the end of the row behind the mirror, Tony O'Sullivan by his side. Stuart broke off from speaking to McPherson when he saw Hamilton come in. He looked at Hamilton warily as he crossed the room and sat down on a chair on the opposite side of the desk.

'My client was subjected to interrogation before I arrived, Superintendent,' McPherson stated. 'The Supreme Court ruling in Crown versus Cadder in 2009 specifically states that the right of a prisoner to have a lawyer present at all times while being questioned applies also in Scotland. May I therefore remind you that anything my client may have said before I arrived is not admissible in evidence.'

'Do you want to file a complaint, Stuart?' Hamilton asked, loosening his tie knot. Stuart gave a surly shake of the head. 'In which case,' he said, 'let's get on with it.' Hamilton switched on the wall-mounted camera and activated the audio recording system. He slid the microphone to the middle of the desk. 'This is the recording of an interview with Malcolm Stuart by Superintendent Nigel Hamilton on Thursday, 30 June, commencing at – ' He broke off to check his watch. 'Commencing at nine fifteen a.m. Also present is Tom McPherson, Malcolm Stuart's lawyer.'

Hamilton took a sheet of paper from his briefcase and smoothed it out on the desk in front of him. 'Malcolm Stuart, you have been formally charged with the murders of Irene McGowan, Zoe Taylor and Pete Johnston, and you will also be charged with the murder of Terry McKay. How do you intend to plead?'

Stuart exchanged a quick glance with McPherson. 'Guilty,' he mumbled.

'To all four murders?' Stuart nodded his head.

'For the record,' Hamilton stated into the microphone. 'The prisoner answered in the affirmative.'

Hamilton referred to the questions on his sheet of paper. 'Is Campbell your real name?'

'My name is Malcolm Stuart. It would have been Campbell – if Anderson hadn't murdered my father.'

'DCI Anderson was instrumental in convicting your father of terrorist-related activities. He had nothing to do with his death.'

Stuart's gaze was steely. 'You have no idea how much I hate that bastard.'

Hamilton held his stare. 'On the morning of 23 June, the day you murdered Pete Johnson, did you phone DS O'Sullivan and send him to Crosshouse Hospital in Kilmarnock on a wild goose chase?'

'Yes.'

'Why did you do that?'

'So he wouldn't have an alibi for the time of the murder.'

'Was it your intention to implicate him?'

'He calls himself a Fenian!' Stuart spat out the words. 'He's a traitor!'

'Consider yourself well and truly put in your place,' Charlie said, as an aside to Tony.

Charlie's attention was grabbed by Hamilton's next question. 'Did you send a letter to DCI Anderson's daughter, threatening her son?' Charlie moved onto the edge of his chair.

'Yes.'

'Did you subsequently phone his daughter and try to frighten her?'

'Yes.'

'How did you obtain her address and her phone number?'

There was a smirk on Stuart's face. 'From Anderson himself.'

'What the hell is he talking about?' Charlie's fists bunched.

'Explain what you mean.'

'The first time I went to see Anderson, he left me alone in his office while he went for a leak – something about a problem with his prostate. He'd left his jacket over the back of his chair, so I took the opportunity to go through his pockets. I came across his address book and I used my phone to photograph all the pages.'

Charlie shook his head in frustration. 'The bastard!' squeezed out from between clenched teeth.

'Is that how you got Sergeant O'Sullivan's mobile number?'

'Yes.'

'Thanks for that, sir,' Tony said.

Hamilton referred again to his list of questions. 'Were you responsible for putting Pete Johnston's amputated hand into Mrs Anderson's shopping trolley in Sainsbury's in the Braehead shopping centre?'

'Yes.'

'How did you manage to identify Mrs Anderson – and how did you know she would be in Sainsbury's at that particular time?'

'I knew where Anderson lived from his address book. I went there intending to post Johnston's hand through his letter box to scare the shit out of him. I parked at the end of his street and I was walking towards his house when I saw his wife coming out and getting into her car. I turned round and went back to my car and followed her to Braehead. When she went into Sainsbury's, I followed her inside and slipped Johnston's hand into her shopping trolley while she was ordering meat at the butcher's counter.'

'Why did you kill Zoe Taylor?'

'She fitted in with the theme. Not her. Her name.'

'How did you know her?'

'I bumped into her in Glasgow – or, to be more precise, she bumped into me,' Stuart said with a sardonic smile. 'She'd given me her address after a minor traffic bump, so I went to her flat with the intention of killing her, but when I got there I saw there were two names on the door. I rang the bell and her boyfriend answered. He told me Zoe was at her work. I made him set up a rendezvous with her in a remote spot. He picked the boathouse in Glasgow Green.'

'And that's where you killed her?' Stuart nodded. 'Answer the question,' Hamilton said, pointing forcibly at the microphone.

'Yes.'

'And the only reason for killing her, and then cutting off her hand was to send it to DCI Anderson?'

'Yes.'

'Why did you murder Irene McGowan?'

'I was due to report for duty in Glasgow on the Tuesday afternoon, so I killed her on the Monday and posted her hand to Anderson from the main post office in Glasgow. I wanted to make sure it would arrive in Pitt Street on the Tuesday morning. I reckoned that if Anderson was involved with the murder, there was a good chance you would assign the SIO role for the enquiry to him. When I had my initial meeting with you, I told you I was keen to get front line experience, hoping you would allocate me to Anderson's team so I could watch the bastard squirm.'

'Why Irene McGowan?'

'I needed to kill a tinker to fit in with the rhyme, so I found the address of a gypsy encampment in Port Glasgow on the Internet and I went down there and knocked on the first caravan door I came to. When an old woman answered, I showed her my ID and told her I was investigating a spate of burglaries from houses in the area. She let me in and I checked to make sure she was on her own before strangling her. I cut off her hand and took it up to Glasgow to post it to Anderson.'

'So you didn't actually know Irene McGowan?'

'Any old tinker would have done.'

'Did you intend to kill Terry McKay?'

Stuart shrugged his shoulders. 'Not much point in denying it. Anderson knew McKay had killed Brady and, with McKay out of the way, I was hoping he would carry the can for the other three murders as well.'

Hamilton gathered up his papers. Announcing the closing time of the interview for the record, he switched off the camera and the recording equipment.

'I must say that was one hell of a rugby tackle he made on McKay,' Charlie said, turning to Tony. 'Barlinnie's gain is Scottish rugby's loss.'

Kenicer and Farrell were waiting for Hamilton when he came out of the interview room.

'Is there somewhere we can talk?' Kenicer said.

Hamilton led the way to an empty office at the far end of the corridor. When they went inside, Farrell closed the door behind them.

'The imminent threat has been contained,' Kenicer said.

'What does that mean?'

'It cost me and arm and a leg, but Bespalov has given me an assurance that the FFF won't be able to use the anthrax.'

'They've got the attaché case – how can he be sure they won't use it?'

'He didn't give me chapter and verse – only a guarantee that he'd take care of it.'

'Can he be trusted?'

'From an ethical standpoint, not at all. But from a financial point of view – yes. When Bespalov gives a guarantee, he always delivers. Otherwise he knows we would never do business with him again.'

Leaving Kenicer and Farrell in the office, Hamilton walked back along the corridor and climbed the flight of stairs to the observation room where Charlie and Tony were waiting for him.

'Did you hear the interview?' he asked. They both nodded. 'Not very clever, Anderson, leaving someone you didn't know alone in your office with access to your address book.' Charlie's cheeks flushed. 'However,' Hamilton continued, 'the immediate danger seems to have been averted. Kenicer has been given an assurance that the FFF won't be able to use the anthrax.'

'How many of Stuart's fingernails did he have to extract to get that?' Charlie asked.

When Kenicer and Farrell landed at Heathrow airport, a driver was waiting for them. Kenicer's mobile rang while they were in the car on the way into London. He took the call.

'It's Nick Thompson, sir,' the caller said. 'We've managed to pinpoint the location of Galway Bay's mobile phone.'

'Where is it?'

'In a left luggage locker in Euston Station. I decided not to call the number as that would've tipped Galway Bay off that Stuart had blabbed. Besides, unless the FFF have a leprechaun sitting inside the locker waiting to take the call, all there's likely to be is a recorded message, giving further instructions.

'I sent for the CCTV footage from Euston Station for the past month,' Thompson continued. 'I've just checked it out and it appears that the locker was last opened a week ago.'

'Do we know who by?'

'Indeed we do, sir. By the same person who switched Stuart's assignment from Manchester to Glasgow.'

'Nice one, Nick!' Kenicer nodded in grim satisfaction. 'Another nail in the bastard's coffin.'

The fishing boat was making steady progress towards Murmansk through heavy seas. Bespalov called across one of his crew and instructed him to take over the wheel. He signalled to Ryleev and they both descended the steep spiral staircase to the captain's cabin.

Bespalov removed his sou'wester and stripped off his oilskins as he crossed to the small fridge in the corner, from which he produced a bottle of iced vodka and two chilled shot glasses. 'An excellent week's work, Dimitri,' Bespalov said. 'We've earned ourselves a drink.'

Filling both glasses to the brim, Bespalov handed one to Ryleev. Bespalov raised his glass to his cracked lips, pausing to allow the vodka fumes to permeate his hairy nostrils before throwing the drink back in one swallow. Ryleev did likewise, then held out his glass for a refill.

'Have you sent the Irish the combination for the case, Roman?'

'Yes, but I think I might have made a small mistake.' Bespalov chuckled to himself as he tipped another measure of vodka into both their glasses. 'Numbers are very confusing in a foreign language, don't you think?'

'What games are you playing now, you sly old fox?'

'When the Irish try to open the case with the combination I sent them, I think it might blow up in their faces.'

Ryleev frowned. 'That stinks, Roman,' he said, throwing back his vodka.

'It's not like you to suddenly develop a conscience.'

'You know what I'm driving at. Depending on where the case is when it explodes, the anthrax could cause mayhem.'

'Not anthrax, my friend.' A smile was playing at the corners of Bespalov's mouth. 'Just a few measly grams of nitroglycerine.' Ryleev's frown transformed into a look of puzzlement. 'Think it through, Dimitri. Our Iraqi friends are already very upset that their shipment was intercepted. They know the Irish were bidding against them for it, and if they were to find out the Irish had acquired a supply of anthrax, they might conclude it was their consignment. And if the Irish knew the combination to open the briefcase, the Iraqis might think I'd double-crossed them. However, if the Irish contrive to blow themselves up by trying to open up a case they'd stolen, without knowing the correct combination, the Iraqis would have no reason to suspect my involvement.' Bespalov downed his vodka and topped up both their glasses again. 'As you rightly say, a random release of anthrax would have been irresponsible, so, as I knew the Irish were going to intercept the shipment, I settled for a lump of lead in the briefcase, along with a few grams of nitroglycerine and a primed detonator – just enough to take care of whoever tried to open the case. The Irish will assume their guy was blown up because he got careless.'

'But surely they'll realise there never was any anthrax in the case?'

'Of course they will.' Bespalov shrugged. 'But that's not my problem. I'm not planning to deal with them any more. They're too strapped for cash these days. It's my Iraqi friends and the British intelligence services I need to keep sweet – they're the ones with the deep pockets. When I next get in touch with Hassam Salman, I'll have another shipment of anthrax available, which he can have as soon as he can get things organised at his end to accept the delivery. If I'm in a generous mood, I might even offer him a discount to make up for his disappointment at losing his last consignment.'

They both laughed as they chinked their glasses and downed the contents.

Kylie carried two pints of Guinness across from the bar in Òran Mór and set them down on the table in front of Charlie and Tony.

'Thanks,' Tony said.

'By the way, Tony,' Kylie said. 'I forgot to mention. Patrick said to thank you for the cheque.'

'No problem.'

'What was that all about?' Charlie queried when Kylie was out of earshot.

'My pal, Pat – Kylie's husband – he runs the youth football team at our old school in Saltcoats. He held a fund-raising event a couple of weeks ago to raise money for a new kit for the boys. I wasn't able to go along, so I sent him a donation.'

'Right,' Charlie said, nodding. Taking a long, slow sip of Guinness, he wiped the froth from his top lip with the back of his hand.

'I was just thinking,' he said as he placed his glass down on the table, 'it's a sad state of affairs that you've had no one back to your flat for weeks, apart from Malcolm Stuart. You really ought to ease off on the work front and socialise a bit more.'

'Thanks a bunch! As a matter of fact, now I come to think of it, there was someone else in my flat last week, but it was someone completely above suspicion.'

'Who was she?'

Tony hesitated. 'A friend.'

'Kylie?'

'I'll ignore that.'

'When will you ever learn?' Charlie said, shaking his head. 'How many times do I have to tell you that no one's above suspicion?'

'Guilty until proved innocent? Is that the way it works?'

'More or less. So, if truth be told, you happened to get lucky. For all you know, it might've been your other visitor, and not Stuart, who planted the evidence in your suitcase?'

'Okay, let's just agree on that,' Tony said, lifting his pint to his lips to conceal his smile. 'I happened to get lucky.'

'Talking about learning things,' Charlie said, 'some of the things Doctor Orr was able to do with her computer module were quite impressive.'

'Don't tell me you're a convert to profiling?'

'Not at all! It's a load of old cobblers. I was referring to what she was able to do with her computer software. When you boil it down, her methods aren't all that different from our brainstorming sessions – structuring data and analysing it to try to identify patterns and pinpoint anomalies. Even though it didn't give us a result this time around, it's not hard to see how her capability to match photos to CCTV images could prove very useful. Can you imagine how long it would have taken us to slog through the footage from Central Station, searching in the crowd for someone we could recognise? Doctor Orr's program allowed her to scan in photographs and search for matches. That's what I call cutting edge technology.'

'I thought your idea of cutting edge technology was Stuart's hacksaw blade.'

'Aye, right!'

'Before you know it you'll be logging onto your terminal and answering your own emails.'

'There's no need to get carried away.' Charlie took another sip of Guinness. 'Nice temperature, by the way. I don't like it when it's too chilled.'

'Weren't you sailing a bit close to the wind yesterday?' Tony said.

'What do you mean?'

'If Niggle ever finds out that you sat through his press conference and remained schtum when you knew all along that Stuart was the serial killer, he'll have your guts for garters.'

'Put yourself in my position. When I got your note telling me you'd found the evidence in your suitcase, it was ten minutes before Niggle's press conference was due to begin. The way I saw it, I had two options. I could either walk into his office and say something along the lines of: "I don't have any firm evidence to back this up, but you might want to consider cancelling your press conference because O'Sullivan thinks a fellow officer committed the first three murders" – or else I could play dumb and let him pontificate about his success, knowing he'd have to eat humble pie later on.'

'Tough call.'

'A touch of humility is always good for the soul. By the way you might be interested to know that Niggle did authorise a search warrant for your apartment, but he withdrew it in double quick time when events took a turn. Barry Crawford tipped me the wink. He'd been told to give your place a thorough going over.'

'The lying git!'

'I've been doing a few enquiries myself,' Charlie said. 'It's all creeping out of the woodwork. I spoke to the estate agent Stuart was supposed to have been with on the morning Pete Johnston was murdered. He confirmed that the lease for Stuart's apartment had been signed the previous day. Stuart made up the story about having to go to the estate agent's so he would have time to get on the London train and take out Johnston, besides which he wouldn't have wanted to risk going anywhere near the post office in St Vincent Street in case he was recognised.'

'Why the baseball cap?' Tony asked. 'Just showing off that he could get away with it?'

'Probably part of the reason,' Charlie said, 'but I imagine he would also have wanted to hide his rather distinctive blond curls.'

'I can't get over the arrogance of the bastard,' Tony said. 'The way he showed off by supposedly solving the smiley mystery.'

'He really had it in for you,' Charlie said. 'He came to me with a spiel about how you were paranoid about being victimised. He told me you played Irish rebel songs when he went back to your place for a drink. He more or less implied you were a fully paid up member of the IRA.'

Tony looked Charlie straight in the eye. 'He was out to nobble you as well, sir.'

'What do you mean?'

'He was doing his best to ruin your reputation.' Charlie looked puzzled. 'He told me he thought you were tippling in the office during working hours.' Charlie's eyes narrowed. 'Why would he say something like that unless he was planning to set you up? Maybe he dropped a similar comment in Niggle's ear? We know what a vindictive bastard Stuart is. I wouldn't put it past him to have stashed a bottle of booze somewhere in your office and tipped Niggle off where to find it.' Tony picked up his pint and took a long, slow pull before placing his glass back down on the table. 'It might be worthwhile checking your office thoroughly in case something's been planted.'

Charlie nodded, his rheumy eyes studying Tony closely. 'Good point, Tony. Thanks. I'll do that.'